Return to Serendipity

SERENDIPITY SUNSETS BOOK ONE

LIZA LANTER

Copyright © 2022 Liza Lanter

ISBN: 978-1-942994-09-1

Published by Ink On My Fingers Publishing

All Rights Reserved

Cover Design by Cassy Roop / PinkInkDesigns.com

No part of this book may be reproduced in any form or by any electronic or mechanical means including information storage and retrieval systems, without permission in writing from the author. The only exception is by a reviewer, who may quote short excerpts in a review.

This book is a work of fiction. Names, characters, places, and incidents either are products of the author's imagination or are used fictitiously. Any resemblance to actual persons, living or dead, events, or locales is entirely coincidental.

Printed in the United States of America

Contents

Also By	V
1. Jenn	1
2. Jenn	13
3. Mel	27
4. Jenn	35
5. Jenn	51
6. Doris	64
7. Jenn	71
8. Randy	86
9. Jenn	107
10. Mel	128
11. Jenn	142
12. Mel	164
13. Jenn	175

14.	Randy	187
15.	Mel	200
16.	Jenn	212
17.	Sinclair	227
18.	Jenn	235
About the Author		241

Also By

SERENDIPITY SUNSETS
Return to Serendipity
Second Chances in Serendipity
Miracles in Serendipity
Revelations in Serendipity
Wedding in Serendipity
New Beginnings in Serendipity
Happy Endings in Serendipity

Chapter One

Jenn

JENNIFER HALSTON LEANED HER head out of the rolled down window of her Jeep Grand Cherokee and inhaled a deep breath of salty evening air. *It smells like home*, she thought. She'd driven the busy corridor more times in her life than she could count. It was a relaxing feeling to drive the four-lane highway to the town of her youth. It conjured happy memories of sunny days of childhood. With every mile that passed, she felt more relaxed. The road led to some of the people she loved, and missed, the most in the world. After spending the bulk of her adult life living in an urban area, Jennifer never imagined that one day she would again be driving the road to the small town—her new home, her new life.

In recent months, many things happened that Jenn, as most people called her these days, never imagined. The past year had been one heart-tugging surprise after another. During the long months of transition, almost daily stress headaches made Jenn long for the soothing sound of the ocean waves and soft sand between her toes. *Be careful what you wish for*. That wish had become a reality in the blink of an eye and the stroke of a pen.

The sun was setting on the distant horizon bathing the landscape in a burnt orange and red hue. She smiled remembering her grandfather's words. *Red sunset, hot day ahead.* Her grandfather would be pleased that her new home was his last residence. The roomy beach cottage Jenn recently inherited was built in the 1970s by Gramps. Carson Frederick was already a sought-after contractor when the coastal acreage where her new home now sat was being developed. In exchange for his expert carpentry and design skills, Carson's childhood friend gave him a prime piece of coastal real estate right next door to the mansion Carson built for his friend.

It took him a few years, but the master builder constructed a spacious beach house that was as unique as Jenn's grandfather's personality. Only a few miles from the house where Jenn grew up, her childhood was filled with memories of spending time at her grandparents' beach house. Once a remote hide-a-way location, the oceanfront property was now prime coastal real estate.

Drinking in another lungful of ocean air, Jenn continued to pass structures that were a mixture of old memories and new development. While she knew that her hometown of Serendipity would always be a place she would return to, Jenn had not imagined that the town of her childhood would ever be her permanent residence again. All that changed when a year earlier, her husband of thirty years decided that he wanted a new life minus Jenn. The ink was barely dry on their divorce papers six months later, when Simon Young married the twenty-plus years younger marketing manager of his company. Since she didn't feel 'young' anymore, Jennifer Halston Young dropped her married title returning to the name her hometown friends would remember. A sign of a future Jenn did not know was ahead.

In the midst of the divorce, Jenn's mother, Paisley Halston, passed suddenly in her sleep sending Jenn another tragic blow. Much to Jenn's surprise, Paisley and Marshall Halston, her parents, had years earlier set up their estate with equal, but different, forms of inheritance for Jenn, her older sister, Renee, and younger sister, Amber.

Jenn's father, Marshall, took over the helm of the Carson Frederick's construction company upon his father-in-law's death and continued to grow the company. Before Marshall's passing, Renee's husband, Neil, joined the business as a partner. The terms of Paisley's will set forth for Renee to inherit the remaining shares in their father's construction company. Amber, their troubled younger sister, would inherit a trust fund to help secure her future despite her battles with addiction. To Jenn's surprise, the will stated that Jenn would inherit the full title to the beach house so that Jenn could 'find her way home,' when she was ready.

While the events in her life had suddenly become complicated and life-changing, Jenn embraced the opportunity to inherit her family's coastal property. The Frederick and Halston families had deep roots in Serendipity. Through the years, Jenn felt a tinge of sadness each time she departed after a visit with her parents. It wasn't just the relaxed lifestyle that the beach town embraced; it was the small town feeling of community and sense of place. Generations of friends and neighbors had decades of common history. They knew one another the way one knows family. They rejoiced together in successes and special moments. Neighbors held each other tight in sad times and heartache.

While in the area for her mother's funeral, Jenn learned that the community newspaper where she got her career start was for sale. Taking this as the third sign leading her back to Serendipity, Jenn made the bold move of buying the newspaper to get back to her roots, in more ways than one. The time she spent at the newspaper as an entry level reporter during the first months after her college graduation was some of the most formidable of her early career. She'd often wondered what her career might have been like if she'd stayed in the 'newspaper business,' instead of letting life take her in a different career direction.

All these reasons fueled why Jenn felt a scary combination of excitement and fear as the ocean wind blew her shoulder-length light brown hair in every direction as she drove down the coastal highway. Pulling a moving trailer with the remaining possessions from her 'Young' life, she was more than ready to reclaim her identity as Jenn Halston.

Flashing blue lights in her rearview mirror roused Jenn from her thoughts and made her heart race. Looking at her speedometer, she was relieved to see that her mind wandering had not caused her to exceed the speed limit. The police cruiser moved into the oncoming lane as it sped by. Jenn breathed a sigh of relief followed by a slight smile thinking about a friend from her childhood in Serendipity. Jenn's mother had kept her informed about Randy Nave's rise in the ranks of the local police department since his return from twenty-five years in the United States Army. Paisley had even sent Jenn the newspaper clipping about Randy's promotion when he became Police Chief.

Randy Nave. It was a name that was imbedded in most of Jenn's childhood memories. The rambunctious little boy who pulled her pig tails and taught her how to throw a football became the teenage high school sports star. The once chubby middle schooler with jet black hair became the muscular and handsome crush of almost every girl within his sight. Randy treated Jenn like a sister. Always friendly and caring, he kept her at arm's length. Other girls would seek her out to learn how they could 'get' him. Jenn was considered the 'Randy whisperer.' It wasn't a role she enjoyed.

Having grown up in the same neighborhood, Jenn was surprised that she didn't see Randy at her mother's funeral. After the service, she learned from his sister, Juliet, that Randy was with his son, several hundred miles away, attending the funeral of his son's maternal grandfather, Randy's former father-in-law. A spray of flowers stood reverently in Randy's place, reminding her that their families' neighborhood connections ran long and deep.

Stopping at the traffic light in the center of town, Jenn took another deep breath of ocean air and looked around at the businesses on the town's Main Street. Quick visits to the area over the decades had not left much time for exploration. As the new owner of the local newspaper, Jenn would need to take the pulse of the business community to make the publication successful from an advertising and editorial standpoint. A big smile crossed her face as she noticed that the neon sign of Quincy's Diner still shone brightly on the corner of Main and Jefferson Streets. A favorite of locals and visitors alike, Quincy's food was classic diner fare, morning, noon, and night. Some of Jenn's most special memories involved sitting at the counter or in a corner booth drinking a thick banana milkshake and laughing until some of it embarrassingly came out her nose. Her mouth watered, remembering the onion rings.

"That will be on my list of first meals, Jasper. I'll bring you a few bites of my hamburger." Jenn spoke to her beloved canine companion, a champagne colored Yorkipoo, while she eased away from the stoplight, slowing down to make the left turn to take the shortcut down Jefferson Street to Ocean Boulevard. "My goodness, I can't believe it. That's Mr. Quincy cleaning the glass on the front door. I had no idea that he was still working at his restaurant. I think he's the same age as Mom."

A wave of sadness hit Jenn's heart with the mention of her mother. Living in the beach house without Paisley Halston would be a hard adjustment. Jenn had forgotten how many memories she would revisit living in the town her mother adored.

While Serendipity was small in population, it was big in name recognition. Two decades earlier, a famous author wrote a fictious emotion-grabbing novel set in the coastal town. The best-selling book became a blockbuster movie and the number of visitors seeking out the beach location rose with each passing year. Not even monstrous hurricanes with merciless paths of destruction could temper travelers from flocking to the area. With it came business growth, but also an attempt to change the community. Her visits, during those years, were a mixture of seeing interesting new businesses being built and hearing the commentary from her parents regarding how growth was changing *their* town.

At last, she made the turn onto Beach Glass Drive. Named by her grandfather, the street snaked through now-large trees he had planted himself in the 1970s. The location was the envy of more than one real estate developer who salivated at the thought of turning the spacious property where the family beach house sat into a tall oceanfront hotel.

Parking her vehicle in between the stilts that elevated and protected the home from flooding, Jenn got out and stretched her legs. Letting Jasper out of his carrier, Jenn watched him run around in circles for a moment, before beginning some serious sniffing. Jenn's sandals sunk into the sand while she walked around the property for a few minutes. Prior to beginning her journey, she had decided to postpone unloading until the morning, packing a small bag to get her through her first night in her new home. It would give her an opportunity to relax and drink in a gorgeous Serendipity sunset from the spacious deck's panoramic view.

Climbing the multiple levels of wooden stairs to reach the wrap-around deck, Jenn's hand felt the initials carved into the handrails. Even on the edge of darkness, Jenn knew what the letters were, as each member of their extended family had left their mark through the years. It was like a family tree dating back to her grandparents—the couple who first made the home possible.

"Wow. This view never disappoints." Jenn stood at the ocean side railing of the deck and gazed into the beautiful orange and red sunset. Her first glimpse of it on the drive into Serendipity was only a preview of the gorgeous horizon that now loomed before her eyes. Taking a deep breath of the ocean breeze, her memory could taste the salt on her tongue. The tenseness in her shoulders from the long drive began to ease almost instantly when her body realized what her mind already knew.

"I'm so thankful to be here." Tears streamed down Jenn's face as the emotion of the past few months caught up with her.

"Oh, Mom, why couldn't you stay a little longer? Maybe you could have lured me down here, and we could have enjoyed these sunsets together." A sob escaped her. The loss of her mother was still fresh in her mind and heart. "You and Daddy have given me the chance to have a wonderful new life, when I needed it most. How I wish you were both here to help me make the right decisions, but how happy I am that you two are together again."

Jenn gulped another deep breath, wiping the tears from her eyes. No amount of wishing would bring her parents back. Yet, she could feel their presence on that deck beside her. The subtle scent of Marshall's nightly thin cigar, only one and only allowed to be smoked outside. His nod to the Rat Pack of his youth. The aroma of fragrant hot tea, most likely chamomile, even in the heat of summer, with a swig of gin—her mother's favorite nightcap.

"I think I will skip the cigar, Dad. But, if I can find the makings of Mom's toddy, I might have one to help me sleep tonight."

As Jenn walked back toward the staircase, she saw a glimpse of light coming from the inside of the house that stood on the left of the Halston's beach house. Jenn smiled, seeing that the property's owner was visible in the room with floor-to-ceiling windows.

"I'm going to enjoy living next to Gladys. Mom was always talking about some crazy story that involved Gladys. Hopefully, we will be neighbors for a long time."

With her tears now replaced by a smile, Jenn climbed back down the stairs to her Jeep. She retrieved her purse and the overnight bag she packed with enough necessities to get her through the first night as well as a small bag of food and toys for Jasper. It was Saturday evening. She had all of Sunday to unpack the moving trailer before her first day at the newspaper.

Making her second trip up the stairs, Jenn quickly opened the tall entryway door into the home. Even though she'd literally walked into the house hundreds of times in her life, *this* moment felt different. Jenn felt a tug at her heart and a speeding up of her pulse—it was a new beginning.

A few weeks earlier, she and Renee had gone through their parents' belongings so that Jenn wouldn't have to face that job when she moved in. Now, Jenn found that the boxes Renee had packed for herself and their sister, Amber, were gone. Cabinets and closets were empty, except for items Jenn was keeping. Much of the furniture in all the rooms remained, part of a grand remodel Paisley Halston did less than five years earlier. The furniture fit the house, so it remained.

Checking her phone, Jenn found many missed calls and text messages awaiting her. Jenn made minimal stops on the ten-hour drive from Atlanta to Serendipity in order to arrive before nightfall. She'd mostly kept her phone inside her purse to avoid being distracted on the busy interstates she was travelling. Stopping only for bathroom and stretching breaks for her and her furry pal, combined with a couple of snacks, meant that Jenn did not answer any of her calls. The natives were restless now. She better check in.

The growling of her stomach reminded her that breakfast was many hours ago. Taking a quick glance in the refrigerator, she was surprised to find that it had been stocked with basic items to feed Jenn for her first week. She immediately knew who should get the first call.

"Renee, that was so thoughtful of you." Jenn's sister answered on the first ring. "I'm so hungry." Jenn pictured her tall, slender older sister with long, auburn hair. Renee's personality matched her hair color Jenn always thought. It was reminiscent of one of their favorite comedienne's, Lucille Ball.

"I can't let my sister starve to death." Renee laughed. "I guess this means you've arrived safe and sound. You meant it when you said you weren't going to check your phone along the way."

"You know how it is. Answer one call and it turns into a ten-minute conversation. Multiply that by a half dozen people and you've lost an hour. I needed to get here before dark. The sun was setting when I arrived."

"Ah, the 'Welcome to Serendipity' sign, a gorgeous sunset. I'm glad you are safely there. I won't keep you past the ten minutes you mentioned. I left you some of the basics for your first couple of days, including a small dish of lasagna and a green salad. The lasagna has been cooked; just warm it in the microwave. I left all of Mom's wine, so I'm sure you can find a nice bottle to pair with it."

"You're the best, Sis. I think I'm going to enjoy being closer to my big sister."

"There's still two hours between us, but it's certainly better than the eight that's been most our adult lives. You are going to be a great excuse for me to spend more time at the beach. Go eat your dinner and get a good night's rest. Call me when you have time tomorrow. Love you, Jenny Girl."

Jenn smiled at the special name Renee gave her at a young age. "Love you, Renee. Thanks again. Goodnight."

Before she answered any other messages, Jenn went back to the refrigerator and removed the small glass dish of lasagna. Taking off the lid, Jenn's mouth watered seeing the contents. A note on top of the lid told her the power setting and length of time necessary to reheat the food. She quickly slid the dish into the microwave across the room, starting the warming process. Jenn opened a can of Jasper's food, filling a small bowl with wet and dry food, placing it on the floor next to a water bowl she'd given him when they first arrived.

After texting her three children quick notes confirming her safe arrival, Jenn carried her bag into the room she'd chosen for herself, formerly a guest bedroom, Jenn took her toiletries and a change of clothes into the bathroom for a quick shower. When she finished, she heard the ding of her phone that she'd left on charge in the kitchen.

"Hey, Mel. I was just about to call you."

"I was beginning to get worried. I know you left early this morning."

Hearing Melinda Snow's voice calmed Jenn's heart. Despite hundreds of miles of distance and almost fifty years of time, Mel was still the closest friend Jenn ever had.

"I barely made it here before the sun set. Wow, it sure was a beautiful one."

"Serendipity's welcome mat."

"Renee said almost the same thing."

"She's obviously seen our marketing. We feature a sunset in all our advertising."

"I forgot about that. You've sent me some of those ads."

Mel was the director of the Serendipity Visitors Bureau, helping to lure thousands of visitors to Serendipity each year. It had been Mel's job for as long as Jenn lived away. Her bubbly personality suited the marketing role. Her dogged determination and creative savvy insured that the town's tourism revenue rose every year.

"I'll get you reacquainted with our branding once you get settled in. I'm so excited that we are going to be working less than a block away from each other. This is a dream come true."

Jenn could almost visualize the energy she heard in her friend's voice. Petite in stature with wavy black hair and emerald green eyes, Mel was a fireball of energy. In her mind, Jenn could see Mel pacing around whatever room she was in, full of excitement.

"Are you hungry? I bet you've moved into a house with an empty refrigerator. I'd be glad to pick up some food and bring it to you."

"Thank you, Mel, but Renee beat you to that. She left me with a stocked refrigerator and a delicious smelling lasagna that is warming in the microwave." Jenn's stomach rumbled at the mention of food.

"That sounds like your organized big sister. I'm standing between you and that food, I bet, so I will let you go. Can I come over tomorrow and help you unpack?"

"Absolutely! I was hoping you'd volunteer. I would love to get the moving trailer unloaded and taken to a drop-off location. Don't worry; I've been careful how I've packed the boxes. No lifting anything too heavy."

"Smart girl! We aren't getting any younger. How about I come about mid-morning in case you want to sleep in? I'll bring some brunch food."

"That sounds wonderful. One of the biggest blessings of this move is that I get to spend the rest of my life within a few miles of my best friend. We've got lots of catching up to do."

"I can't wait! You get some good rest. I'll see you in the morning."

A feeling of contentment came over Jenn after the call ended. *Peace, I feel peace.* Jenn's emotions were raw in ways she knew it would take months and years to heal. However, being in a home that only held loving memories for her, with the backdrop of the relaxing beauty of the ocean, in a town which held her heart, with friends who meant the world to her, and the prospect of building her dream job for herself, would help with the healing. What more could a girl want?

A new love who would embrace the new her. Jenn didn't dare let her broken heart have that dream yet.

Chapter Two

Jenn

"Your lasagna put me into a food coma."

Jenn stretched while answering Renee's call.

"Mission accomplished! After a long, stressful drive that's followed long, stressful months of life, you needed your first night in your new home to be blissful, restful, and rejuvenating. That means you needed a dose of the best Italian sedative."

"Sister knows best."

"I've waited your whole life to hear you say those words." Renee cackled like a witch in a Disney movie.

"It's my lasagna hangover talking." Jenn swung her legs out of bed and sat up. "What are you doing this fine day? I'm unpacking, and then I'm unpacking."

"If I didn't have a doctor's appointment bright and early on Monday morning, I would be right there with you to make sure you organize the 'Paisley-way.' Followed by sticking my feet in that warm ocean water."

"Doctor's appointment? What's that about?"

Jenn rose from the bed, walking around the room in circles. *Where's the door?* The first day in a new home was confusing.

"Oh, you know, checkup time. Procedures that invade your personal space, the collection of body fluids, and that dreaded machine that equates numbers with gravity's hold on us."

"It's the worst, the necessary worst. Treat yourself to something that has excessive calories when you're done." Finally finding the door, Jenn walked out of the room in the direction of the bathroom.

"That's a distinct possibility. Will you be going into the newspaper office on Monday?"

"I will. I have this excited nervous feeling about it. Almost like it's the first day of school."

Looking at herself in the bathroom mirror, she saw a tired fifty-something woman. Under brighter lighting than at her previous home and in a mirror, Jenn saw extra strands of gray in her hair and more lines on her face. The cries of her bladder overruled a closer inspection of her reflection. Jenn hoped that sound didn't travel via a cell phone.

"Do you know much about the staff? What was the former owner's name? I can see his face."

"Mr. Sebastian. Several of the core staff have been there for many years. The office manager is a lady named Doris who has worked the newspaper's front desk for almost forty years."

"I know Doris. She's Aunt Rachel's friend."

"Yes! Doris is quite the character. Knows everyone and has a mind like a steel trap."

"I'm sure her knowledge will be of great benefit to you, especially when it comes to the people inside and outside of the business who you will encounter."

"I do intend to rely on her. I had a brief chat with Aunt Rachel the week after Mom's funeral when I was first thinking about purchasing the business. I wanted to see if there was anything she might know from Doris that would be a red flag. Aunt Rachel said that Doris was so excited that I was even considering buying it and that she would do everything in her power to help me make it an even better operation." Jenn washed her hands and left the bathroom.

"I think Doris would have revealed any negatives. She and Rachel are like sisters and that makes Doris family."

"I enjoyed working with her all those years ago. Nothing got by Doris. Mr. Sebastian even had to toe the line. One of the first things I intend to do this week is have a long heart-to-heart with Doris and ask her to help me develop a plan of strategy for my first six months."

"That's my smart sister talking."

Jenn could hear her brother-in-law's voice in the background.

"Listen, sis, I've got to go. Neil is heading out to play golf in a few minutes. Don't strain yourself unpacking."

"Mel is coming over in a while to help me. We will be careful. I didn't do any heavy packing. All boxes that one person could manage and just a few pieces of furniture. I'll make sure to call you tomorrow evening to find out how that doctor's appointment goes and to tell you about my first day."

"First day as the owner of your own newspaper! Woo hoo! Dad would be so proud."

"I hope so. Talk to you soon."

Since she'd let Jasper out at the edge of dawn and he was still sleeping in his bed, Jenn made her way into the kitchen to brew some coffee. She was certain that her coffee-addicted sister had left a delicious selection with the supply of staple items stocked in the kitchen. She found a bag of blonde roast and a variety box of Keurig cups in the cabinet above the dual coffeemaker on the counter. The combination pot and Keurig coffee maker was one of the last gifts Jenn bought her mother.

Since Mel was coming over and it would be a long day, Jenn decided to brew the largest pot she could. After hitting the start button, Jenn saw Jasper stretching as he made his way into the kitchen. She slipped on her shoes to let him out and retrieve a couple of her suitcases. She'd only packed pajamas and toiletries in her overnight bag.

Jenn was greeted by the beautiful sunshine of a Serendipity morning. She was itching to put on running clothes and begin the day with a jog down the beach. It was just a little after eight o'clock. Maybe she could take a half hour and start her resolution to run on the beach every day.

After bringing the suitcases and Jasper back into the house, Jenn dug through a suitcase and found some clothes that would be suitable for running. She thought hard, trying to remember what box she'd packed her running shoes in. Grabbing a cup of the freshly brewed coffee while she walked back outside to the moving trailer, it didn't take long before she found the right box.

"Duh, Jenn." She laughed. "The box that's labeled 'shoes' might be a good place to start." Pulling off the tape and digging into the contents, her running shoes were about midway in the box. "I must have been asleep when I packed."

Back inside the house, Jasper flopped down on his big pillow Jenn had brought upstairs the night before. Jenn finished her first cup of coffee before lacing up the shoes and heading out via the sliding glass doors onto the deck. Jenn quickly made her way down the deck steps and onto a sandy path leading to the beach. Another set of wooden stairs led her closer still to the beach. Jenn saw no one in either direction. This did not surprise her because most of the homes on that stretch of beach were spaced apart and privately owned.

Stretching first, Jenn soon began to run near the ocean toward the property to the right of her house. This was the mansion location—the home that her grandfather built for the friend who gave him the land Jenn now owned.

Oasis. The name of the mansion suddenly came to her. Looking up at the majestic building, she could see why it was so named. Surrounded on two sides by large stately trees, the two-story structure peaked in the front with an expansive second story deck. Jenn glanced a couple of times at the home as she jogged past. The glare of the sun obstructed her view at times, but she thought she saw someone on the deck stand up and began to walk down the stairs toward the beach. Continuing her run, a few minutes later, she heard someone coming up behind her.

"Hello!"

The male voice caught her off guard. A familiar feeling of apprehension overtook Jenn. In her haste to get a run in before Mel arrived, Jenn had forgotten to get her pepper spray from her purse. She quickly thought about the self-defense training she'd taken, so she suddenly stopped, turning in the direction of the man behind her.

He immediately stopped and began backing away from Jenn when he saw her defensive move.

"Hold on. I'm sorry if I spooked you. No harm is intended, I assure you."

With the sun now behind her, Jenn had a clear view of the man's face. There was only one word that came to mind, beautiful.

Jenn remained silent, standing still and watching the man. He was at least six feet tall with an athletic, slender build. Blondish-brown hair, slightly long, lay in a tousled wave with sprinkles of gray throughout.

A serious expression was on his face. *He looks a little afraid.* For some reason that thought amused Jenn. She hid that reaction.

"I heard that I was getting a new neighbor this week. Would that be you?" Jenn remained silent. "I wanted to come over and introduce myself. I don't suppose you remember me. It's been a long, long time—our whole lives actually—since we last met."

Jenn tilted her head, furrowing her brow. The man neither looked nor sounded familiar to her. His statement led her to believe they had met as children. She did not remember.

"My name is Parker Bentley. My grandfather was Walter Bentley. Our grandfathers were—"

"Friends."

For a split second, Jenn traveled back in time to that same beach. She'd spent the entire summer on that beach when she was six, the summer before she started school. Amber had been born prematurely in early June. It had been a difficult birth for her mother. Both mother and baby remained in the hospital for several weeks before they came home. Renee was sent to stay with their father's sister in Charleston. Jenn spent the summer with her grandparents at the beach house. She'd spent the whole summer playing with a little boy named Parker. After that summer, Jenn never saw the little boy again.

"Yes, our grandfathers were friends and did business together."

"It's nice to meet you again. I'm Jenn Halston. I remember you, Parker."

"You and I were friends, too, a lifetime ago."

"We were playmates one summer. Why have I never seen you here in all the years since?"

The happy expression which filled the handsome face quickly vanished, replaced by the sound of a deep sigh and a frown.

"Right after that summer, my father moved our family to Europe. Dad took a new job with a large European company. My grandfather didn't like it. He and my father had a falling out. It lasted the rest of my father's short life. He died young, in his forties. My mother and I stayed in Europe. She remarried. I only returned here a few years ago. Shortly before my grandfather died. We reconnected. It was too short of a time. Despite the years of estrangement, he left me everything. I own the Oasis now."

This time it was Jenn who backed away from him, not in fear, but shock.

"I had no idea. I don't remember my mother mentioning anything about it, except that your grandfather had passed."

"The Bentleys are not ones to idly speak about family matters. I doubt that your mother knew whom the property had passed to, unless she inquired. I did not visit your mother on any of my trips here before my grandfather passed. No one has lived in the house until I came a few weeks ago."

"Are you planning to sell it?" A feeling of apprehension began at the pit of Jenn's stomach. Only their two families had lived on the properties since the homes were built by her grandfather.

"I'm evaluating the situation. That's why I'm here. The work I do can be done from anywhere in the world. I thought I would see how I liked living here again."

Jenn looked at her watch. It was getting close to nine.

"It was nice to see you again, Parker. I'm sorry that I was startled when you approached. It's been a long time."

"Indeed. It's been a lifetime, in more ways than one. I hope to see you again, neighbor." Parker smiled.

For an instant, Jenn saw a glimmer of the little boy she once knew. Jenn became lost for a moment in the memory.

"Maybe you and your husband could come over for dinner one night."

The statement jerked Jenn back to reality.

"Thank you, Parker. I'm divorced."

"Oh, I'm sorry."

Parker's words did not match his expression. Jenn swore she saw the edges of his mouth turning up in a smile. She chose to ignore it, turning to head back.

"I'm glad I ran into you. I hope to see you again."

Before there could be anymore dialogue, Jenn turned and began running toward her house. She didn't look back in Parker's direction until she reached the beach stairs to the house. Jenn saw that Parker was still standing in the same spot, watching her. She raised her hand and waved. He returned the gesture, then walked up the beach and began climbing his own stairs back to the Oasis.

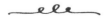

"I cannot believe that we are actually going to finally live in the same zip code again."

The grip of Mel's hug grew tighter with each second that passed.

"It's incredible. I still don't believe it myself, and I'm the one who's done all the moving."

"It's like everything in the universe has lined up for this wonderful time."

Mel's words hit Jenn between the eyes. She gave Mel one last squeeze before she wiggled out of the embrace.

"Oh, Jenn, I'm sorry. I didn't mean it exactly the way it came out. I know that there have been so many horrible circumstances that led up to you moving here. That was so selfish of me to only focus on why it's wonderful for me. I'm being a bad friend." Mel lowered her head. Her normally bright expression turned sullen.

"No, Mel. Don't beat yourself up. I understand what you meant. I'm happy to be here with you. I'm sad about the series of events that has led me here at this precise time. Aside from Mom's sudden passing, I cannot say that I was totally surprised at what occurred. It's been a long time since I would have described Simon and I as being happy."

"He's a jerk, Jenn. He had the best wife in the world, and he didn't appreciate her."

"Oh, Mel. I wasn't the perfect wife. But I did try to make Simon's and the kids' lives as perfect as possible. I think in the process I lost myself. Maybe that's why he went looking for someone else." A lone tear fell down Jenn's cheek. Emotional reactions seemed to be the only type she had these days.

"Don't you dare blame yourself for Simon's stupidity. I'll not tolerate negativity directed toward yourself when there are plenty of other directions that it can be directed." Mel rolled her eyes, giggling. "Enough of this sad talk. I've brought enough food for us to eat for days, all your favorite brunch items." Mel pointed at the kitchen counter where she'd placed several bags of food. "Take that shower you were heading toward when I arrived. I'll start creating the buffet."

"Perfect. I won't be long."

A few minutes later, Jenn found herself enjoying the multiple pulsating showerheads of the large walk-in shower her parents installed with their last remodel. It felt like an answered prayer. Yesterday's long travel day combined with busy weeks leading up to it made every muscle in

Jenn's body hurt. The run would have helped if she'd been able to complete it. The encounter with Parker only left her feeling more confused and mentally tired. She wanted the water to wash the confusion away and give her a clear vision about the next steps of her new life.

True to form, Mel created a brunch spread that would rival a restaurant. Thankfully, the portions were not too huge, more like one person servings. Jenn's mouth watered seeing eggs benedict, breakfast meats, cinnamon rolls, English muffins, fresh fruit salad, hash brown potatoes, and several other items. Mel knew all of Jenn's favorites and brought them to welcome her home.

"Mel, you're going to make me gain five pounds my first day here." Jenn leaned down and took a whiff of the delicious aromas. "It's okay. That gives me even more reason to get my butt up early each morning and run on the beach."

"Your own private beach on one of the most exclusive sections of property in the area."

"Honestly, that concerns me a little bit." Jenn began filling her plate with samples of everything. "I just ran into the owner of the Oasis. From our conversation, I'm wondering if he might be planning to sell it. I can only imagine that he would get the best price from a potential commercial owner."

"What? Owner of the Oasis? Wait a minute. Isn't it still owned by the Bentley family? It's not been that many years ago since Walter Bentley passed away. I think he was close to one hundred years old when he died. Wasn't he friends with your grandfather?"

"Yes, Walter Bentley was like a brother to my grandfather." Jenn sat down at the small table in the kitchen area while Mel filled her own plate. "They grew up together on neighboring farms in central North Carolina. My grandfather started building his contracting business while

Walter went off to work in the corporate world. Walter was led by a mentor to make some extremely profitable investments. It's one of those rare stories where someone becomes a millionaire overnight."

"I remember a little bit of this story." Mel filled a mug with coffee and placed it in front of Jenn. "Didn't Mr. Bentley also build some companies himself?"

"Yes, he took a portion of the money and purchased several companies that he then built to success. Around that same time, he bought this coastal property. It was right before the area started developing. He held on to it for several years before convincing my grandfather that they should build homes here. Mrs. Bentley wanted to have a huge house because she wanted to have a large family. The Bentleys ended up only having one child, a son. Sadly, there was a falling out in the family, also."

"Now, you're getting to the juicy part, the family drama." Mel sat down across from Jenn and began eating.

"I can't remember the son's first name. It's on the tip of my tongue." Jenn took a big sip of coffee. The warmth was soothing. "Anyway, Mr. Bentley and his son disagreed about his future. Jearl! The son's name was Jearl. I learned this morning that Jearl and his father became estranged because of that move to Europe. Sadly, Jearl died young, without reconciling with his family."

"Oh, that is sad. How did you learn that this morning?"

"While I was running on the beach this morning, I ran into the man who owns the Oasis. He's Walter Bentley's grandson, Jearl's son. His name is Parker. He and I were playmates one summer. The summer before I started school."

"The summer before you met me!" Mel's green eyes sparkled with excitement.

"Indeed. I had no idea what was ahead of me."

"I seem to recall you talking about a little boy who was your friend. I thought he was imaginary since I never got to meet him when I'd come with you to visit your grandparents."

"I think I might have thought he was imaginary, too. I never saw him after that summer until this morning."

"Really? He never came back to see his grandparents. That seems strange."

"I guess it was until you heard the story. Parker's father was estranged from Walter. They were living in Europe when Jearl died. It seems that Parker's mother remarried, and they stayed in Europe. Parker didn't have any contact with his grandfather until a short time before Mr. Bentley passed."

"It's a wonder you didn't hear this story from Paisley. Your mother seemed to keep up with the lives of her friends."

"Remember, Mr. Bentley was a generation before Mom's. He was friends with her father. I don't recall hearing much about him in those later years, other than Mom occasionally cooking some food for him, or something like that. I remember that Mr. Bentley liked my grandmother's strudel. My grandmother taught Mom how to make it. I think Mom would make some for Mr. Bentley occasionally."

"I guess the news about an estranged son and grandson didn't make friendly coffee talk. I don't imagine he looks too much like his six-year-old self."

"He doesn't." Jenn became lost in her thoughts for a moment, remembering the morning encounter. "I remembered him though. It was like being transported back in time. We had so much fun that summer."

"I do remember you talking about him when we first met. I was a little jealous of that little boy who seemed to be your best friend. I wanted to be your best friend."

"It didn't take you long to fill that role." Jenn reached over and squeezed Mel's hand. "You've been the undisputed champion of that position every day since."

"Looking back, would you say that Parker was your first crush?"

"Oh, I don't know. I think my first crush was a man named Perry who was on my father's construction crew. I thought Perry hung the moon." Jenn pushed her plate away. "I'm so full."

"I guess I went a little overboard on the brunch menu." Mel picked up both plates and headed toward the kitchen sink. "What you don't know is that I didn't put all of it out."

"Mel!"

"I know. We have something different to eat later in the day after we've done all that unpacking. It's mostly lunch-type foods like salads and such. I've put them in the fridge already. Renee really did a nice job of stocking it for you."

"She did. I'm very grateful. I think this week will be extremely busy on many levels. There are a few things that I need to do related to this house, like having different services switched to my name. I can't even imagine what's ahead of me at the newspaper. I think my learning curve may take a while."

"Doris will be extremely helpful."

"That's what I was telling Renee. I believe that one of the first things I should do is give Doris a raise."

"Well, that's one way to build an allegiance from the start." Mel began putting away the leftovers.

"I think that Mr. Sebastian wasn't around the office much over the last few years before he passed. I don't think his health was conducive to that. Doris had to have picked up a lot of the slack. She's way past retirement age. I don't need her to get the idea of quitting in her head anytime soon."

"Doris is a woman of loyalty. She's a fixture at that newspaper. Personally, she's always been close to your Aunt Rachel. That personal allegiance will translate to you."

"I hope so."

"I know so." Mel wiped her hands on a dishtowel. "Disposable plates and utensils make for easy cleanup. I made sure that you are stocked up on those. Just think of it as Mel's China." Mel did a little flourish with the towel, bowing.

"I've missed you, Mel. We're going to have so much fun." Jenn laughed, bowing in return.

Chapter Three
Mel

"You were wise to dispose of most of your furniture in Atlanta." Mel stood behind Jenn at the opened moving trailer in the driveway. "You had beautiful furnishings, but they were a completely distinctive style than this house."

"Absolutely. I really lucked up. One of the bidders on the house asked if they could buy some of the custom furniture that I had created for the house years ago. They were a young couple who were moving to Atlanta because of a job promotion. They have one child and one on the way. I quoted a price that I thought might start a negotiation. They accepted it without hesitation. I was thrilled that the furniture could stay with the house."

"I'm still amazed that Simon gave you the house, free and clear. That's way more generous than I expected."

Mel smirked. She had never liked Simon much. Jenn had not been as happy in that relationship as she should have been, in Mel's opinion, because Simon did not treat Jenn as an equal in the marriage.

"Simon made a deal that benefited him. He was fair in some of the financial portions of our divorce. But don't get the impression he was generous. It's not true." Jenn pulled a couple of lamps out of the back of the trailer, handing them to Mel.

"You're going to need to explain that." Mel took the lamps, heading up the sidewalk.

"Simon wanted to retain all his retirement accounts. My lawyer wanted all our assets to individually be split 50-50." Jenn followed Mel with a large box that had the word 'linens' written on the side. "I knew the division of those retirement accounts, his and mine, would be a point of contention. I also knew that he could care less about the house because he already had a high-rise condo in the city. Simon never enjoyed life in the suburbs."

"You poured so much of your creativity into that home." After setting the lamps down on the floor, Mel headed back outside.

"I was fortunate that even before working remotely became cool, I was able to work at home four days a week."

"Remind me again how that came to be. I thought that was so strange when you started doing that." Mel laughed. "You were a trendsetter and didn't know it."

"I was at the right place at the right time. It was about fifteen years ago. The public relations company I was working for had just merged with another firm. They didn't want to have to rent another floor of expensive Atlanta office space to house all those new employees. The internet made computer connectivity seamless from about anywhere. One of the firm partners had already made it known that he was going to work from his beachfront house in the Gulf. I'd been with the company for almost ten years at that point, so I asked my boss if I could work remotely. She knew that I had three kids that were elementary and middle school age. She approved it."

"That's amazing. You were still doing that when you resigned recently, right?"

Mel and Jenn began to carry the largest piece of furniture that Jenn brought. It was a beautiful, and quite heavy, bookcase. Mel hoped that neither one of them got a hernia from the experience.

"How did you get this bookcase loaded?"

"I paid the teenager who mowed the grass. He made it look easy. He mows every yard in the cul-de-sac and is on the football team."

"You should have brought him with you. He sounds handy." Mel let out a groan once they got the bookcase inside the house. "Where do you plan to put it?"

"I'm not sure. I just could not bear to leave this piece. Do you remember me talking about our neighbors, the Bybees, who lived next door when the kids were small?"

"Oh, yes, you had some interesting stories about them. I remember meeting the lady. I don't think I met Mr. Bybee. Do I remember correctly that he worked for the Secret Service?"

"Yes, both were retired by the time we moved there. Delightful couple; they were like grandparents to the kids. Joe was a character. He did not like Simon from day one. Told me that I should divorce him."

"I think I would have liked Joe. Sounds like a smart man." Mel rolled her eyes.

"Joe could see right through people."

"What do they have to do with this bookcase?"

"Joe had a quick bout with cancer and passed in his early sixties. Carole, his wife, decided to move to Virginia to be closer to family. I helped her pack. She did some major downsizing. She gave me this bookcase.

When her first book was published, Joe made her this bookcase and told her that she couldn't quit writing until she filled it."

"That's a big goal. I didn't realize you had a neighbor who was an author!"

"She made the goal. She wrote enough books to fill that bookcase."

"What type of books did she write? I don't think I've ever heard of her."

"Oh, you've heard of her, in fact, I'm pretty sure you've read most of her books."

"What?"

"She wrote under a pen name—Caroline Bibbs."

"Oh, my goodness! The Queen of Cozy Mysteries! That's how you got me all those autographed copies! You said you got them at book signings."

"It wasn't a lie. There were books and Carole signed them."

"I remember meeting her at a barbecue you had during one of my visits." Mel covered her face. "Mrs. Bybee and I talked about books. I told her that Caroline Bibbs was my favorite author."

"Do you remember what else you said?"

"Yes." Mel moaned. "That's why I'm covering my face. I told her that Caroline Bibbs was my favorite author even if she told the same story over and over again. Oh, how could I say that? She must have thought I was an idiot."

"Quite the contrary! She was delighted to meet you. Carole said you were one of the smartest fans she'd ever met. She said the secret to her success was writing a story that her readers enjoyed. She said she did that one time and then spent the rest of her career replicating that first story. She made a fortune doing so."

"Why didn't you ever tell me?"

"Because she swore me to secrecy. We lived there at least five years before she shared her secret. Carole joked that both she and Joe were in 'secret service.' Simon still does not know. When she moved, she gave me this bookcase and all the books in it. They are in those boxes you see in the back of the trailer. A first edition of all her books, signed by her on the day she received the copy."

"Wow! That's an incredible collection you have."

"They are all yours now."

"What?" Mel's eyes filled with tears. "You can't do that. They are worth a fortune. She gave them to you."

"I have her blessing. She said that I could give them to you after she passed."

"Oh, no! When did that happen? I bought a new Caroline Bibbs book about six months ago."

"Carole passed away two years ago, at the age of 92."

"I don't understand."

"Carole told me that she stopped writing when she was in her late seventies. But, beforehand, she authored enough books that one could be released every year until she was one hundred. I'd say there are a few more that her publisher has in their vault."

"That's incredible. She was quite prolific."

"Carole told me she could write books faster than her publisher wanted to release them. She started stockpiling manuscripts so that she could retire whenever she wanted."

"I can't believe it."

"I'm sorry that I couldn't tell you that my neighbor was your favorite author. Carole valued her privacy. I valued her friendship. When I told her that I would like to give the collection to you, Carole said that she hoped that would help smooth things over and that she enjoyed her conversation with you about your favorite author."

Mel pulled Jenn into a hug. "You are the best, my friend. After almost fifty years of friendship, I can forgive you one secret."

Mel watched Jenn scrunch her face like she had something else to confess.

"What? Another secret?"

"I'm afraid so. I don't think that I've ever told you that my dentist's name is George Clooney."

Mel pushed Jenn away and stomped off, shaking her head and laughing.

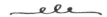

"I met Jenn on the first day of the first grade."

Mel arrived to work extra early on Monday morning so that she could be at the newspaper to greet Jenn before Mel opened the Visitors Bureau at nine o'clock. Doris was arranging a beautiful bouquet of flowers that sat on the high top of her reception desk.

"I remember you girls coming in here on a field trip when you were young. I'd say it was maybe when you were in the third or fourth grade."

It was a popular local opinion that Doris could have been the twin sister of television actress Florence Henderson. No one was quite sure whether it was intentional or an accident, but Doris also seemed to get her fashion style from Ms. Henderson's most famous role—Carol Brady. From the 1970s polyester pantsuits to the cute flip of her bottle-blonde hair, Doris was trapped in a time-warp, and she made it work. She made retro look cool, even for a woman who was old enough to have worn the outfits when they originally came out.

"Yes, that trip was when Jenn fell in love with journalism. After that, she started her own newspaper."

"Goodness, I remember that. Her Aunt Rachel gave me a copy of it once to show Mr. Sebastian." Doris stopped arranging the flowers for a moment. Her eyes darted back and forth, like she was trying to find something. "You stay right here a minute, Mel. I'm going to check something in Mr. Sebastian's, I mean Jenn's, office."

Before Mel could say anything further, Doris scurried away from her desk and into the large corner office to her left. Mel walked to the front door to see if she could see any sign of Jenn.

"I hope she gets here soon. I've got to open my office."

"Who are you looking for?"

Mel jumped when she heard and felt Shaun Hardy come up behind her. Shaun was the newspaper's sportswriter.

"I'm looking for your new boss, Shaun. You scared me half to death."

"I'm sorry, Mel. Is that today? I forgot our new boss was coming today. She's a friend of yours, isn't she? You'll put a good word in for me, won't you?"

"Do a decent job and you won't need a word from me."

Before Shaun could say anything further, his phone rang, and he walked away to take the call. Doris returned to the front desk moments later with something framed in her hand.

"Come here, Mel. Hurry before Jenn gets here."

Doris turned the frame around so that Mel could see what was behind the glass.

"Oh, Doris, that's Jenn's newspaper!"

"When you mentioned it, I remembered that Mr. Sebastian had me purchase a frame so that he could hang it in his office. I'm sure that Jenn saw this when she worked here years ago. I think she will love having this in her office."

"Definitely! I'm so happy that my friend is living her dream. After all that she has been through the past couple of years, it's wonderful that a little happiness is coming her way."

"She's lucky to have a friend like you." Doris pulled Mel into a quick hug. "Your friendship reminds me of the bond that Rachel and I share. I couldn't love her more if we'd been born into the same family."

"I'm thankful that Jenn and I have managed to stay connected all these years. It was more difficult before cell phones, email, and all the other forms of technology that we have today. We made it work though. Even when Jenn's children were young, we had at least one night a year away together. Most of the time, it occurred when she was here, visiting her parents. Paisley always made sure that we had our best-friend time."

"Paisley was so devoted to her daughters. I wish that her time with Amber could have been more pleasant. That poor girl can't seem to get her life together."

"I'm hoping that Amber will get straightened out soon. I think she was on a better road until Paisley passed so suddenly. Renee and Neil quickly got her back into rehab. I haven't asked Jenn about her in a while."

"Those three girls are each so different. Sometimes it's hard to imagine that they grew up in the same family." Doris glanced out the window. "What does Jenn drive?"

"A Jeep Grand Cherokee."

"I think she's arrived."

Mel walked to the door. Looking across the street, she saw Jenn parking her vehicle. Mel's heart skipped a few beats with excitement. Her best friend's big day was about to begin.

Chapter Four

Jenn

Jenn parked her vehicle in the public parking lot across the street from the *Serendipity Sun* office. Her heart was racing. *It does not seem real.* How could it be that the little girl who walked through those doors on a field trip would now have the word 'Publisher' after her name on the mast? Jenn tingled all over with excitement. A goofy grin was on her face that she would have to bite her bottom lip to conceal.

For once in her life, Jenn put herself first. It was a risk to invest every dime she had received in her divorce settlement on a business venture. Her post-college self would have taken the money and toured the world. The 'Helicopter Mom' version might have set up trust funds for the grandchildren who didn't yet exist. The most recent Jenn wanted her to hand the money over to a financial advisor to pad her retirement fund.

There was no doubt, *this* Jenn Halston was resurrected from the deepest corners of a little girl's heart. From the place where stories were created that only had happy endings. A hundred miles beyond the rainbow, where every dream came true.

A tap on the passenger side window jolted Jenn out of her thoughts and to the wide smile of her best friend. Jenn opened her door and stepped out, feeling the beams of the morning sun on her face like a spotlight.

"I came to work early so that I could be waiting inside your office when you walked through the door." Mel met Jenn at the front of the Jeep. "Do you realize you've been sitting out here for ten minutes? Why are you still out here, girlfriend? Your future is waiting beyond that front door."

"I know. I'm scared. I keep hearing my mother say, 'Be careful what you wish for.' I'm worried that once I go inside, it will become real, and the reality might ruin the dream."

"That's certainly possible, Jenn. It's also possible that it will be even better than you imagined." Mel moved behind Jenn and turned her to face the street. "I think the person who has the most control of that is you. The Jenn I know is fearless. She's nurtured this dream her whole life. She's put everyone else ahead of herself all these years. It's your turn, my friend. Go get it."

Jenn nodded, pulling her friend into a quick embrace before she looked both ways and crossed the street. Jenn didn't look back when she reached the door, she knew Mel was watching her every step of the way.

Taking a deep breath, she turned the knob of the old door and opened it to the inside.

"Good morning, Jenn! We're so happy you're here." Doris stood up from behind her desk with her arms outstretched in welcome.

Jenn looked up on the wall behind Doris and saw a big banner with 'Welcome Jenn' in big multi-colored letters. It surprised her.

The layout of the newspaper office was not new to Jenn. She had been there a few weeks earlier when she met the lawyer for Mr. Sebastian's estate to look at the property and go over the assets. She was surprised at how little the building had changed in the thirty years since she worked there. Old brown paneling still lined many walls. Those painted needed a fresh coat. Most of the flooring was tile with a few offices, including her own, that had industrial-style carpet. It would be a long time before she would be able to afford any remodeling. She did have in mind, though, a few touches, here and there, to breathe new life in the old structure.

"You've received all sorts of calls over the last few days." Doris came from behind the desk and led Jenn toward her office. "I've taken the liberty of setting up an email address for you and have encouraged some of the callers to email you. I've also sent the phone messages to you via email."

"That's very efficient, Doris. You must be quite computer savvy."

"It is something that I have endeavored to become proficient with. Just because I'm an older model doesn't mean I can't upgrade my software." Doris tapped her temple. "I may not understand how the computer does its work internally, but I can study and experiment to learn how to make it work for me."

"I'm truly fortunate to have you on my team, Doris. I hope you know that I'm depending on you to teach me what I need to know."

"Jenn, you are kind." Doris blushed, opening the door to Jenn's office. "I'm humbled by such a compliment. I'm ready to help you in every way I can. I wasn't sure whether I would continue to work here with the new owner. I promised Mr. Sebastian though that I would at least stay until someone bought it. I only imagined that I would help with a transition or that I might be shown the door even before then to make room for someone younger."

"Never!" Jenn shook her fist in the air. "No replacing Doris, ever!"

"Ever is a long time, Jenn." Doris stood in front of the door and motioned for Jenn to enter the office. "Welcome to your new office. Besides giving it a thorough cleaning and removing some of the personal items for Mr. Sebastian's family, the office was given a fresh coat of paint. All of Mr. Sebastian's files and general office items are where he left them. I considered cleaning out the files and can still do that, if you wish. I thought that, perhaps, you might find some of them useful or interesting."

Jenn looked around the room in amazement. Its appearance was virtually identical to her memories from thirty years ago when she worked at the newspaper. *I wish I could talk to that version of myself.*

"I'm sure I will find lots of beneficial information. Maybe I can go through it gradually and weed out the things I don't think I'll need."

"Certainly. We can get you some boxes for the things you want to throw out."

"Oh, I can bring some boxes from home. I've got lots from my move." Jenn walked toward the desk.

"I guess you would. I forgot about that." Doris began to leave the room. "There's a mini fridge in the corner. I've stocked it with some assorted beverages. There's also a Keurig coffee maker, in case you want some coffee."

"Somehow, it's hard to imagine Mr. Sebastian using a Keurig. I remember him having an old Mr. Coffee."

"You have a good memory. That was his standard; it was a 12-cup model. He made a new pot every morning and drank it all day until it was empty." Doris took hold of the doorknob and began to pull the door closed. "I had an extra Keurig at my house. I'll be right out here if you need me."

Without another word, Doris began closing the door behind her.

"Oh, I'm going to need you, Miss Doris." Jenn spoke loudly, and then whispered. "I'm going to need all of the help I can get."

The morning passed like a blur as Jenn combed through dozens and dozens of messages and files. Mel brought her a deli sandwich midday. Jenn ate her lunch at her desk with the office door open so she could hear the office sounds—the whirl of the copier that stood in the back corner, the ring of the phone system with continuous phone calls, the clang of the bell that hung over the front door. One voice caught her attention, making her stand up from her desk.

Jenn followed the sound of the male voice out of her office and into the lobby. A whispered gasp escaped her lips when she saw a tall, dark, middle-aged man in a police uniform standing in front of Doris' desk. There was something quite familiar about the man. *It can't be.* In an instant, she was transported back in time to the same lobby decades earlier, when a man in an Army dress uniform stood in the same spot.

"I'm here to see Jenny—." The man stopped talking and turned in her direction as his shortened version of her given name rolled off his tongue.

Jenn became slightly dizzy, and the world tilted for a moment, flashing before her eyes was a younger version of this man, so handsome, it took her breath. Surely, it could not be the same one she knew so long ago. A smile slowly replaced the man's somber expression confirming what Jenn knew in her heart.

"Randy."

Still standing in the doorway of her office, it was all Jenn could say. Her feet did not want to allow her to move. Glancing in Doris' direction, she could see the older woman was in rapt attention, eyes darting back and forth between Jenn and Randy, waiting for what would happen next.

"I heard that you bought the newspaper and were moving back. I wanted to be the first to welcome you to Serendipity." Randy did not move from his spot in the foyer of the small lobby.

Jenn's thoughts flew back to a day shortly after she graduated from college when she was a new feature writer for the newspaper. She came walking toward the front from the pressroom in the back and saw Randy standing in the lobby in his full-dress Army uniform. The sight had taken her breath then as it did now.

The blaring sound of a dispatch call coming in on the radio clipped to Randy's left hip broke the spell. Randy immediately lifted the radio to his face, made a brief reply, and returned it in one fluid move.

"I've got to go." Randy turned back to Jenn. "Welcome Home, Jenny. It's good to have you back."

"Bye, Randy. It's great to see you." Jenn was too shocked to say much more.

With a tip of his uniform hat to Doris, Randy disappeared out the door.

"Age has only made that man handsomer." Still looking out the doorway, Doris verbalized what Jenn was thinking. "He is such a good human. I don't know what our town would do without him."

Jenn became lost in memories again. It was a surreal feeling.

"I've seen that same look on your face before." Doris smiled. "Only you were standing in this doorway." Doris pointed to the door over her right shoulder that led to the back of the building.

"I remember that day."

"Same boy, same girl. Then, as now, he left too quickly and didn't get to convey what he came to say." Doris went back to opening the mail on her desk.

"I don't remember him leaving quickly that day." Jenn walked to the large front desk that Doris occupied. "He came to drop off a press release about completing his first stint in the Army and to have his photo made to go with the article."

"Mmm, hmmm. Yes, he did those things." Doris did not look up at Jenn.

"Was there something else that he came in for?" Jenn leaned over the desk to try and make eye contact with Doris.

"I guess you'll have to ask Randy that." Doris glanced briefly at Jenn.

"Why would I ask him such a question all these years later?"

"Because now I've piqued your curiosity and the girl you were then wants to know."

"I suspect that you already know the answer to that question, Doris. Why don't you tell me?"

"My answer would only be speculative, not concrete facts like you could learn if you asked Randy. Remember what Mr. Sebastian used to say."

"The facts deserve the work." Jenn had never forgotten the man's mantra. Now those words stared at her in cross stitch from behind a frame in her office. A creation of Doris', no doubt, which remained after Mr. Sebastian's passing.

"It certainly doesn't matter what Randy's intentions were for coming here then. I'm sure it had nothing to do with me. Therefore, it's really none of my business." Jenn turned away from the desk to walk back to her office.

"Perhaps." Doris muttered under her breath, continuing to open the mail. "Perhaps not."

Jenn kept walking, not turning around until she reached her doorway. Looking back at the receptionist, while closing her office door, Jenn could see a mischievous smile cross the woman's face for a moment, before the sound of an incoming phone call drew Doris' attention back to business.

"She knows something." Jenn muttered once she'd returned to her desk. "Like Mr. Sebastian, Doris will make me find out for myself."

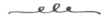

Near the end of her first official day as publisher of the *Serendipity Sun*, Jenn asked Doris to gather the staff in the middle of the building for a brief meeting. Many years previously, when Jenn worked there as a young woman, the area was divided into several cubicles for those who worked in advertising. Jenn noticed that the bustling department she'd known was now down to two people.

Walking around that area and the space behind it, Jenn reminisced about those days. She remembered a hum of busy advertising salespeople talking on the phone. Long before computers dominated the work, graphics and layout staff physically put the news and advertising on large sheets of paper which would be sent to a large camera, and then those negatives were ultimately burned onto plates to go on the press. There was always someone moving around, the chatter of co-workers talking, or possibly swearing if something or someone was wrong.

Jenn was struck by the quiet, it was eerily quiet. The lack of sound was sad. There were less people working in each department and all of them were stationed at computers. The loud press was silent in the back of the building. The *Serendipity Sun* was printed in another location and shipped back to town twice a week.

Gazing at the area which she remembered housing the darkroom and big press cameras, Jenn smiled to herself remembering the interesting people who once filled the space. In her memory, she could hear the hearty laugh of Mr. Charles, the old pressman who'd long since passed, and the sarcastic comments of Mr. Garland, the persnickety man who laid out every page of the newspaper for over thirty years. *I will miss them.* Jenn longed to travel back in time to the newspaper as it was then.

"Miss Halston, are you ready for us?"

Doris' formal comment interrupted Jenn's memories. She turned to find a small group of people standing in the open area of the room. Taking a deep breath, Jenn put on a big smile while walking to join them.

"Yes, Doris, thank you. Hello, everyone. As I'm sure most of you by now are aware, I'm Jennifer Halston and I've recently purchased the *Serendipity Sun*. Please call me Jenn. Over the next few weeks, you may see my office door closed a lot as I try to learn what I need to know about our operation. I want you to know that even though you may see it closed, my door is always open to each of you. I'm anxious to hear your thoughts and ideas regarding how we can move forward together and become a stronger organization."

"Jenn, if you don't mind a suggestion, why don't you allow each of us to introduce ourselves and tell you what we do." Doris winked, shaking her head affirmatively.

"That's a wonderful idea. Why don't we start with you, Doris?" Jenn sat down in a nearby chair, motioning for everyone else to do the same.

"No one probably wants to hear my tired old story." Doris laughed softly, sitting in a chair that someone placed for her, directly across from Jenn. "My name is Doris Hudson. I came to work at the *Serendipity Sun* when I was in my early twenties. That was almost fifty years ago. I've spent my whole life working here and I can honestly say I've loved every minute of it. That's mostly because of the people whom I've worked with, including these fine folks who are here now."

Jenn looked around the room, watching the staff individually smile and nod at Doris. A little buzz of chatter ensued for a few moments. The group grew silent, causing the woman next to Doris to speak. Jenn thought the woman was probably close to her own age, but she didn't remember meeting her before.

"I'm Betsy Lawson. I've not worked here quite as many years as Doris, but I have been here most of my working life. I started when I was still in high school, helping Doris with the billing and bookkeeping. I returned after I finished business school. That was about thirty years ago. I currently oversee the advertising department. I handle most of the online sales and supervise any special sections we do."

"That's a lot of responsibility, Betsy." Jenn furrowed her brow, looking at Doris. "I worked here about thirty years ago. Did we work together?"

"Betsy is a few years younger than you, Jenn. When she was working here part-time during her high school years, you were probably in your latter years of college. If I remember correctly, she came to work here full-time after you left."

"I went to school just over the border in Sullivan County, but we really lived closer to the coastal towns than the heart of the county. Yes, it is a lot of responsibility, but I enjoy the work we do here. I hope you allow us to continue to do it."

"I need *everyone* as we move forward together. It seems like such a smaller staff than I worked with years ago."

"A lot of that has come with technology, Jenn. Mr. Sebastian tried to change with the times." Doris shook her head. "Sometimes the times changed him. He hated sending our paper to another operation to print. It became hard to find the parts to keep our press running and even harder to find someone who knew how to keep it going."

"When I first toured the building before I made the purchase, I was surprised to see that the press was still back there. The area looks like it's frozen in time, like a museum."

"Mr. Sebastian held out hope that we could one day resume printing our newspaper here again. He went to the expense of having a company to come in once a year to service the press and run it, so that it would remain in working order." Doris raised her eyes. "I suppose you will have to decide whether you want to continue the expense of having that done or try and sell the press."

"Another thing to learn about." Jenn forced a smile. "Who's next?"

"I'm Shaun Hardy. I'm the sportswriter and photographer. I've worked here less than two years. I learned last night that you went to school with my mother."

"Oh, what is your mother's name?" Jenn searched the young man's face to see if there were any features she might recognize.

"Lisa."

"Shaun, I think you're going to have to be more specific." Doris chuckled. "I'm sure Jenn has known several women named Lisa."

"Lisa Hardy."

"Your mother's maiden name, Shaun. Her name when she was going to school." Doris rolled her eyes.

"Oh, yeah, sorry. Lisa Patton."

"Goodness! I remember Lisa Patton. Lovely girl. She was Miss Serendipity one year. I think she went on to the state pageant."

"Yes, ma'am. Mom came in first runner up. She says that's why she married Dad. If she'd won, she would have ended up in Hollywood. Instead, she married her first date." Shaun smirked.

"Tom Hardy! It just hit me that Lisa dated Tom through most of our high school years." Jenn squinted her eyes while trying to think back. "Does your grandfather still own the hardware store?"

"No, Grandpa passed away when I was small. Dad has Hardy Hardware now."

"And you didn't want to help run the family business?"

"I've got an older brother who is doing that just fine. I'd rather write about football games and take photos of kids scoring points. I hope I get to continue to do that."

"I've been looking at some of the recent editions of the paper. You seem to be doing a fine job, Shaun. If it's not broke, we aren't going to fix it."

Jenn enjoyed seeing a broad smile come to the young man's face. In that smile, she saw the young Tom Hardy she remembered.

"My name is Ellie James." A young woman, perhaps in her late twenties, was sitting next to Shaun. "I work with Betsy. I sell advertising. I've worked here about four years."

"Ellie is a strong salesperson." Betsy spoke up. "I think she could certainly help us develop more accounts, if she had a little help. She has a large territory to cover."

"Do you agree, Ellie?" Jenn questioned the young woman.

"I think we could be the biggest newspaper in the region, if we could spend some time developing new accounts up and down the coast. Maybe even creating some guides for the Visitors Bureau to use."

Jenn's ears perked up, hearing the mention of Mel's office.

"I'd like to hear more about these ideas. Ellie, perhaps you and Betsy could put those ideas into a proposal that I could review. It sounds like there would need to be some work on the editorial side of that equation, too." Jenn looked at the others who hadn't spoken yet. "Who are my reporters?"

Two people, a man and a woman, raised their hands. The man looked to be in his twenties. The woman was, perhaps, in her forties.

"We do not have an editor, at this point, Jenn." Doris' expression was stern. "We've not been able to retain one during the transition. We've had several good editors through the years. One of them called a few weeks ago. I'd like to tell you about him, when you have time."

"Certainly. First, I'd like to hear from my existing editorial staff." Jenn nodded at the man and woman.

"I'll go first. I'm Helen Berry. I've been a newspaper reporter for my entire adult life. I've worked at this publication for almost ten years. Since there are just two of us now, Tyler and I cover all the beats. When we had more staff, I mainly handled government and business writing, and editorials." Helen nodded to Tyler.

"I'm Tyler Murphy. I came here fresh out of college about three years ago. I do most of the feature writing and handle the police beat. I, also, sometimes help Shaun cover some games."

"You three are juggling a lot of writing each week. Who does the layout of the paper?"

There was one person left who had not spoken. The woman raised her hand.

"I'm Marella Yarnell. I do all of the editorial layout and most of the graphic design for ads for Betsy. I've been here fifteen years."

"You are certainly a busy person, too." Jenn looked at each of the people she'd met. "It sounds like all of you are juggling a couple of jobs.

I'm sure that is because revenues have been tight. I know that it is hard to find good people who want to work in this industry these days. I want each of you to feel secure in your positions. Doris told me about each of you before I decided to purchase this newspaper. You can imagine that I needed to feel secure, too, about what I was investing in. We will no doubt still have some tight and hard weeks ahead. I want to give you my assurance though that I'm committed to making improvements and increasing our staff when we can figure out how to offset that with more revenue. I would like for each of you to take some time over the next few weeks to think about that and email me any ideas you have on how we can do this together. This is a strong team. I don't intend to merely own the *Serendipity Sun*. I will be an active working member of this team."

Jenn stood up, feeling she needed to reinforce what she wanted to convey.

"Some of my fondest working memories occurred here years ago. I know how hard the days can be. Skills I learned here have shaped my entire career. It's a dream come true to be back. It's beyond my wildest dreams that I will be in the driver's seat. I expect excellence. In return, I will give you nothing less."

After the meeting ended, one-by-one the staff left the building with only Doris remaining. Jenn came out of her office while Doris was shutting down her computer.

"I think the meeting went well. They all seem like wonderful people."

"They truly are. Each one has their own strengths and weaknesses, like we all do. These different people come together each week and put out a great product that our readers enjoy on Wednesday and Saturday."

"I want them to feel secure. I can't ensure that security without their dedication."

"They are concerned about losing their jobs, Jenn. A few of the potential buyers had the nerve to have conversations about eliminating all the existing staff right in front of them. When I heard that you were interested in buying the paper, I gave them all a pep talk. I told them that if Jenn buys it, everything will be okay." Small in stature, Doris had a commanding presence. Her conviction made you believe.

"I hope you're right, Doris. We've got to get more revenue flowing."

"I suggest that you listen to Betsy's and Ellie's ideas. I think they are also correct that we need another salesperson. The other position I think you need to fill sooner rather than later is the Editor role. Our reporters need some help. They can handle creating the stories. We need someone to polish them, handle the editorial page, and run interference for touchy issues."

"I agree. Tell me about the former editor you mentioned that called recently."

"His name is Lyle Livingston. Lyle moved here to help care for his father about a dozen years ago. His father's illness progressed slowly. Lyle was the Editor for several years. After his father passed, he stayed around until the estate was settled and the property sold. Mr. Sebastian was sad to lose him. We've not had anyone as good since."

"Where did he move to?"

"Out West somewhere, I believe it was Nevada. I remember forwarding some mail to him once."

"Why do you think he's interested in coming back?"

"I'm not sure. He said that he thought the newspaper might have been bought by a larger media group and wondered if they needed someone to run it. He's interested in moving back to the area. He didn't say why. I always got the impression that he liked living here. I don't think he is currently working for a newspaper. Perhaps his circumstances have changed."

"I assume that he's left some contact information."

"I wouldn't let him get off the phone without doing so." Doris took a piece of paper off a small corkboard that was hidden under the top of her desk, handing it to Jenn. "You also have an email message about him calling."

"Your emails are fabulous, Doris. I hope I get to work here long enough to read them all."

Jenn chuckled until she saw a scowl cross Doris' face.

"That's not funny. Don't even joke about leaving, Jenn. We need you." Doris took hold of Jenn's hand, squeezing hard.

"Don't worry, Doris. I've basically invested my entire future in this operation. I've got to make it work."

"Well, today you met the people who will help you do that."

"I already knew one of them. Aunt Rachel has great taste in friends."

"Rachel has a fabulous niece." Doris put the strap of her purse over her shoulder. "If you can hire Lyle and get one new ad rep, I think you will see a big difference in everything about this operation."

"And you will delay your retirement a few more years."

"Honestly, Jenn, I will probably be sitting at this desk on my last day of life. My financial situation is fine. I truly love it that much."

Chapter Five

Jenn

"Are you going to work late on your first day?" Mel held the door open for Doris as she left.

"Tell her about it, Mel. This is a marathon, not a sprint. She didn't even eat all the sandwich you brought her." Doris waved. "Goodnight, girls."

"Goodnight, Doris. Thank you for making my first day fabulous." Jenn gave Doris a big smile.

Doris blew kisses before she began to cross the street to the parking lot.

"Did you have a good day?" Mel walked into the foyer.

"It was a great day, except the overwhelming part." Jenn closed the front door, locking it.

"When was it overwhelming?"

"Pretty much all day." Jenn laughed. "I'm kidding, sort of. It's a lot to take in. I went through a ton of the files that were left in the office. I met the staff. I am beginning to understand where the holes are. The holes are going to cost me some money."

"You've got to spend it to make it. Or so they say."

"Words uttered by the woman who lures people to the area to spend their money and leave. Someone mentioned an idea that involved the Visitors Bureau."

"I bet that was Ellie. She's talked to me about a special section that would be given to our visitors, once they are here, to help them explore the region."

"Interesting. I assume it would be paid for by advertising."

"Since it is Ellie's idea and she sells advertising, I would assume you are correct." Mel cackled.

"Okay, smarty pants. Be nice to your friend. Her brain is tired. It's full of lots of new stuff."

"Okay, girlfriend. If Doris is right and you didn't eat your lunch, your brain probably needs some nourishment."

"True. I can probably throw something together for an easy dinner."

"I've already solved that problem. I asked Mom to make us some of her chicken noodle soup and rolls." Mel rubbed her stomach.

"Oh, your mother's soup is wonderful. It's been a long time since I've had it. That's exactly what I need after today."

"That's what I thought. She agreed. I'll go pick it up on my way to get Princess Mia. I believe that Mia would like to see her 'Auntie Jenn' and her new pal, Jasper. Mia feels like she was left out of the festivities this weekend."

Princess Mia was Mel's sweet little dog. The solid black Pomeranian-Poodle mix was a rescue animal that Mel adopted several years previously. Jenn wasn't sure which one was more devoted to the other, Mel or Mia.

"I cannot imagine that Mia would have enjoyed the countless back-and-forth trips we made from the moving trailer to the house. She would enjoy taking a walk on the beach with her new buddy, Jasper. Her mother would, too."

"That sounds like a wonderful ending to a great day. I can catch you up on what I've learned so far, including a visitor I had today."

"I'm intrigued. Let me out of this building and get yourself out of here soon."

Mel and Jenn walked toward the door. Jenn turned the bolt lock and opened the door.

"I'll just be a few minutes. I want to gather a few files that I can read before I go to bed tonight."

"Don't dilly-dally. Mia and I will be upset if you're not there to greet us when we arrive."

"I'll beat you there, I promise."

Jenn locked the door again after Mel left. Taking a deep breath, she looked around the front office area while walking toward her office. She hadn't taken the time to look at every plaque and framed photo that was left from Mr. Sebastian's time. For some reason, one framed item in the corner farthest from her desk drew her attention. Moving closer to it, Jenn gasped when the contents became clear. It was one of the copies of her own version of the *Serendipity Sun,* the newspaper she created after her third-grade field trip to the newspaper. She didn't remember seeing this in his office years ago. Then again, she always went straight to his desk to receive the critique of whatever article or editorial she'd written that week. She wouldn't have dared to take the time to look at anything on the walls.

"Dreams do come true." Jenn whispered. "Now, I've got to concentrate on keeping the dream alive."

"Do you remember Randy Nave?"

After her second bowl of Mel's mother's soup and two rolls, Jenn wished she had put on pants with an elastic waistband.

"Police Chief Randy Nave? Sure, he stopped in the office one day last week to see if I had a map of Virginia. He must be planning a trip."

"Oh, silly me, I forget that you've lived here a while."

"Just my whole life. Is this the yeast rolls talking, or did you fall and hit your head today?" Mel leaned over the table, staring intently at Jenn.

"I'm tired. I guess my brain is fried from all the stuff I read today." Jenn started to stack the dirty dishes on her side of the table, refusing to make eye contact with Mel.

"Oh, no, you're trying to hide something. Have you been wondering about Randy since you returned to Serendipity? Is that old crush reviving? He's as handsome as ever."

"I know." Realizing what she'd said, Jenn put her hand over her mouth.

"You do? How do you know that?"

"Randy came into the office today. What do you mean 'old crush'? When did I have a crush on Randy Nave?" Jenn picked up the plates, rising from the table.

"You've probably had a crush on him since you first met, probably in your backyard on Danner Street. Did you say that Randy came into the newspaper office today? Your first official day back in Serendipity? That's interesting."

"Yes, he must have had some business there. I saw him briefly." Jenn took the dishes into the kitchen.

"What did he have to say?" Mel followed, carrying her dishes.

"Randy was polite. He welcomed me back. I'm sure that is something he does as the Police Chief. He welcomes new business owners to the community."

"I don't think so. I've never heard of him making a point to welcome a new business. It's not as if the Police Department is on the Welcoming Committee or anything. That's usually done by the Chamber of Commerce or the Mayor or even me."

"As Police Chief, I'm sure he wants to have a good relationship with the Publisher of the local newspaper."

"I bet he does." Mel smiled from ear-to-ear.

"Stop it, Mel. I'm sure it was merely a polite gesture."

"Jenn, I've worked with Randy on many different projects and initiatives since he moved back to Serendipity, a dozen or more years ago. Yes, Randy is cooperative and professional. He's also a tough police chief. Even in a small town like ours, there's a lot more crime than anyone wants to admit, especially since we are a transient community. Through the travel season, our population doubles. Most of those people simply want to enjoy themselves with their family and friends. A few enjoy themselves too much."

"Yes, he's a serious person doing a serious job." Jenn loaded the dinner dishes into the dishwasher.

"Exactly. He's also doing it with limited resources. Randy doesn't have a lot of time for social calls. He made a point to come to your office today." Mel folded her arms in front of her, leaning against the counter.

"If that's true, I appreciate it. Randy is an old friend."

"A handsome, eligible bachelor old friend who *always* had a soft spot for you."

"Like a sister. He thought of me like a sister. We were buddies." Despite what Jenn was saying to Mel, she could feel her temperature rising and her pulse quickening.

"I told you then and you wouldn't listen to me. I'll tell you again now. Randy Nave saw you as more than a sister. For some reason, he never acted on it. But there were many of us who could see his feelings. Maybe he didn't even realize them himself."

"Even if that was true, which I don't think it is, that was a long time ago. We were young. We've both experienced many things since then. I'm recently divorced, so I'm not interested in a relationship yet. I've invested almost all my financial resources in a gamble on a dream. I've got to stay focused."

"I understand that." Mel walked over to Jenn and took hold of her hands. "Promise me though that you won't give up on the idea that you could have a happy relationship. You've spent a lot of years with someone who wasn't worthy of you. There! I've said it! Simon was not worthy of you. You can't turn back the hands of time. You can choose better for the future."

"What about you, Mel? When are you going to take that advice?"

Mel released Jenn's hands and stepped back. "I'm always on the lookout for Mr. Right. I've been looking for him all my life. I've not found him yet. But I've also not given up hope that he might be around the next corner."

"I hope so." Jenn pulled Mel into a hug. "You deserve someone to sweep you off your feet."

"Until then, I'm going to bask in the joy of finally having my best friend nearby and cheer her on in a new adventure."

"Fabulous! And feed me like this any time you want to. Now, let's take Princess Mia and Jasper for a walk on the beach and you can tell me everything you know about my new staff."

"Did you hear that, Mia?"

The small dog scurried toward them, wagging her tail in excitement. Her new buddy, Jasper, was not far behind.

Jenn and Mel spent about an hour leisurely walking on the beach. Mel shared many stories about the people Jenn would be working with. It gave Jenn renewed confidence that she was surrounded by a strong group of professionals who would work together as a team to make the newspaper even more successful.

The sun was beginning to set when the beach house came back into view. Just before it, the Oasis glowed with many lights beaming from within.

"I don't suppose you've heard anymore from Parker Bentley." Mel looked in the direction of the large beach house.

"Believe it or not, that was only yesterday when I saw him."

"That's right. Goodness, you've crammed a lot of different things into these last two days that you've been here."

"Indeed. It's been a whirlwind. I've got to slow down and let it all sink in."

"Walks on this beach will be good for that." Mel twirled with her arms outstretched, splashing along the edge of the water. "I envy you having the beach as your backyard."

Just then, a seagull swooped overhead, landing on the water's edge in front of them. Jenn watched it for a moment, marveling at how comfortable the bird was so close to humans. The crashing of the waves lulled her into relaxation. She hoped for many such moments with her friend.

"You need to consider yourself right at home here, Mel. Honestly, I wouldn't be opposed to you moving in with me. There are several extra bedrooms and plenty of space."

Jenn joined Mel in her twirling and splashing. They both began giggling like teenagers. Mia and Jasper skirted the edge of the water, seemingly unsure of getting their paws wet. The women's laughter grew in intensity until Jenn turned around and saw someone approaching them.

"Hello, ladies. It's a beautiful evening for a walk."

Hearing the voice, Mel turned around from her splashing.

"Oh, Parker, hello. You've caught us playing in the water." Jenn laughed, giving Mel a side-eye glance.

"Playing in the water is a great thing. Those little fellows seemed to be enjoying it, too." Parker looked down at the dogs.

"Parker, this is my dear friend, Melinda Snow. We've been friends since childhood. She's the Director of the Serendipity Visitors Bureau on Main Street."

"Hello, Melinda. I'm Parker Bentley. I own that glowing monstrosity up there." Parker pointed to the Oasis. "It's a beacon to high electric bills."

"Hi, Parker, please call me Mel."

"Mel, I might like to have a chat with you about how viable the Oasis might be as a vacation rental property."

"Oh, there's no doubt that it would make a great rental location. I'm sure you could get top dollar for it."

"Is that what you've decided to do with the Oasis?" Jenn wondered what that would mean for her new home.

"I've not decided anything yet. I'm trying to get a good handle on what my options might be. Selling it would probably be the easiest solution. I can't seem to wrap my mind around that yet. I guess my family connection to this property is stronger than I thought." Parker made eye contact with Jenn. "I've got some wonderful memories from years ago. Most of them include Jenn."

After a few moments, Parker broke his gaze.

"It's nice to meet you, Parker. Feel free to stop by my office, if you'd like more information about the market for vacation rentals."

"I'll do that, Mel." Parker nodded. "Jenn, it's nice to see you again. Maybe we can share a meal sometime soon and catch up on the last fifty years."

"Fifty years, that sounds like a lifetime." Jenn shook her head.

"And, yet, standing here on this beach, it seems like yesterday." Parker smiled. "Goodnight."

Jenn and Mel continued to walk toward home not speaking until Parker was out of earshot.

"I see why you talked about that little boy so much, Jenn. Parker is charming. He obviously remembers you fondly."

"That seems like two lifetimes ago. I don't know how I feel about him selling or even renting the Oasis. These two homes have always been in our families. It doesn't seem right for that to change. It would certainly open the door for more development in this little corner of paradise."

"First Randy and now Parker, I'm getting rather jealous of all these handsome and charming men who are swarming around you."

"There might be another one. Doris said that one of the previous editors wants his old job back. A man named Lyle Livingston."

"Oh, my goodness, I certainly remember him. There's another charmer. You know him, too."

"I do? He wasn't working at the newspaper when I did back then."

"No, but you knew of him in high school." Mel's wide-eyed look did not give Jenn any clues to the man's identity. "You knew Lyle Livingston. He was from a nearby high school. Remember 'Lyle the Smile?'"

"You're kidding me?" Jenn put her hand over her mouth in shock. "I didn't remember his last name. I would never have figured out that was him. I don't remember you mentioning him when he was in the Editor role. Being right down the street, you must have worked with him."

"I did. He was great to work with, very cooperative. I didn't become too friendly with him though. He had a girlfriend, an older woman, who was very standoffish and didn't like him being too friendly with other women. Several of us in the business community got that vibe from her at different social functions she would attend with Lyle. He seemed oblivious to her behavior. We left well enough alone."

"Is she the reason he left here?"

"Probably so. You may know that he came here to take care of his father." Mel paused, narrowing her eyes like she was trying to remember something. "I can't remember what her name was. Several of us called her Cruella."

"Oh, Mel, that's not nice."

"Hey, it fit. You had to know her." Mel shrugged her shoulders. "Anyway, after Lyle's father passed, Cruella got on her broom and flew back to where she came from. Lyle wasn't far behind."

With Mia on her heels, Mel began to climb the steps to the house. Jenn followed with Jasper.

"Well, perhaps that relationship has ended. Doris said Lyle wants to move back to the area. She's encouraging me to call him. She thinks he's the leadership we need in the newsroom."

"Lyle is a great newsman, no doubt. Without Cruella, he's probably a different person, too. When he was here, that smile was certainly still intact." Mel winked.

"Lyle the Smile in my newsroom. Wouldn't that be something?"

When Jenn reached the top of the stairs from the beach, she saw Gladys waving from her own deck. The woman motioned for Jenn to come over. Jenn gave Gladys a thumbs up sign.

"Mel, Gladys just motioned for me to come over. I haven't visited her yet. Would you like to join me?

"As much as I would love to have a hug and a chat with the craziest celebrity lookalike we have in Serendipity, Mia and I better get home. This is only Monday, remember?" Mel gathered up her belongings. "Please tell the Divine Miss Gladys that I send my regards."

"I will certainly do that. Thanks so much for helping me celebrate my first day. Please tell your mother how much I enjoyed the soup. I will make a point to stop by and see your folks one day soon."

"If you can catch them between vacations. I believe their passports are burning a hole in their pockets." Mel moved toward the doorway. "Mia, tell your buddy Jasper goodbye. It's time to go." The word 'go' made Mia's tail begin wagging with excitement.

Leaving Jasper behind on his big pillow, Jenn followed Mel and Mia out, waving goodbye as Mel drove away.

Following a path of eclectic stone pavers designed by Gladys, Jenn admired the immaculate landscaping that surrounded her neighbor's home. Jenn always loved the multi-layered small decks which led to a large one that surrounded the ocean side of the house. While it was not the handiwork of Jenn's father, it had been designed by Renee's husband, Neil, and built by a team from the family's construction company. Gladys had owned the property for over two decades and had been a close friend of Paisley's during her final years. That closeness was reflected in Renee calling Gladys the oldest Halston sister, knocking herself out of the role by the loving neighbor who was Renee's senior by a few years.

"I've restrained my hugs for as long as I can!" Gladys shouted in excitement when she came onto her deck through the opened sliding glass door. "I've had to do strong meditations to the gods of patience since you arrived on Saturday night. I've worn my ceremonial garb in your honor."

Jenn held out her arms to Gladys while taking in the vibrantly colored outfit she was wearing. The flowing kaftan in bright, earthy colors had geometric shapes throughout the fabric. It gently moved with the breeze as the woman walked. The movement made Jenn a little dizzy. The feeling was quickly forgotten when Gladys pulled Jenn into a hug. Gladys' hugs were powerful. Jenn felt like it was almost a healing experience to be embraced by her. You had to be careful not to get too close to her jewelry though. The chunky pieces, made mostly of wood carved and painted by the woman herself, could be painful if you happened to get knocked in the head by one. Jenn's mother often joked that Gladys weighed ten pounds less without her heavy jewelry and the bright clogs that frequently adorned her feet.

"I have felt the welcome vibes you've been sending me, Gladys. They have been full of love and papaya juice." Jenn giggled, remembering that all of Gladys' signature beverages contained the tropical fruit.

"I am currently in the season of watermelon, my dear." Gladys released Jenn from her embrace, holding her at arms' length. "I'm still mad at the papaya for not giving our dear Paisley the nutrients she needed to stay with us."

Jenn remembered that during her last week of life, her mother spoke of the evening cocktails she enjoyed with Gladys.

"We drank the juice nightly on your deck." Gladys closed her eyes, shaking her head.

"Don't blame the juice, Gladys. Mother enjoyed it immensely."

"Your mother enjoyed the vodka, Jenn." Suddenly, Gladys' eyes bugged out with surprise. "Maybe it was bad potatoes."

"What?"

"Maybe the vodka was made with bad potatoes!" Gladys face palmed herself. "I had not considered that."

"Oh, Gladys, I don't think your beverages had anything to do with Mother's sudden departure. Her heart was ready to be reunited with the love of her life."

"Your father was indeed a heartthrob." Gladys raised her eyebrows, grinning. "He had a little James Dean swagger. I am happy that Paisley and Marshall are reunited. I wish he could have returned to his former address instead of her traveling to his new one."

"Me, too, Gladys. Me, too."

Chapter Six

Doris

"Yes, Mr. Arnaz, we have plenty of extra copies of Wednesday's edition. You can stop by anytime during our normal business hours and purchase them. If you want to let me know how many you would like to have, I'll have them here at my desk. Congratulations, on your daughter's wedding. Thank you for calling."

Doris leaned back in her chair and looked down the hallway that led to the newsroom. She could see Shaun Hardy, the sportswriter, typing at this computer.

"Shaun, could you come here when you have a moment?"

Shaun pulled the earbud out of his ear. Looking around a moment, he finally saw Doris waving at him. He jumped up and walked to the lobby.

"Hey, Doris, did you need me?"

"Yes, Shaun. Mr. Arnaz, you know him, don't you?"

"Yes, he teaches Spanish and Chemistry at the high school and is also a baseball coach."

"Yes, that's the one. His daughter got married a few weeks ago."

"Oh, yes, Josephina is beautiful. I tried to get her to go out with me a few years ago. She turned me down multiple times. I think she married Arnie Davenport. It's a good thing that guys don't take girls' last names. He'd be Arnie Arnaz now." Shaun laughed heartily at his own joke.

"Yes, Shaun, it would a tragedy." Doris shook her head. "Let's get back on topic, shall we? The wedding announcement with Josephina's photo was in yesterday's paper. Mr. Arnaz will be coming in here before the week is over to buy ten copies. Could you go to the backroom and get those for me?"

"Sure, Doris. I'll be right back." Shaun started walking away, then stopped. "Did you say last Wednesday's paper or yesterday's?"

"Yesterday's."

"Gotcha." Shaun made a pistol-shooting gesture, winking before he quickly headed to the back.

Doris continued to shake her head, chuckling under her breath.

"What are you laughing about, Doris?" Betsy, the advertising director, asked as she came around the corner.

"Sometimes, I forget how young some people can be. I don't normally feel too old myself until one of those moments."

"I hear you. The other day, I was listening to the oldies station in my cubicle. The station was playing an hour of Elvis' music. Ellie came in and asked me if Elvis Presley ever actually existed or if he was just a character from history. I couldn't wrap my mind around what she was even asking me. Maybe the generations that were before ours had strange conversations with us, too, when we were young."

"I don't think they were quite that confusing. All I can say is, bless their hearts."

"Spoken like the fine Southern lady that you are."

Betsy and Doris laughed together. A few moments later, Shaun appeared again with a stack of newspapers in his arms.

"Here you go, Doris. I've got to head over to the high school to take some photos of the teams practicing for this weekend's games."

"Thank you, Shaun. It's a beautiful day for you to get some good photos."

After he went back to his office, Betsy resumed talking.

"I've barely seen Jenn outside of her office since our meeting Monday afternoon. Is she okay?"

"Yes. She's been carefully going over the bookkeeping to see how the revenue and expenditures have been playing out over the months during the transition." Doris glanced around, lowering her voice. "Jenn is taking to heart what we've suggested to her. I think she wants to try to bring one person on in the newsroom and one in advertising. She is trying to be as cautious as she can. This business didn't come with a big nest egg of money, you know."

"I understand. I'm thankful that she's willing to even consider our suggestions. I've never mentioned this, and I bet Jenn will not realize it since she's lived away for so long, but my sister-in-law, Cecile, has been the bookkeeper for Jenn's father's construction company for years. She's mainly worked with Jenn's brother-in-law, Neil, but she fondly remembers Marshall Halston from her early years with the company."

"Oh, I don't think I've ever met your sister-in-law."

"No, I wouldn't think so. The construction company office is now about an hour west of here. That move occurred during Marshall's years. Neil has grown the company's construction projects in the direction of Raleigh."

"Interesting."

"I tell you this because the Halston family has a reputation for being astute businesspeople."

"Absolutely. Even though Jenn has spent her career working for other companies, I expect her to have that same level of business savvy that her family is known for. She's always been one of the sharper pencils in the box."

Betsy laughed heartily.

"What's so funny?"

"I can't imagine what Ellie and Shaun might think that expression meant."

"Touché, my dear. That's a conversation for another day."

"Doris, how would I find some of the editorials that Lyle Livingston wrote while he was Editor?"

She's stealthy like a cat. Doris was going to have to figure out a way to better detect when Jenn left her office. The woman's steps were so light that it was the third time this week that Jenn was at Doris' desk before she realized it.

"I remember when I worked here, we had bound copies in the room Mr. Sebastian called 'the morgue.' I went back to where I thought I remembered that room was located earlier today and found the area is now a breakroom."

"Yes, you are correct. Mr. Sebastian begrudgingly embraced technology. Mainly because we couldn't get the newspapers bound in those big books anymore. He subscribed to the microfilm service that puts all our editions on those little film things that you look at on a special machine."

"What happened to the bound copies?"

"They were donated to the historical society and are in their research library."

"Oh, well, that's good." Jenn paused for a moment. "So, where do I find the microfilm files? Do we have a machine here?"

"Absolutely! I'm sorry that I do too much explaining and not enough answering. The microfilm machine is in the newsroom in the far back corner. If you remember, it's where the machine was in the newsroom that the typesetters used to type your stories."

"The Comp Junior."

"You have an excellent memory, Jenn. It's been a long time since one of those was around here." Doris nodded. "That's where the microfilm reader is located. Helen is quite proficient with its use. We have every edition of the *Serendipity Sun* in our archive. It has a good search function. You should be able to find all of Lyle's articles and editorials."

"Excellent! I'll go see Helen."

"I think you fill find that Lyle's editorials were thorough and thought-provoking. He put the newspaper in the middle of several controversial local issues. It didn't necessarily make him any friends doing that, but he earned a lot of respect for giving in-depth looks at both sides. You will find it interesting, Jenn, since you knew Mr. Sebastian, that he and Lyle would often butt heads on the stance that the paper would take. But Lyle could be so thorough in why he was taking a certain side that often Mr. Sebastian would allow him to be the voice of the newspaper, even when he disagreed with him."

"That's quite an open-minded position for the Publisher to take. I'll have to ponder that for the future. In the meantime, I'm going to do some quick studying about Mr. Livingston. I remember my mother saving me some of his editorials. I don't remember what the issues were or his writing style."

"Paisley was a fan of his. I remember her and Rachel having some long discussions about some of the positions Lyle took."

"Good to know." Jenn looked up at the clock above the front door. "I'm supposed to be somewhere this afternoon. It's Thursday, isn't it? I feel like I've forgotten something."

"You have a three o'clock appointment with your new attorney. Mr. Crewe's office is on the corner of Jefferson and Hedrick Streets. I suggest that you be on time. His waiting list is long. He is continuing to handle the newspaper's affairs out of respect for Mr. Sebastian."

"How in the world did you find out that information so quickly?"

"It's my job, Jenn. Keeping up with your calendar is one of my top responsibilities. That's why I set up your calendar. I have the same information on my computer. If you don't want me—"

Jenn held up her hand. "Thanks, Doris. I knew I needed you here with me. You are proving that every day."

Doris watched Jenn go back to her office. Within a few minutes, she came out with a briefcase full of files in one hand and her purse in the other.

"Doris, I don't think I will be back today. After my meeting, I'm going to head home. Text me if anything comes up. Otherwise, I'll see you in the morning. Have a good evening."

"Hope your meeting goes well. I'll hold the fort down."

Jenn turned to open the door.

"One more thing, Jenn. The Police Chief called today and asked if he could have a meeting with you. I'll send you his email address. I told him that you would have to look at your calendar."

Jenn did not respond, just smiled, and walked out the door.

Doris watched Jenn cross the street through the glass front door. A relaxed feeling came over her. In only four days, Doris saw Jenn begin to transform from anxious new owner to educated entrepreneur. There would no doubt be ups and downs. That was inevitable. But Doris was convinced that Jenn had the backbone and integrity to take the newspaper in the direction it needed to go.

Doris hoped that Jenn would also recognize her need to create a happy life for herself. Rachel's version of Jenn's life with Simon was less than complimentary. She knew it wasn't in her job description, but Doris thought she might need to help keep up with that calendar as well.

Chapter Seven

Jenn

"I've studied the past finances of our company and the future financial projections. This information has led me to the conclusion that the suggestions some of you have given me are beneficial for our future."

Midday Friday, after the deadlines for the Saturday edition had been met and the 'submit' button had been pushed for the final version to be sent to the press, Jenn called her team together again with a fresh pot of coffee, prepared by Doris, and some mouth-watering baked goods Jenn picked up at The Frosted Goddess, a cool bakery in the downtown.

Jenn glanced around the room to see several smiles, some nodding heads, and a couple of confused looks.

"I'm planning to hire two people as soon as possible. Someone to help Betsy and Ellie with advertising, and an editor for our newsroom."

"Will this be an entry level position in advertising?" Betsy raised her hand.

"Not necessarily. I think the suggestions that you and Ellie put together are some great ideas for how we can increase advertising. It seems to me that we probably need someone with at least a few years of sales experience to be able to see this growth in a reasonable amount of time. It may not be crucial that the person have advertising sales experience, but the best candidate should have a proven track record in sales."

"I'm happy to hear you say that, Jenn. There will certainly be a learning curve for whoever is hired. If we must completely train someone the principles and practices of sales, it will take us months to see a return on the investment." Betsy looked at Ellie, smiling and nodding.

"Exactly. First thing next week, I would like you to draft a job description and advertisement for this position. Let's make a goal to try to hire someone within a month. Based on my experience, I have some suggestions about where we might post this ad for some strong results. We'd certainly want to use some local and regional outlets, including our own newspaper, as well."

"We won't let you down." Ellie beamed. "Thank you for taking our suggestions seriously."

"I've spent most of my life in the corporate world. One thing I've observed repeatedly is that the best ideas come from the people who are doing the work. I cannot promise that I will be able to carry your ideas out in every situation since someone must make the tough calls, but I do promise that I will always listen to them."

Stopping for a moment to take a sip of her coffee, Jenn did a quick glance around the room. Doris was busy taking notes. The three members of the news staff seemed a little nervous. Barely in her view was a woman in the back corner behind Doris.

"Excuse me, Doris. I don't believe that I have met the lady behind you."

Doris glanced over her shoulder, raising her arms up in the air. "I don't know what's the matter with me, Jenn. I've forgotten about Alice! Come out from behind there, dear. It's way past time for you to meet your new boss."

Jenn furrowed her brow, trying to figure out what role this woman played at the *Serendipity Sun*. Jenn was so concerned about filling the slots on the advertising and news teams, she must have forgotten about other aspects of the operation.

Alice stood up from behind Doris and walked toward the circle of other staff. Jenn guessed that the woman was close to her age, give or take a few years.

"Jenn, this is Alice Ziegler. Alice's title is bookkeeper. She is way more than that though. She handles accounts receivable, accounts payable, as well as our payroll. She's the money lady around here."

"Goodness!" Jenn jumped up from her seat, walking straight to Alice and shaking her hand. "It is your precise records that I've been studying for the past week." Jenn looked at Doris. "Didn't someone tell me that our bookkeeper was out for medical reasons?"

"I was." Alice finally spoke. "This is my first day back. Monday will be my first day back at my desk. I came in today because Doris thought it would be a good for me to be here for this meeting."

"Can we tell Jenn what you did earlier in the week?" Doris stood up and pulled Alice into a hug.

Slowly, a smile brought her frail-looking face to life. "I rang the bell. My cancer treatments are over. I got to ring the bell."

Everyone in the room stood up and applauded. Alice was overcome with emotion, wiping tears from her face.

"While it's been many weeks since Alice has been able to be with us here at the office, she's continued to do all her work from home. We've taken turns delivering things to her and picking her work up. So much can be done electronically these days. Mr. Sebastian would be so proud of you." Doris hugged Alice again.

"I'm so happy that you've come to this meeting, Alice. Your financial records are so clear and precise. Numbers are not my specialty, I'm more of a 'words' person. The way you've set up the reports made everything make sense to me. I'm very grateful."

Alice smiled, bowing her head. "Being able to continue to do my job made all the difference in the world for my recovery. I live alone. With my immunity compromised because of the chemo, I had to limit my interaction with others. Every day, even if it was only for an hour on some days, I could spend time with my numbers. I could put my illness out of my mind for a little while and dive into the order of our financial records. It was a haven for me."

"Thank you for your dedication. It's wonderful that you can now be able to be here with us. We've got more obstacles to overcome, and we will do so together, as a team." Jenn returned to her seat. "As I mentioned a few minutes ago, I've also decided to fill the Editor position. I will begin that process next week as well. I appreciate how hard everyone in the newsroom has worked without a team leader. Helen, you have obviously done an outstanding job stepping up to handle editorials and making assignments. Anyone who wishes to be considered may let me know privately."

Jenn took a moment to look around the room again, reflecting on the week.

"It was exciting for me to watch the Saturday edition being put together this week. As most of you probably know by now, I worked here when I was in my early twenties. While the main goals are still the same today as they were then, the process is certainly extremely different. It amazes me." Jenn took a deep breath. "What most of you do not know is that I walked in this building for the first time when I was in the third grade. It was a field trip. I was enchanted by the fact that words and photos could come to life and create a world in black and white. From that day forward, I dreamed of having my own newspaper. Like many dreams that each of us has, I never imagined the dream would ever come true."

A weekend of moving followed by a full week of long work hours and intense concentration came to a halt about six o'clock Friday evening. Everyone had long since left the newspaper office, even Doris waved goodbye to Jenn a little after five.

Jenn was happy to hear that Mel had a date that evening with a gentleman who was opening a new business in town. That meant that Jenn would be dining alone and the basic supply of food that Renee left her was dwindling. Jenn would have to go to the grocery store.

Realizing that her tired brain and hungry stomach would make her buy things she didn't need and forget grocery items she needed, Jenn took a few minutes to write down a list that would hopefully make her time inside the store shorter and more efficient. From Jenn's visits with her parents through the years, she knew that there were several good grocery store options in the area. She opted for one of the larger stores that would likely have more of the items she was accustomed to purchasing.

After locking up the building, Jenn made the short drive to the store. Happy to see that the parking lot was not as crowded as she expected, Jenn checked several items off her list after spending a few minutes in the produce and deli sections. Jenn enjoyed cooking. It made her happy to see that the store's variety and quality of products would allow her to easily find ingredients whenever she found time to cook again.

Jenn turned the corner, catching a glimpse of a tall muscular male frame at the end of the aisle. A pronounced limp hindered his approach. Heavy black eyebrows forming a line in his furrowed brow reminding her of a long autumn wooly worm. Jenn chuckled, realizing that she knew the man. It was Randy. He appeared to be unsuccessfully searching for an item on the shelves.

"May I help you, sir?" Jenn altered her voice slightly.

"Yeah, I'm looking for a can of green chiles. I thought I would find it with the other canned vegetables." Randy kept looking toward the shelf.

"I think you might find that with the Mexican food on the next aisle over." Jenn bit her lip to stifle a laugh.

"Thank you. That makes sense." A shocked expression crossed Randy's face when he finally made eye contact with Jenn. "Oh, hey, there. I didn't realize that was you, Jenn. Were you trying to trick the old trickster?"

Randy's smile was wide, genuine, and irresistible. Exactly like Jenn remembered from high school.

"I wouldn't do that. You must be making a Mexican dish this evening." Jenn shifted her mind to a safe topic.

"This weekend, I am going to attempt to make a chicken enchilada recipe that I got from one of the dispatchers. She made it a month or so ago for a staff potluck lunch. It was delicious." Randy paused for a moment. "Hey, maybe you might like to come over and share it with me? If you aren't afraid of my cooking."

"Oh, I don't know. I've still got a lot of unpacking to do. It's taken more time to get settled then I expected." As if on cue, Jenn's phone buzzed. Pulling the cell phone from her purse, Jenn saw that the call was from Emily, her daughter. Still in graduate school, Emily's calls were not frequent. "I better take this. It's my youngest. Excuse me."

Randy nodded and motioned in the direction of the Mexican food aisle. He smiled and waved before turning to walk in that direction. Jenn watched him limp away, wondering how her friend had been injured, while she pushed the answer button on the phone.

"Hello, sweetheart. What's up?"

"Mom! Has Dad told you his latest news?" Emily's voice was up at least an octave from her normal tone.

"Emily, your father and I don't talk often now. With the divorce being final, we are past that point." Jenn rolled her eyes imagining what this latest tidbit would be. Perhaps Simon had bought a sports car or some other midlife crisis symbol. He already had the trophy wife.

"He's pregnant!"

"He's what?" Jenn looked around, realizing her tone matched her reaction.

"Well, I guess that's not exactly right."

Jenn would certainly agree that there was something not right about her fifty-five-year-old ex-husband being pregnant. A giggle escaped before she realized it. As tired as she was, the mental image of Simon pregnant might cause her to go into an uncontrollable fit of laughter in the canned vegetable aisle. There was nothing funny about the canned vegetable aisle.

"Kenzie's pregnant." Emily corrected herself. "My father, who is old enough to be a grandfather, is going to be a new dad, again. I can't even stand it."

Jenn's initial reaction of tired giggles quickly turned to full on amusement. She was certain that Simon enjoyed having a young wife. She was equally certain that he would not enjoy having a new baby. While he'd been a good father, the baby stage was not the portion of his children's childhood where he shined. Despite having three children relatively close together, Simon never got the hang of diapers or middle-of-the night feedings. The bulk of the responsibility of caring for the needs of their children fell on Jenn. It was the main reason she enjoyed working remotely before it was a normal business practice.

"Well, that's certainly some interesting news. I wish them well." Jenn shook her head. "Is everything okay with you, Em? Are you doing well in your classes?"

"Yes. I'm covered up with three projects and mid-terms looming. How can you be so calm about this? Dad's going to be a father."

"Simon is already a father. He knew how he became one. Maybe this was a planned addition." Jenn knew the development wasn't part of Simon's plan. Kenzie obviously had another agenda.

"Oh, no, they were both on the Facetime call when Kenzie told me. I could tell that he didn't even want her talking about it. Dad had the look he gets when a business deal falls through."

"His 'oh crap' face." Jenn knew the expression well. She could see it in her mind.

"Exactly. This was not in the Simon Young plan. I hope Kenzie knows what she's gotten herself into."

Jenn had thought the same thing several times over the last few months. "She's an adult, a married woman." The words left a bad taste in Jenn's mouth.

"She's barely older than me, remember?"

Jenn remembered. How could she forget that her husband of more than thirty years left her for someone who wasn't even born yet on their wedding day? Simon had made his 'baby bed,' he was going to have to sleep in it. Or, rather, not sleep because a real baby would keep him awake. There was some poetic justice in that thought. It made Jenn smile.

"Listen, honey, it's been a long week and I'm in the grocery store. Can we continue this conversation later?"

"Sure, Mom. I'm sorry. I didn't think about what you might be doing. I couldn't hold this news in any longer. Don't mention it to Claire or Foster. I think Dad plans to call them this weekend. We don't want to rob them of this shock. At least, I won't be the baby in the family anymore."

Emily's words hit a tender spot in Jenn's heart. "You will always be my baby, sweetheart. There's no chance of that changing."

"I love you, Mom. Have fun in the grocery store. Buy some wine in Dad's honor. I'll call you later. Bye."

Before Jenn could say anything further, she heard the beep of the call ending. She was still holding the phone in her hand when Randy's voice roused her from the fog of her thoughts.

"Is everything okay, Jenny?" Randy's calm voice, using her childhood name, made a warm feeling pass over Jenn. "You're in the same spot where I left you."

"Yes. I'm fine." Jenn looked up into Randy's dark brown eyes. His presence was soothing after such shocking news.

"That was your youngest child on the phone?"

"Yes. My daughter, Emily. She's in graduate school. She had some interesting news to share." Jenn looked down at the overflowing grocery basket Randy was carrying. "It looks like you found all the ingredients for your enchiladas."

"I think I've got them all." Randy glanced in his basket. "It seems like a simple recipe, but the ingredient list is long. I'm glad to hear everything is okay with your daughter. The offer still stands to come over for dinner. Half the ingredients I needed were in the Mexican food section. I might not have even been able to make the dish without your help. You've earned a serving."

Jenn's eyes met Randy's and she saw that same youthful spirit that touched her heart all those many years ago. The schoolgirl who still lived inside her felt a thrill of hopeful excitement. Glancing down at the phone she still held in her hand, Jenn was reminded of the news she just learned. Thinking of the young woman who now shared her ex-husband's life, she imagined that this former football star that stood in front of her was probably being polite to an old friend. She was certain that the handsome police chief had his pick of women to share his enchiladas with.

"That's kind of you, Randy. As I mentioned earlier, I've got quite a bit of unpacking to do."

"I understand. Can I see your phone a minute?" Randy held out his hand.

"My phone? Why do you want to see my phone?" Jenn looked from Randy to her phone and back to him again.

"You know, as the police chief, I'm concerned about citizen safety." His tone changed from friendly to stern.

"Certainly. I didn't mean to imply—." Jenn stumbled over her words, feeling foolish as she handed the phone to him.

Randy set his grocery basket on the floor between them. Angling the phone screen so that he could see, Jenn could not tell what Randy was doing as he typed on her screen, until a few seconds later when she heard the phone on his belt buzz. He punched another key on her phone before handing it back to her and cutting off his own.

"Now you have my phone number, for safety reasons, of course." Randy's stern expression changed to a humorous one as he lifted one eyebrow and winked.

"And you have mine." Jenn raised both her eyebrows and tilted her head.

"Can you think of a reason that you would not want the police chief to have your phone number?" Randy waited a few seconds before he continued. "It's for your own good. Now you'll know who it is, if I call you. It's up to you whether you decide to answer."

Her schoolgirl self could not think of a 'cool' response. The adult version decided to remain silent.

"Thanks for your help, Jenny. Sorry, old habits, I believe you go by Jenn now. Have a great first weekend back home. Take care." Randy picked up his grocery basket.

The beautiful smile Jenn remembered so well returned to Randy's face. Watching him walk away, she wondered if she'd been too quick to turn down his dinner offer. They were old friends, after all. Once he was out of sight, she began to put her phone away. Seeing the number he called, she decided to save his number, simply typing 'Randy' in her contacts. Jenn could not imagine that the name would ever come up on her screen. The young girl who remembered a sweet young boy couldn't help but wish for it though. Maybe she needed a friend like Randy to help her navigate life in their hometown.

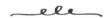

By the middle of Sunday afternoon, Jenn had done all the unpacking she could bear. While there were still boxes piled in the small room off the kitchen, she had managed to unpack the bulk of the necessary items for her immediate day-to-day life. Since Jenn's older sister, Renee, had taken their mother's China dishware after her passing, Jenn worked on unboxing and washing her own set to fill the empty dish cabinet.

She was pleased to see that her heavy stoneware successfully made the move without any broken pieces or even chips. While her twelve-piece set was way more than she needed for everyday use, she hoped that her children would come and fill her large dining room table as often as their schedules allowed, bringing their families or friends for gatherings.

"I'm going to have to figure out something for us to have for dinner." Jenn's small dog, Jasper, raised his head for a moment in acknowledgement of the prospect of food. "I hope I don't have to go back to the grocery store again soon." Jenn grabbed a piece of cheese out of the refrigerator. With her first bite, she heard her phone buzz.

"Where did I put my phone, Jasper?"

Jenn hurriedly picked up empty boxes off the kitchen table while the buzzing continued. Finally seeing it under a stack of bubble wrap, she grabbed the phone and looked at the screen. Her heart skipped a beat when she saw 'Randy' beaming in big letters. Jenn bit her bottom lip and took a deep breath.

"Hello." Jenn could hear the hesitancy in her voice. She hoped Randy didn't notice.

"Hey, Jenn. This is Randy."

"Hi, Randy." Jenn tried to sound upbeat.

"For a second, I wasn't sure if you were going to answer. I guess I shouldn't have mentioned that you had an option." Randy chuckled. "Have I caught you at a bad time?"

"No. I was getting a snack and taking a little break. I've been unpacking all weekend. For some reason, it seems to be taking longer to unbox things then it did to pack them."

"I imagine part of that extra time is figuring out where to put things."

"Yes, I think you're right. Just because my mother had her things in a certain order does not mean that I must do the same."

"Somehow, I think that the Paisley Halston I knew would not agree with that statement."

"You've got a point. I'm the rebellious daughter though. I break the rules."

"That's not the Jenny Halston I remember. The girl I grew up with walked the straight and narrow. She was a little bit of a goody-two-shoes."

"Ouch! I felt the sting of those words, Mr. Nave."

"No harm intended. You were a good girl. Trust me, in my line of work, I see too many people who are the other extreme. The straight and narrow is a good life."

"That may be the girl you remember, but in my house back then, I was the rebel. Renee was the Straight-A student with the full Yale scholarship and Amber was a star athlete. I was the weird middle child."

"The irony of that does not escape me. Renee earned her Ivy League degree and then never used it that I'm aware of, and Amber's life hasn't exactly been a championship season. How's she doing, by the way? I've lost track of her."

"Amber is back in rehab. She'd been doing somewhat better until Mom passed. Renee couldn't reach her for about a week and called Amber's son. She relapsed. No matter where she ends up living, there always seems to be someone within proximity who will feed her addiction."

"That's another scenario I see way too often." Randy was silent for a moment. "Listen, Jenn, the reason I called was that I'm about to put a huge dish of enchiladas in the oven. You may have thought that I was kidding the other day, but I would love to invite you over to share them with me. Consider it a welcome home dinner with local law enforcement."

"Is this a regular service that you offer to all new residents of Serendipity?"

"Well, no, it's reserved only for girls I didn't date in high school."

"That would be a short list then."

"Ouch! Now who's handing out the low blows?"

"Randy, let's face it. You were the most popular boy in school. You were dating a different girl every week."

"Hey, I didn't want to play favorites."

"You knew you could date every girl you wanted. You worked that advantage."

"I wouldn't say that I dated every girl I was interested in. It appears that I may have lost my touch, because it sounds like you are about to turn me down."

Jenn let those words hang between them for a few moments. Her younger self was screaming 'Accept, you idiot!' The mature version could not imagine why Randy was inviting her.

"Okay, Jenn, you are being too quiet. I don't want to make you uncomfortable. I may be overstepping my boundaries. Please forgive me; I only wanted the chance to reconnect with you after all these years."

Ugh. She'd made him feel bad. What was wrong with her? She needed to undo this damage.

"Honestly, Randy, I'm mostly concerned about food poisoning."

"What?"

"I had home economics with you, remember? It wasn't pretty. I believe the fire department had to be called the day you made a cake."

Randy howled with laughter, reminding Jenn of the fun person she knew long ago. She had to stop second guessing and allow him to become her friend again. A male friend would be good for her at this point in her life.

"Oh, Jenny, after the weekend I've had, I needed that laugh. I promise you that my cooking skills have improved immensely. They are so good that sometimes the fire department asks me to come over to their station and cook for them. It's what happens when you return to bachelorhood unexpectedly."

"Okay, I would be happy to accept your gracious invitation. Is there something I can bring? I haven't stocked my pantry much yet, but I'd be glad to stop on my way over and pick something up."

"Yes, there is. I planned to make a dessert, but I've spent most of this weekend working. Could you stop at Dippers Creamery and grab a couple of pints? Pick whatever flavors you like."

"Absolutely! Dippers is one place that I've stopped at through the years when I would visit my folks. You can't beat their frozen custard. What time would you like me to come?"

"As soon as you can. The enchiladas are in the oven now and I'm about to make a pitcher of margaritas. My address is 286 Barrett's Landing."

"I'll take a quick shower and head your way. Thank you, Randy."

"Jenn, I'm looking forward to spending some time with you. It's been too many years. See you soon."

Chapter Eight

Randy

The mirror in his bathroom was still foggy from a quick shower as Randy put on his jeans. Picking up his towel, he quickly wiped a circular spot so that he could see his reflection for shaving. His gaze caught a glimpse of the scar on his left shoulder. Like the limp in his stride, it was a reminder of his life's work and a rare occasion when a criminal got the upper hand in a situation. The scar was fading with the passing years, but the limp was becoming more pronounced with age.

Randy doubted that Jenn saw the young quarterback she knew when she last lived in Serendipity. That guy may have seemed to be full of confidence, but he never found the nerve to ask out the one girl who could have claimed his young heart. The fact that she would be eating dinner with him in his own home made his heart skip a beat in a way he didn't think he would ever feel again.

Checking to be sure he hadn't missed a spot with his shaving, Randy splashed on some of the cologne his son, Bryson, gave him for Father's Day. The name on the bottle said 'Sexy.' Randy hadn't felt like that in a long time. Most days, he felt old. He knew he was still too young to feel that way, but he couldn't shake it. The life of a police officer was heavy like the layers of armor and weapons he wore. He needed to lighten up. Dinner with an old friend might be precisely the medicine he needed.

The buzzer of the oven timer went off. Randy quickly pulled his polo shirt over his head while walking toward the kitchen.

"I can't let Jenn's concerns about my cooking prove true." Randy laughed as he opened the oven door. "Good, it's not burned. I better get them out though." Putting on oven mitts that looked like lobster claws, another gift from Bryson, Randy slid the casserole dish of chicken enchiladas out of the oven and carried them to the dining room table where he placed them on a hot pad. Quickly, he retrieved the lid and covered the dish.

Randy glanced around his house when the doorbell rang. He strived to keep things neat and clean but was unsure if it would meet a woman's criteria for good housekeeping. It had been a long time since Randy had shared a home with anyone other than visits from Bryson.

Peeking out the window on the side of the door as he approached it, he saw the profile of Jenn's face. She was looking in the direction of his lawn while she waited. Randy's heart skipped a beat and butterflies began to fight in his stomach. Here he was the Chief of Police, encountering criminals almost every day, and he was nervous to have dinner with a woman he'd known since childhood. Randy tried to shake off the feeling, opening the door with a big smile.

"Welcome, Jenn!"

"Hi, Randy, this is a lovely area. I didn't realize that you lived on the water. Although, I suppose the name 'Barrett's Landing' should have given that away."

"I lucked up when I came back from the service. This little house was owned by one of the previous police chiefs. He was the last of his family without any heirs and had stipulated two things in his will—the property had to be purchased by a police officer and the proceeds from the sale had to go to a fund to help retired police officers. I paid the appraised value of it, which was a little more than I'd planned spending at the time. Knowing where the money was going made it worth it. I knew it was a special place."

"This is sounding familiar to me now. I think my mother told me about this. Would she have known?"

"One of the reporters interviewed me when I first moved back, and the article told the basics of the story. I'm sure Paisley read it."

"I think Mom read every issue from cover to cover. I sure wish she was here to read the newspaper now that it is mine."

Randy gave Jenn an understanding smile. The loss of her mother was still fresh. The grief was still sharp.

"Come on in, Jenn." Randy stepped out of the doorway. "I'll take that bag of ice cream and put it in the freezer. The food is ready."

"Great." Jenn handed the small bag to Randy as she stepped inside. "You mentioned on the phone that you spent a lot of time working this weekend. May I ask what happened?"

"Tyler can pick up my full report on Monday, Madam Publisher."

"You caught me, Chief. The real reason I'm here is to scoop a story. The promise of a delicious dinner was merely a way in." Jenn winked.

"Typical." Randy laughed. "Here's the quick version of the story. About twenty guys came down from Raleigh for a bachelor party for their buddy. After way too much alcohol consumption, they lost their common sense and started taking dares from each other. The level of dares progressed to the point that they broke into a local business and then led my team on high-speed chases in three directions. One of them ended up wrapping a car around a tree with the future best man being thrown through the windshield. He's going to make it, but I doubt he walks again."

"Oh, Randy, that's awful."

"You're a mother so you will understand. Seeing young people in that state takes years off your life. It's a parents' biggest fear."

"I understand. That sure makes for a tough day off."

"Which is even more reason that I said a little prayer before I called you. I need to have a happy evening."

"Roger that, Chief." Jenn gave him a little salute. "I can smell dinner. I'm so hungry. I've snacked all day while unpacking."

"I hope you like it. I enjoyed the dish so much at the staff potluck that I had to have the recipe. The ingredient list was long, but it was easy to put together."

Randy led the way through the house to the dining room and kitchen area. After putting the ice cream in the freezer, he turned to find Jenn looking at the framed photos that were hung on the wall between the living and dining rooms.

"That's the Wall of Bryson." Randy laughed.

"Randy, he's the spitting image of you. At first, I thought that some of these were photos of you when you were young. It's incredible."

"I know. It's amazing. I feel sorry for the poor kid."

"Right. It's a horrible thing to look so much like the handsomest boy to ever live in Serendipity."

Randy saw Jenn bite her bottom lip while a blush appeared on her cheeks. He looked away from her, smiling inside. He never thought that she saw him that way.

"Thankfully, he didn't inherit his father's cowardly habits of jumping from one girl to the next. Bryson has been dating the same girl since high school. They are planning to get married next summer."

"That's wonderful. What do you mean by cowardly habits? 'Coward' is the last word I would use to describe you. You never seemed to be afraid of girls, if that's what you mean."

"No, not afraid of them, afraid of having a relationship with one. I didn't go out more than once or twice with any girl because I was terrified of what was next and how I might screw it up. I'm thankful that Bryson doesn't have any of that. He's like his mother. Even though she divorced me, Bryson's mother is a stick-to-it type person." Randy knew he should change the subject. "What would you like to drink?"

"I believe on the phone you mentioned margaritas or am I mistaken?"

"You are not. I have a pitcher in the refrigerator. Would you also like iced water with your meal?"

"That sounds perfect. Need to keep that hydration level."

"Especially when eating Mexican food and drinking margaritas." Randy walked toward the kitchen to begin preparing the beverages. "Please have a seat, Jenn. Everything is on the table except our drinks."

"It smells delicious, Randy. I also see some sort of corn and rice dish and what appears to be homemade salsa."

"Corn and rice fiesta is the name of that dish and it is another recipe from the same lady who shared the one for enchiladas. I bought the locally made salsa at the farmer's market." Randy set two glasses of iced water in front of their plates.

"Moving back to Serendipity is not going to be good for my waistline. Earlier in the week, I dined on Mel's mother's homemade chicken noodle soup and rolls."

"Mrs. Snow's rolls? Those are like heaven with butter." Randy made his final trip from the kitchen with the pitcher of margaritas. "Please have a seat."

"You've had her rolls then." Jenn sat down opposite where Randy was still standing.

"There are good things about being in law enforcement. One of them is that appreciative citizens sometimes treat us to homemade food. Every year on the day before Christmas, Mel's parents bring two huge baked hams and dozens of Mrs. Snow's homemade rolls to the station for the officers who are working to enjoy on their Christmas shifts."

"I bet you volunteer to work every Christmas." Jenn laughed.

"Only because I want my officers who have children to be home with their families." Randy sat down. "And because there's ham rolls. Mostly because there's ham rolls. There's another local lady who brings us a dessert called Ho Ho Cake. It's chocolate heaven."

"It's nice to know that even a job as dangerous and difficult as police work has some perks and people show gratitude."

"For the most part, police work is a great job. You get to truly help people when they need it the most." Randy took the lid off the dish of enchiladas and handed Jenn a serving spoon. "Please help yourself."

"I hope you cannot hear my stomach growling. When you took that lid off, it sounded to me like a lion roaring."

"I'm starving, too. We are old friends and should not be embarrassed by eating large portions of food together. I'm thrilled that you are here to share this meal with me."

Randy took the spoon from Jenn after she served herself. Taking a heaping portion, Randy put the lid back on the dish. He was about to reach for the corn and rice when he noticed that Jenn was staring at him instead of serving herself.

"What's wrong? Did I forget something? You have silverware, don't you?" Randy looked around the table, trying to figure out what was missing.

"Nothing is missing. You amaze me." Jenn tilted her head in a questioning gesture.

"I don't understand."

"I'm having trouble wrapping my mind around the idea that you eat a lot of meals alone. From where I sit, I see an older version of the charming boy I knew in childhood. What's changed?"

"Oh, Jenn." Randy took a deep breath. "You know how life goes. I'm sure you are not quite the same person I knew either. You may still see me as the boy who dated all the girls. I was serious when I said earlier that I was afraid then. You knew my parents. Everything probably seemed happy from the outside. I never heard a harsh word spoken between my parents. It was a civil household. My parents weren't happy though. They married too young because of yours truly. They stayed married and made the best of things because that's what people of their generation did. I didn't grow up seeing the love between two people that I saw in the homes of some of my friends. When I got old enough to date, I knew there was a difference. I didn't want to be like my father."

"How?"

"I didn't want to marry the wrong girl." Randy's words left a taste of regret in his mouth. "I think that's why I never had a steady girlfriend. I didn't trust my own judgment."

They both began to eat. Randy allowed the silence to hang between them. He could tell that Jenn was either deep in thought or at a loss on how to respond. A few minutes later, he caught her staring at him again.

"Was it growing up and life in general that made you change that philosophy? You obviously married Bryson's mother. How did that happen?"

"Jenn, I'm not so sure that this is the most appropriate time to have this conversation, the first time we've talked in such a long time."

"I'm sorry, Randy, I shouldn't be prying into your life. You've shown me kindness. Invited me into your home for a friendly meal. It's none of my business."

"That's not what I said, Jenn. It is your business, in an indirect way. Or at least, it could have been your business years ago."

"I'm not following you. What could it possibly have to do with me?"

"I hadn't planned to have this conversation so soon. It was hard enough convincing you to have dinner with me. I want us to be friends."

"I want us to be friends, too. Maybe I'm misinterpreting what you are saying. I don't understand what your marriage to Bryson's mother has to do with me. I never met her."

"Jenn, I was a mixed-up kid when I left this town and joined the Army. I was going to see the world and never look back. The only problem was that I didn't realize that I'd left a piece of my heart here. It took me several years, but the first chance I got, I came back here to see if I could claim it. That was the visit when I came to the newspaper."

"I remember that day. I was so happy that I happened to be there. I'd just come in from covering some government meeting. If you'd come any earlier, I would have missed you." Jenn took another small helping of the enchiladas. "These are so good."

"You wouldn't have missed me. I would have come back."

Randy clinched his teeth. A habit that caused too many trips to the dentist in his life. Could he tell Jenn the real reason he'd been at the newspaper that day long ago?

"I heard your voice in the front lobby. Doris was talking about Jennifer, so I assumed you were there to see me." Jenn broke eye contact with Randy and looked down at her plate.

"I was. Only I said Jenny, like I always called you. Doris must have gotten confused as she said Jennifer with a name I didn't recognize."

Jenn met Randy's eyes again. A surprised look crossed her face. "Oh, goodness. I bet the name was Jennifer Reynolds. She was an advertising rep then. More people came to see her than me in those days. No wonder Doris got mixed up."

"Well, I heard a different last name and assumed that you must have gotten married."

"Really? Why would you assume that?" Jenn tilted her head, causing her hair to fall toward her eyes.

The action made Randy want to reach up and push the beautiful lock of hair away. It reminded him of what a good listener Jenn always was. She'd tilt her head and listen like there was no one else in the world.

"I knew you'd graduated college by then. I figured you met some guy who wasn't good enough for you and brought him back to Serendipity. Those years were during some of my first tours of duty overseas. I didn't get home much. Mom was going through her first bout of cancer, so that was the most frequent topic of conversation when I called home. I was behind on the neighborhood gossip."

"Your mother was special. I miss her."

"She loved you."

Randy moved the food around on his plate, deep in thought. Jenn seemed to be lost in her thoughts as well. He took a deep breath before resuming the story.

"From that deep breath, it sounds like you're about to say something serious."

"You might say that. I'm about to say something foolish, probably." Randy looked into Jenn's eyes. He saw concern.

"I came to the newspaper that day to see you."

"Yes, it's not every soldier who has his own personal reporter to write an article about him." Jenn giggled.

"That was a great article. My mother loved it so much that she framed it." Randy laid his napkin in his plate. "I know I came in carrying a press release. That was just an excuse. I think the Army had already mailed it to the Editor. It was standard practice back then for notices regarding promotions in rank to be sent to a soldier's hometown newspaper."

"You needed a photo to go with it."

"Not really. I believe my official photo was sent, too."

"I don't understand then. Why did you come?" Jenn picked up her margarita glass and took the last sip.

"I wanted to see you. I'd heard you were working at the newspaper. I wanted to ask you out."

"What?" Jenn spewed the margarita as she spoke. Much of it landed on Randy's face. "I'm sorry."

Randy picked up his napkin, wiping his face, laughing. He was happy that something lightened the mood.

"Randy, did you say you came to ask me out? I don't understand."

"I'd spent the previous four long years all over the world. The military is a busy life. It's also a solitary one. You make friends with other soldiers and form bonds that last a lifetime. You learn all types of skills and see unbelievable parts of the world. It's a long way from home though. In your bunk at night, you've got a lot of time to think. The people and places that are important to you rise to the top. Of all the people I left behind, you were the one I missed the most."

Randy wasn't sure that he dared to watch Jenn's reaction. Yet, one way or another, he had to know. He could see realization in Jenn's eyes as they filled with tears. She bit her bottom lip.

"I'm sorry I stopped writing to you."

"Yeah. During my first year in the service, I got dozens of letters a week. The guys called me Elvis because they said I got bags of fan mail.

I couldn't possibly respond to all of them. Sadly, many of the girls who wrote those letters I couldn't even remember knowing."

"You were the most popular boy in high school for years. Even our classmates' younger sisters were in love with Randy Nave."

"That's not how I saw myself. I couldn't understand why all these girls were writing to me. At first, I was happy to receive the mail. Then, it became overwhelming. I wasn't good at letter writing. I wanted to write to you, but I didn't think I had anything interesting to say. I tried to send you photos or postcards from wherever I was stationed. I wanted to keep in touch with you."

"I got them. I had a bulletin board in my dorm to hang them on. One of my roommates made a 'Where's Randy?' sign that hung on the top. I think she wrote you letters, too." Jenn laughed for a moment, before her expression became somber. "You stopped writing, so I stopped, too. Our lives were moving in different directions."

"It's true. Parts of my life were standing still though. I was caught up in my military life. I didn't pursue much of a social life. I met a couple of girls along the way. Nothing stuck. I'd spent all those high school years going from girl to girl, trying to not take any of it too seriously." Randy closed his eyes, summoning the nerve to make his confession. "Those long nights lying awake in my bunk made me face the fact that there was one girl I'd never pursued. The one who my heart was drawn to was too close for me to realize. Then, she was a world away."

"Randy, I am honestly shocked to hear this. Never in a million years did I think you saw me as anything more than a sister, a buddy. I can't imagine how I would have reacted had I heard this then. Why couldn't you tell me?"

Randy looked deep into Jenn's green eyes. "Honestly, I thought I was out of your league."

"What? I'm sorry. That doesn't make sense. You're out of *my* league?" Jenn shook her head, furrowing her brow. "I think it was the other way around. You may have been the most popular guy ever in our high school. You were voted most athletic and most popular. I was voted most studious. I was the one who was out of your league."

"You were smart and confident. There was no doubt in my mind that you were going to follow in Renee's footsteps and go to an Ivy League school and be a big success. Why would you want to date a football player with barely average grades? The only way I was going to college was by throwing a ball."

"Why didn't you do that? I've always wondered. I know you got offers."

"You may remember that I had an uncle who played professional football. He didn't have the best stories. He made a lot of money for a short time. But, once it was over, that was the only career he'd known. His body was shot. For the rest of his life, he was on painkillers. I didn't want that. Too bad no one told me that law enforcement could do the same thing."

"Randy, I'm still finding it hard to believe that you came to the newspaper to ask me out. Weren't you on leave to visit because your mother was sick?"

"Yes. I was also nearing the end of my enlistment. I had decided that if you were still around and interested, I wouldn't re-enlist. You probably don't know this either. On a previous visit home, your father offered me a job with his company. You remember I worked for him every summer during high school. That was the one job I especially enjoyed. I liked working construction. Your father was a craftsman. I knew I could learn a lot. You might have seen me in a different light."

"See you in a different light? Oh, Randy, you have no idea. From the time we were in the sandbox in my backyard, I thought you hung the moon. All through high school, every time you went out with a new girl, it broke my heart. I was your pal, your sister. Girls came to me for Randy advice. It was horrible."

Jenn bit her bottom lip again. It was a habit Randy remembered from childhood. When Jenn said something she wasn't sure she should have, she'd bite her lip.

"Now you are shocking me. I didn't know any of that." A million thoughts swirled through Randy's head. He never saw interest in Jenn's interaction with him.

"We were always good friends, you and me. It was something I valued very much. If I couldn't be the girl on your arm, at least I knew that I was the one you often confided in. I was happy to see you that day at the newspaper. I missed our friendship. While I was taking your photograph, you congratulated me. I thought you were talking about me getting that job. I'd not been there long. You knew that I had always wanted to be a writer. It might have only been an entry level position at a small-town newspaper, but it was a dream job to me."

"I knew it was a dream of yours. We would often go by the newspaper office on those days we walked home from school together. I could only imagine that you would move up in the ranks and that you would want to build your life here. I was full of cautious hope and excitement until I heard that last name."

"Was that the reason I couldn't get you to smile for the photograph? You said that soldiers don't smile. That wasn't the Randy I knew."

"Looking back, I think my heart broke a little that day. I wouldn't have admitted it at the time. That was the day everything changed. There were many aspects of Army life that I enjoyed. I didn't really want to make a career of it though. After that day, I came to the decision that since I didn't have anything, or anyone, to stay in Serendipity for, I would have a secure future staying in the Army. I was good at it. I would move up the ranks. So, I decided to re-enlist." Randy grew silent, remembering that day. "Mom was so sick. I didn't even tell her that I had been to see you. I didn't tell anyone. If I had, someone would surely have told me that you weren't married."

"I was dating someone then. Simon, the man who I would end up marrying. We met in college. I had applied for the job at the newspaper on a lark. Simon wanted me to apply for positions at a book publisher or a big city public relations firm. When I got the job here, I thought it was a sign that I should come home. Maybe there was a reason I was being drawn back to my hometown."

"Oh, Jenn, don't tell me that." Randy shook his head.

"I learned a lot from Mr. Sebastian while I worked at the newspaper. Simon got a job at a big company in Atlanta. He kept asking me to join him there. I applied for three or four jobs and got interviews for all of them. As much as I loved the newspaper business, I guess I thought that my life was going to be with Simon, so I accepted one of the positions and moved to Atlanta. Until this week, I've lived there ever since."

"But you've been happy, right? Up until your divorce." Randy searched Jenn's expression for what he hoped to be the truth. "I've heard a few people mention you through the years, it's always seemed like you were living a good life."

"I've been content. I've had the things that every little girl dreams about—a successful husband, healthy children, a beautiful home, a thriving career. It was all picture-perfect on the surface. I didn't realize there could be anything different."

Randy furrowed his brow, thinking about her words. He didn't want to pry. He hoped she would reveal what was below the surface.

"Then, one day, someone pulled the veil away from my eyes and I saw the reality of my life. My children were grown and off into their own lives. My career, while successful, had grown stale and lost its challenge. My husband was in love with a woman who was the age of our daughters. When Mom made her sudden exit, I knew it was a sign. It was time to start over. If I was going to truly start over, then I thought I needed to go back to the beginning. When I found out the newspaper was for sale that was all I needed to hear."

"It's amazing sometimes how the universe will lead us if we just pay attention. I'm glad you've come home. It was a decision that I never imagined I would make either. All roads led here. I'm glad I made the trip."

"You've been back quite a while. How long has it been?"

Randy sensed that Jenn was trying to shift the conversation away from his feelings for her. He would follow her lead.

"I left the Army after twenty-five years. It's weird to retire when you are forty-three. I'd been divorced about ten years by then. My ex-wife, Roxanne, was from North Carolina. After we divorced, she moved back to where she grew up and married her high school sweetheart."

"That's an interesting turn of events. How did that make you feel?"

"The Army life was hard on her. Roxy is a good person. We weren't right for each other. I'm glad she's happy. Her husband is a good man. He's always been good to Bryson. By the time I retired, Bryson was in his teens and had a little sister. I wanted to move somewhere to be close enough to Bryson so that I could see him often, but not so close that I messed up Roxy's life. Serendipity seemed like as good a place as any."

"That's a healthy way of looking at the situation. I've got to say though that when Mom told me you had gone to work for the police department, I was more than a little surprised."

"It was the main work I did in the Army. I ended up working in military investigation. When a crime was committed within the ranks, I would investigate it."

"There's a television series about that. Simon used to watch it all the time. Was it NCIS?"

"Yes, that's the Navy's version. The Army calls it CID, Criminal Investigation Division."

"That sounds more advanced than working for a small-town police department."

"It was. The principles of the work are the same. Even though Serendipity is a small town, it's a popular coastal community. The area has more crime than you might expect. You remember Greg Palmer, don't you?"

"Sure, the second most popular boy in high school." Jenn laughed. "Who also happened to be one of your best friends?"

"Yeah, that's the one. Greg was the Assistant Police Chief when I was hired. The police department was two investigators short at the time. Greg encouraged me to apply. I did and got the job. It was early summer—a life-changing summer for me. Before I started the job, I took Bryson on a long vacation to the Keys. We spent ten days deep sea fishing and being beach bums. It was a great time of bonding for us. We've done a shorter version of that trip every year since. It's made us closer as I've watched him grow into a man."

"What a crossroads of your life!"

"Indeed. It sounds like you are at one of those crossroads, too."

"I think I am, Randy. I hope I am making the right decisions."

"I'd like to say there's a magic formula. It isn't true. My best advice is to watch for the signs and go with your gut."

"That's what I've done so far. I do believe that things happen for a reason. Sometimes we think the timing is horrible or heartbreaking, but that doesn't mean there won't be something good come of it." Jenn played with the spoon next to her plate, rolling it back and forth on the table. "My mother passing so soon after my marriage ended was hard to accept. It led me back home though, right when the newspaper was for sale. Having an old friend drop by during my first week was a happy accident, too." Jenn gave Randy a smile that went straight to his heart.

"Jenn, it wasn't an accident that I came to the newspaper. I stopped by the day after I heard you had bought it. Doris told me when you were planning to move back."

"It's nice to be remembered by old friends."

Randy heard hesitation in Jenn's voice. It was probably too soon after her divorce for her to consider a relationship.

"The newspaper could use someone who will give it a new focus. Especially someone who has a respect for the area and its citizens." Randy heard his 'police voice.'

"I'm probably in way over my head. I spent most of my career working in public relations. Being on the media side is a different world. I do like the idea of telling a good story though. Being fair and honest, showing both sides of a situation. I want to give local citizens and businesses the information they need to keep current in their community and make good decisions for their lives."

"The growth in the area has spurred a lot of controversy. Big portions of coastal property have been sold by the younger generations who've inherited it. I'm afraid they've been more concerned about the dollar amount on the check rather than the historic preservation of the structures or environmental issues associated with the land."

"Doesn't the local government have ordinances in place to protect the properties in those ways?"

"Jenn, you are going to find out that there are some in key positions who have their own agendas. Serendipity is still small enough that things get swept under the rug if they don't suit someone in power."

"How did Mr. Sebastian handle that in the newspaper's coverage of those situations?"

"Mr. Sebastian was in poor health for the last ten years. The man you knew who made sure every local issue had its day in court on the front page gradually slipped away from us. When I first joined the police department, Lyle Livingston was the Editor. His editorials did not mince any words regarding local corruption."

"Mom told me about some of his editorials and the dozens of Letters to the Editor that would be printed later, in agreement or argument with whatever side he'd taken. I'm surprised to learn that this Lyle is the same one who we knew in our high school days, 'Lyle the Smile.'"

"I think every female with a pulse knew who Lyle was when we were in high school. Even though he was a few years older than us and went to a neighboring high school, it didn't change his popularity. It's hard to believe that a hardnosed journalist was once a local teen heartthrob. Now there's one person who was more popular than me, back in the day."

"Only barely. It was that blonde-haired blue-eyed thing. Most girls thought Lyle looked like Shaun Cassidy."

"He had the whole surfer look down. Lyle could ride the waves, too."

"Am I remembering correctly that he was in an accident?"

"Yes, our senior year in high school was his senior year in college. He was in a motorcycle accident coming home for Thanksgiving. If I remember correctly, he broke his back, an arm, and a leg. He was laid up for a long time. Had dozens of surgeries and years of therapy. Lyle was majoring in journalism in college. When he was finally able to go back, he really dove into it, as I understand. He worked for a couple of big city newspapers before he came back to the area about fifteen years ago to care for his ailing father."

"All roads lead home, don't they?"

"It seems like it. Lyle lived in the area while he helped care for his father. After his father passed, Lyle sold the family home. As I understand, he followed some woman out West. Still a ladies' man, I guess."

"That must not have worked out for him."

"Why do you say that?"

"Doris told me that Lyle called a few weeks ago asking who had purchased the newspaper. She said that he thought it might have been bought by a larger media group and wondered if they needed someone to run it. He's interested in moving back to the area."

"Too bad for him that there is an owner who wants to manage the place herself."

"Yes, but I've been thinking about calling him. I've been looking at the business' financial statements. Most newspapers are struggling, especially local ones without corporate financial help. I think that my time will probably best be spent focusing on advertising and other ways to generate income. That would mean that I could use someone to handle the news side of the equation. Unless there are some red flags that I don't know about, a former Editor would be an ideal candidate."

"I guess you're right. Lyle was a great journalist. I believe that the bottom line suffered somewhat because of that though."

"That doesn't surprise me. If you take a stance on issues, there's always an opposing side. I've got lots of things to think about. At least, it gives me an option." Jenn looked down at her phone. "I didn't realize how late it was getting. I know that you are tired from working that emergency. I've spent a lot of time working myself. Monday morning will come early." Jenn rose from the table.

"Oh, we didn't have dessert."

"That's okay. You can enjoy some ice cream when you come home from work this week. I'm stuffed from that wonderful dinner. Someone needs to call Mrs. Jackson and tell her that you would pass home economics now."

"That would be nice if she hadn't passed away about ten years ago."

"Goodness! Are all the adults who were in our lives back then gone now?"

"Well, you've got to remember. They were about our age now when we knew them and that was almost forty years ago."

"Are you trying to say that I'm getting old?"

"You'll always be young in my eyes, Jenny." Randy reached out and took hold of Jenn's hand. "We are growing old together."

Jenn laughed before releasing Randy's hand, rising to leave.

"I'm sorry, Jenn, I didn't mean to be forward. I was just—."

"You were being the sweet Randy I always knew. It's fine. I'm not used to a man taking hold of my hand or cooking me dinner." Jenn walked through the house to the doorway

"You mean, since you and your husband divorced." Randy followed her, turning on the porch light and opening the door.

"I mean I'm not used to it, period. Simon is not like you." Jenn forced a smile. "Thank you again for your hospitality. I enjoyed the evening very much. Goodnight, Randy."

"Goodnight, Jenn."

Randy pondered Jenn's words while he watched her get into her Jeep and drive away. How could a woman as wonderful as Jenn end up with a man who wouldn't even hold her hand? He understood that her wounds were still fresh. He could be patient, especially if it meant that he might have a chance at a relationship with the love of his life.

Chapter Nine

Jenn

"I've been trying to reach you all evening, Jenn. I was about to call the local police."

Jenn almost laughed aloud at Renee's words.

"The police could have told you exactly where I was. At least, the Police Chief could have."

"What are you talking about? Has something happened? Are you okay?"

Jenn regretted making a joke that caused her sister to be concerned.

"I'm sorry that you couldn't reach me, Renee. I didn't pay any attention to my phone until the end of the evening. I was having dinner with an old friend."

"Okay, that sounds nice. What do the police have to do with it?"

"I had dinner with the Police Chief. You remember Randy Nave."

"I most certainly do. No wonder you forgot you had a phone. I would probably forget to put on my hair if I had a date with Randy Nave."

From the tone of Renee's voice, Jenn could imagine the expression on her face. Renee was enjoying this information.

"It wasn't a date. I ran into him in the grocery store on Friday evening. I helped him find the ingredients for the dish he was making. He kindly invited the new person in town to dinner."

"Uh huh. Randy, the handsomest male who has ever lived in Serendipity. The same Randy who grew up a few doors down from us. The same one who you were in love with since you were both in diapers."

"Why does everyone think I was in love with Randy? We were close friends growing up, like brother and sister."

"I'm not sure who 'everyone' is, but to those who lived in the same house with you, it was obvious. It was equally obvious to this big sister that it wasn't one-sided. The real shame is that you had to live with Simon all those years when you probably could have lived happily *ever* after with Randy."

Renee's words hit Jenn in the heart. She couldn't dwell on it. Jenn didn't have time for regrets or a relationship. There was serious work to be done. She needed rest.

"I'm sorry that I worried you. I spent most of the weekend unpacking. Tomorrow starts my first week of making some real decisions and changes at the newspaper. I'm going to say goodnight."

"Sure. I understand. Call me later in the week."

Jenn noticed a change in Renee's tone. Before she could say anything further, the call ended.

"Hello, this is Jennifer Halston. I am the Publisher of the *Serendipity Sun*. Is this Lyle Livingston?"

After answering a few emails and getting an update on the planned front-page stories for the Wednesday edition, Jenn was ready to begin the process of filling positions.

"Yes, this is Lyle Livingston. Thanks for calling. Congratulations on purchasing the newspaper."

"Thank you, Mr. Livingston. I'm excited about having the opportunity to take the *Serendipity Sun* to a new level. I'm looking for some excellent people to help me do so."

"Please call me Lyle. I'm interested in being one of those people. I understand that the paper currently does not have an Editor. Is that correct?"

"Yes."

"I'd like to have the opportunity to be considered for that role."

"I've heard some positive things about your previous time here. I've gone back through our archives and read some of your editorials. I see that you are not afraid to tackle controversial topics head on."

"You've certainly done your homework. That is correct. Under Mr. Sebastian's leadership, I took on some key issues that were facing the citizens and businesses of Serendipity. He and I did not always agree, but we did see the importance of giving the citizens a clear view of all sides of an issue."

"I learned that many years ago when I worked for Mr. Sebastian."

"Oh, I did not realize you were a former employee of the paper."

"It was a long time ago, my first real job. I would like to interview you, Lyle. I understand though that you live in a state in the West."

"I did. I'm in the process of moving back to the East Coast. In fact, I was planning to begin driving a moving truck in that direction in a few days. If you could possibly give me a week or so to travel and get temporarily settled, I would welcome the chance to be interviewed in person. If that does not work, I could be available for a video interview within the next few days."

"I can certainly wait until after you move. Where are you planning on living?"

"In Serendipity, if I get this job." Lyle laughed. "I don't have any plans past that. I would like to live in the South. I thought I would wait until I was on the East Coast before I started applying for positions."

"Okay. Please let me know when you get settled and we will set up an interview. Before then, I would like to ask if you would go online and review some of the recent issues of the paper and send me some bullet points of suggestions for improvements. You don't have to do this before you move. But I would like to receive it before we schedule your interview. When you send that, please attach a current resume and some recent writing clips, if you have them."

"Happy to do all of that."

Jenn gave Lyle her contact information and ended the call. It felt good to begin the process. Turning toward her computer, she clicked on her inbox and was surprised to see the most recent email was from Lyle. He had already sent all the items she requested, including the bullets about improvement.

"How in the world did he know I would ask for that?" Jenn laughed under her breath. "Because he's probably the right person for the job."

The rest of the morning consisted of a variety of business duties for Jenn. Every so often, she'd get this worried feeling about Renee. Something didn't seem right to her about their conversation the night before. Right before noon, Jenn dialed her sister's cell.

"You've reached Renee. I'm a busy lady. Leave me your number and I'll call you back."

"Hey, Sis. Just wanted to chat with you. Give me a call when you have some time. Love you."

Reaching out to one sister, made Jenn think of her other one. She'd not talked to Amber since their mother's funeral. Renee's husband, Neil, had been the one to arrange for Amber to enter rehab again. There were restrictions as to when they could be in contact with her. Like a movie Jenn had seen years earlier, they had to wait twenty-eight days before they could see or talk to Amber. Maybe since Jenn would be closer geographically to her younger sister, she could help her work through some of the issues that fueled her addictions. So much of that responsibility had rested on Renee's shoulders for too long.

A knock on her door brought Jenn out of her thoughts.

"Jenn, there is someone here who would like to apply for the advertising position." Betsy appeared in the doorway. "I wasn't sure if you were accepting applications yet, but since the person was here, I thought I would let you know." Betsy stepped into the office and lowered her voice. "Her name is Sutton Berkley. She worked here in ad sales about ten years ago. Her last name was Carmichael then."

"We don't even have a job description ready yet. Do you know how she found out about the position?"

"Ms. Berkley says that she saw someone from the newsroom in the grocery store over the weekend. I would bet it was Helen. They began working here around the same time."

"Okay. Well, that makes sense. Did she work for you back then?"

"No, someone else was Advertising Director then. Sutton was good at her job. She left because she had a difficult pregnancy, which I'm sad to say resulted in her losing the baby."

"I'm sorry to hear that. Betsy, I've got a phone meeting in about five minutes. Why don't you give Sutton one of our standard applications? We have some, don't we?"

"Yes, they are on Doris' desk."

"Ask her to fill one of those out and leave it with Doris. We can call her for an interview later."

"Okay, I'll tell her. Thanks."

As Betsy was closing the door, Jenn's phone buzzed with a text message.

"Hope the enchiladas didn't give you bad dreams." An emoji with a sombrero hat was at the end of Randy's message.

Jenn smiled. She intentionally had not allowed herself to think about last night. It would be too easy to pick apart each aspect and get caught up with old feelings.

"I'm still not hungry." She typed back. "It was a wonderful meal. Thank you."

"Hope you're having a great day. I enjoyed our time." This time a smiley face ended the message.

Her cell phone rang, taking her eyes away from the message, but not her heart.

"Hello, Mom. Have I caught you at a bad time?"

"No, Claire, I just got off the phone with my attorney in Atlanta. All the paperwork for the closing on the house is finally complete."

"It's sad to think about our house belonging to another family. I'm excited to visit you in your new home though."

Claire was Jenn's oldest child. She couldn't deny that in looks and personality, her oldest daughter was a carbon copy of Jenn. Stable and level-headed, Claire had a creative side, using her artistic eye to represent artists in gallery work. Claire had spent the five years since graduating college working her way up the ladder at one of Atlanta's most prestigious art galleries.

"Can't wait to see you."

"Since you've finished with the closing on the house, does that mean you've talked to Dad?"

"No. Since I am retaining the proceeds from the sale of the house, all Simon had to do was sign the final papers. My attorney took care of having that done."

"So, I guess you haven't heard his news?"

Jenn could hear the hesitation in Claire's voice. Unlike Emily, who was comfortable blurting out news, good or bad, Claire's tender heart would want to cautiously reveal something so shocking.

"I've not heard the news from your father. Your sister filled me in."

"Emily has never been able to keep a secret. Oh, Mom, I can't imagine how it must have made you feel."

"To be honest, honey, I find it amusing. I'm certain that this was not in Simon's plan for his new life. I hope Kenzie is ready to shoulder the load of childcare. Your father never got good at diaper changing, even after having three children."

"It's crazy, Mom. He's old enough to be a grandfather."

"That, he probably could handle."

"We shall see. I called to check on you and see how things are going with the newspaper. How does it feel to be a publisher?"

"I'm not going to sugarcoat it, Claire. It's an incredible challenge and more than a little scary."

"You've got this, Mom. Has it ever stopped being your dream? Even your children know that."

"I always taught you three the importance of having dreams. I'm not sure that I talked much about the reality of them coming true." Jenn stopped when she heard the beep of another call coming in. It was Mel. "I've got to say though that all the staff seems to be top-notch and dedicated. I've got a couple of spots to fill, but I don't think that will take long."

"My Super Mother will take Serendipity's newspaper to new heights. It sounds like you've got another call coming in."

"I do, it's Mel. I'll call her back. Was there anything else you wanted to chat about?"

The silence from normally chatty Claire answered Jenn's question.

"What's wrong, Claire?"

"I do have something I want to talk to you about. It's long and complicated though. I'm wondering if maybe I can come for a visit in a couple of weeks. Would that be too soon?"

"You could have met me at the door when I arrived, and it wouldn't have been too soon. I would have put you to work unpacking though." Jenn chuckled. Claire was silent.

"Honey, do you need to talk to me now? I've got the time."

"No, Mom. It's fine. I've got to get back to work. I'm going to a buying show in New York on Thursday. I will be there for about four or five days. I will try to call you from the Big Apple."

"Please do. I'd like to know that you get there safely. Are you travelling alone?"

"No. Two others from the gallery are going as well. We are going to stay an extra day or two and go to a couple of shows."

"That's wonderful. You have a great time. Thank you for checking on me, honey. It's great to hear your voice."

"I miss you being close by. I'm happy as can be for your new life, but I wish it wasn't so far away."

"We will make lots of fun beach memories, and I'm only a phone call away."

"I know. I'm looking forward to it. Love you, Mom."

"I love you."

Jenn laid down her phone and took a deep breath. As a mother, she tried to not pry in her children's lives, but she kept a watchful eye and a listening ear. Even when they were young, Jenn learned that observation would allow her to learn more about their lives than questions often did.

There was something off about the conversation with Claire. It was more about what she didn't say than what she did.

"Did you skip lunch again?"

Mel's voice startled Jenn. Looking up she saw her friend standing in the doorway. She was a welcomed sight.

"Guilty. If it makes you feel any better, I have been having a hearty bowl of oatmeal with my morning coffee and I bring a piece of fruit to eat mid-morning. There's no chance that I will waste away."

"I'm not worrying about you wasting away. I am concerned that you have enough brain fuel to make important decisions." A serious look crossed Mel's face. "Some of these decisions include math and we know you never excelled at that."

"Said by the girl who won the Math Award every year of high school. The girl who also interestingly doesn't use much math in her career."

"Hey, I use math every day. I count visitors and tourism revenues."

"Okay, Math Queen. Are you here to take me out to lunch?"

"Absolutely! I had a long webinar that started at noon. When Imogene came back from lunch, I tried to call you. When it went straight to voicemail, I knew you must be on a call. Since your Jeep is in the lot across the street, I figured it was a good chance that you had worked through lunch."

"What are we hungry for, Melinda Sue?"

"Cheeseburgers, Jenny Lee."

"That can only mean one place. Quincy's Diner!"

Both jumped up and down, waving their arms in the air.

"When I drove into town my first night back, I saw Mr. Quincy cleaning the glass door out front. I had no idea he was still involved with the business." Jenn walked around her desk, picking up her purse.

"He works a couple of days a week doing different little jobs. You know that he always liked keeping that door clean."

"Indeed. I vowed when I passed it that night that I would make sure to eat a meal there my first week. I'm several days late on that vow."

"All the more reason that we've got to go. I've been craving onion rings."

Jenn picked up her phone, slipping it into her purse. Her thoughts went back to Claire.

"What just crossed your mind? I see worry lines on your forehead."

"I was on the phone with Claire when you called."

"Is something wrong?"

"She didn't say there was. In fact, she's heading to New York in a couple of days for a gallery buying trip with some of her coworkers."

"That sounds like fun. Your mother radar picked up something else though."

"Yes. It's probably nothing. It may even be that she's only missing me. I feel like she wanted to talk about something that she didn't."

"Maybe you can catch her before she leaves for another chat. Claire's a strong girl. She'll talk when she's ready." Mel walked toward the door. "I'm ready for a milkshake. Let's get out of here before Doris tries to give you a call."

Doris looked up at the sound of her name with a big smile and a shaking finger in Mel's direction. Jenn came up behind her.

"We're going to Quincy's, Doris. When I return, I'll be like a walking zombie in a food coma."

"I'm happy to see that you are leaving the office to eat a meal, even if it is a greasy one." Doris went back to typing on her computer. "If you love ole Doris, you'll bring her back a strawberry shake."

"My pleasure. We shouldn't be long."

"At least an hour, that's why they call it a lunch hour." Doris looked up again, overtop of the reading glasses perched on her nose. "Everything will be fine here. We are a well-oiled machine."

"It's a beautiful day." Mel walked out the door in front of Jenn. "Why don't we walk to Quincy's? We can work up an appetite going and walk off some calories on the way back."

"Sounds perfect. This will also give me an opportunity to interrogate you about your date last weekend."

"I intend to do the same once we get to the diner. I want to be sitting across from you so that I can see your face."

"I didn't have a date."

"Sure, you didn't. You just had a home-cooked meal in the home of Serendipity's most eligible bachelor. No more talking about it until we are in our booth. In the meantime, I will tell you about my date. It was like the other two million dates I've gone on in my life, it was disappointing."

"I thought this guy sounded promising from what you told me."

"Good on paper, but that often doesn't turn into a fun experience. This guy was nice enough, successful, and okay in the looks department. What he lacked in personality, he made up for in ego. It made for a long evening."

"I do not understand why a wonderful girl like my Mel doesn't have a dozen wonderful men fighting over her." Jenn pulled Mel into a sideways hug while they continued to walk.

"My mother says I'm too picky. I say, I have taste."

For the remainder of the walk to Quincy's Diner, they chatted about the different businesses they passed along the way. Mel filled Jenn in about management or ownership changes for older businesses and stories about entrepreneurs who had converted old storefronts to thriving new businesses.

"There's nothing quite like being given a tour by the local tourism director." Jenn beamed at Mel, proud of her knowledgeable friend.

"As long as I've had this job, if I don't know this town, it's my own fault. We're finally here. I've really worked up an appetite. I'm afraid we might have to wait though. Even from the outside, it looks packed."

Opening the door and going inside, Jenn saw that Mel was right. At first glance, it appeared that every booth, table and counter seat were full. Jenn took a deep breath and her mouth watered. There's nothing quite like the nostalgic smell of a diner. It wasn't health food by a long shot, but there sure were a mountain of memories within the little restaurant. She could not imagine how many childhood hours, especially during her teens, that she spent at Quincy's with her friends and family.

"I remember sitting at the counter with my father, eating hot dogs and drinking root beer floats." Jenn's heart caught a moment when she saw what appeared to be a father and daughter sitting on stools at the end of the counter.

"Ladies, there's about a twenty-minute wait." The hostess came over to where they were standing. "But there's a gentleman back at that corner booth who says you are more than welcome to join him."

Jenn looked to where the hostess pointed. Leaning out of the booth toward the aisle and waving was Randy. Jenn bit her lip, trying not to laugh.

"Well, well, well, look who our knight-with-a-booth-spot is." Mel's voice was dripping in sarcasm.

Jenn rolled her eyes. Mel couldn't ask questions about her evening with Randy with him sitting right there. At least, Jenn hoped not.

Randy stood up when they reached the booth.

"Won't you ladies join me? I'll be the envy of every man in here."

"Thank you, Randy. I think I'll sit on this side of the booth." Mel slide into the booth, sitting in the middle. "Why don't you sit next to Randy, Jenn?"

With her back to Randy, Jenn gave Mel a wide-eyed look, not unlike ones she'd given Mel during their teen years in similar situations. Randy stepped out of the way, so that Jenn could slip into the booth before him. Out of the corner of her eye, she could see that he was trying hard not to laugh.

The waitress brought Jenn and Mel menus before Randy could even sit back down. Jenn quickly began studying the menu refusing to make eye contact with Mel. A shiver ran down her arm, when Randy sat, slightly bumping into her. Catching a whiff of his cologne, Jenn bit her bottom lip. *He smells so good.*

"Thanks, Randy, for coming to our rescue." Mel pulled on Jenn's menu that was in front of her face. "We sure are happy to not have to wait for a table. Aren't we, Jenn?"

"Yes, thank you, Randy."

"I'm happy to have the company. I've not been here long myself. All I had for breakfast was coffee and I've had a craving for a Quincy burger."

"I've forgotten about that one. Remind me what that is." Jenn scanned the menu to see if she could find the description.

"I don't think I knew any of this when I was a hungry teen who ate one at least once a week. But the Quincy burger is a nod to Mr. Quincy's Italian heritage. It's a burger stuffed with ricotta cheese, smothered in marinara sauce, served open-faced on garlic bread and topped with mozzarella and parmesan cheeses."

"Now, I remember. My father called it the lasagna burger." Jenn giggled.

"It's probably not something that I should eat in the middle of a workday, but here I am."

"This is Jenn's first visit to Quincy's since she's been home." Mel turned her attention back to the menu. "I heard that she had a delicious dinner the other night at a place called 'The Chief's.'"

"Delicious? Did she say the meal was delicious?" Randy smiled.

"I told you that. It was fabulous."

"Maybe she said the chef was delicious." Mel peaked over the top of the menu.

"Mel, cut it out." Jenn narrowed her eyes at Mel. She could feel the heat growing on her face.

Randy remained silent, but Jenn could hear a chuckle that he was trying to hold in.

"Are you ladies ready to order?"

Jenn could have hugged the waitress for appearing at that moment.

"I think we are." Mel laid her menu down. "I would like a grilled cheese with bacon, lettuce, tomato, and mayo, an order of onion rings, and a large diet soda."

"Does the diet soda balance out the rest of your order?" Randy chuckled.

"It does, Chief." Mel smirked.

"What would you like, ma'am?" The waitress turned her attention to Jenn.

"I'll have a patty melt with crinkle cut fries and sweet tea."

Jenn handed back her menu as the waitress picked up Mel's from the table.

"Chief, would you like me to hold your order until the ladies' orders are ready?"

"That will be fine." Randy nodded to the woman before she walked away.

"Slow day for police work in Serendipity, Randy? It sure seems busy enough in here." Mel looked over her shoulder toward the door. "I don't often see you eating lunch in a restaurant."

"It's been a different day for me. I had to assist with the transport of someone we arrested over the weekend. We took him to a regional jail near Raleigh."

"Isn't that something that your patrol officers normally do?" Jenn smiled at the waitress when she placed Jenn's tea in front of her.

"It would be. We are a little shorthanded this week. I've got two officers on vacation and one whose wife went into premature labor last night. That meant I had to pull some transport duty. That was an early morning."

"Oh, and after having me over last night. I'm sorry. I bet you would have gotten more sleep if I hadn't been there so late."

Jenn regretted the words as soon as they came out of her mouth. When she dared to look at Mel, she could tell that her friend was trying hard not to say anything.

"No worries about that, Jenn, I loved having company. After that full plate of food with those margaritas, I slept like a baby. If I had been there by myself, I probably would have had a bologna sandwich and a beer."

"That combination would have affected your sleep, for sure."

Jenn was relieved that was the only comment Mel made.

"Early mornings and late nights come with the job. I'm thankful to have a good team of officers who take it easy on this old man. It's rare for me to have to do a transport."

Randy waved at someone. Jenn looked in the direction of the entrance to see a man who seemed a little familiar to her.

"That man you waved at looked familiar."

"That was Sinclair Lewis."

Mel turned around so fast to look behind her that Jenn feared she might get whiplash. About that time, Jenn realized what Randy had said. Sinclair Lewis was a boy they went to school with. He was Mel's boyfriend their senior year. He was also the one who broke Mel's heart. Jenn scanned Mel's face to judge her reaction. Mel craned her neck to look out the window to the street.

"He's not been to Serendipity since they buried his mother."

"Haven't you heard? Sinclair has moved back here." Randy took a sip of his drink.

Jenn locked her attention on Mel. Randy's last statement seemed to be causing all sorts of reactions to Mel's expression. She looked surprised, angry, and slightly happy, in quick succession.

"Why? When?" A confused expression returned to Mel's face.

"A couple of weeks ago. Sinclair bought a vehicle dealership in Tyrell County." Randy nonchalantly replied.

"Am I remembering right? That's the next county west of here." Jenn had an idea.

"Yes." Randy answered while the waitress began serving their food.

"I'll have to remember that. If those dealerships don't currently advertise with us, having Sinclair as the new owner might help make that happen." Jenn continued to watch Mel. Keeping idle chat going at the table would give her friend the opportunity to process what she had just learned. She couldn't imagine how Mel was feeling.

"I would think so. There are a lot of people who would remember Sinclair. He was quite the basketball player."

Jenn watched Mel closely. She could almost hear her friend's thoughts from the expression on her face. Mel was starting to look a little sick. The server was approaching again. Jenn hoped this would distract Mel.

"Goodness, Randy! That is some sandwich." Jenn looked at the huge plate of food in front of Randy. "I'd forgotten what it was like. I was always amazed that my thin father would eat every bite."

"I don't allow myself to get it often. When I do, I usually get it to go and take it home for dinner. Truth be told, it takes me two nights to eat it. It would be a great meal for two with a salad." Randy made eye contact with Jenn.

"These fries are exactly like I remember." Jenn changed the subject. "They make you want to eat too much ketchup."

"Is there actually such a thing as too much ketchup?" Randy turned his attention back to his food, getting his knife and fork ready to cut into the open-faced sandwich.

"Ketchup contains a lot of sugar." Jenn glanced at Mel. She seemed to be staring at her food. "Mel, are you okay? Is something wrong with your food?"

"No. It's fine." Mel picked up an onion ring, and then set it back down. "So, Sinclair moved back here with his family? Doesn't he have several children?"

Jenn could see a troubled look forming in Mel's eyes.

"As I understand, Sinclair is divorced. I think his children would be grown by now." Randy took the first bite of his meal.

"Divorced? When did he and Dana get divorced? They've been married since we got out of high school." Mel kept questioning Randy.

"I think Sinclair said he's been divorced almost two years." Randy was still chewing his first bite.

Jenn's mind drifted back to what happened between Mel and Sinclair. The two started dating right before the junior prom. They dated steadily throughout their senior year. A large group of seniors, including Sinclair, Dana, and even Randy, went on a trip to Florida the week after graduation. Mel's parents wouldn't allow her to go. Jenn didn't go because Mel wasn't going.

Upon returning from the trip, Mel started telling Jenn that Sinclair was acting strangely, a little distant. Sinclair was supposed to be going to the same college that Jenn and Mel were attending. A couple of weeks before they were supposed to move, Sinclair broke up with Mel and told her he wasn't going to college. Mel was devastated. In a phone call a few weeks later, Jenn's mother had told her that Sinclair Lewis had married Dana Thompson. Dana's mother told Paisley that Dana was expecting Sinclair's child.

"Excuse me. I'm going to the restroom." Mel did not make eye contact with Jenn or Randy before she left the table.

"I forgot about them." Randy lowered his voice, turning to Jenn. "It's been so many years ago. It just hit me. Mel looks upset."

"It was a long time ago. But Mel really took their breakup hard. Sinclair getting married right away made it all so final. There wasn't much hope for them to reconcile then. She was a mess for a long time after that.

The only good thing about it was the timing. We were a couple of hours away from Serendipity, busy with classes and college life."

"I remember a little about it. I wasn't close friends with Sinclair, but we used to hang out some. I don't think he went on that trip planning to hook up with Dana or any other girl. I think it was a first taste of freedom thing. He was mad because his girlfriend wasn't there. Young and stupid. I think he loved Mel. His father made him 'do the right thing,' as it was called back then."

"If I remember correctly, Sinclair has lived a couple of hours away."

"When I saw him the other day, Sinclair told me that he got into the car business a couple of years after he and Dana got married. Dana had an uncle who was a partner in a dealership in Raleigh. They moved there after their first child was born and Sinclair went to work for Dana's uncle. You remember that Sinclair had an outgoing personality. He moved up the ladder, ultimately becoming a partner in that same dealership. When he and Dana divorced, the uncle bought him out. Coincidentally, the dealership over in Tyrell County was for sale. Sinclair decided that maybe he should come home. His older sister and younger brother still live nearby."

"Any idea why he and Dana divorced?"

"One strange thing about being a police officer, people tell you things. Often it isn't more than gossip. In Sinclair's case, without prompting, he told me his life story practically. I never realized that it might be useful. Sinclair said that he and Dana had a decent marriage. They made the best of the situation. Had two good kids. He found out about three years ago that Dana had been having an affair with the finance manager of the dealership for over ten years."

"Oh, my."

"Yes. So, he decided it was time to cut his losses. Because of the circumstances and his long record with the company, Dana's uncle was generous with his exit package."

"Mel's been gone quite a while. Maybe I should go check on her?"

Randy started to get up to let Jenn out when Mel returned to the table, sitting down and nodding at Jenn.

"Are you okay?"

"I'm fine. Just a little surprised."

"Is something wrong with your food, ma'am?" The waitress returned to the table.

"My food is fine. I've lost my appetite. Maybe you can bring me a container to put my meal in?"

"Make that two." Jenn raised her hand.

"Let's go for three." Randy hadn't even eaten a third of his meal.

"I also need a strawberry milkshake to go." Jenn almost forgot Doris' request. "Doris is thirsty."

The waitress quickly returned with the boxes and three checks. "The shake will be waiting for you at the register."

"I've got that, ladies." Randy quickly scooped up the bills.

"Randy, that's not necessary." Jenn tried unsuccessfully to reach for the bills.

"If anything, we should be buying your lunch for allowing us to join you." Mel put her untouched food into the Styrofoam container.

"What I should have done was not wave to Sinclair." Randy shook his head, frowning.

"Randy, it's a small town. Sooner or later, I was going to find out. I'd rather hear it from you then some loudmouth in the grocery store. At least, Sinclair did not see my reaction. I have time to digest this information and have my game face ready."

"It's been a long time. People change." Randy closed the lid of his full box.

"Randy's right. Maybe you and Sinclair can be friends." Jenn ate one more of her fries before she slid them into the container.

"Do you think you and Simon will ever be friends, Jenn?" Mel rolled her eyes.

"Who knows? I might even send him a case of diapers for his new baby."

Jenn's comment provoked a snort out of Mel. It was a welcomed sound.

"Wait a minute. I thought Simon was your ex-husband." Randy furrowed his brow.

"He is. Simon and his new wife are going to be parents."

"Well, there's a twist to that story." Randy shook his head. "That will make for interesting holidays with your children."

"That will make for an interesting life for Simon." Jenn looked at the reminder that had come up on her phone for an appointment in ten minutes. "I've lost track of time. Mel and I walked here. Any chance that the local police chief might give us a ride back?"

"You'll have to sit in the back." Randy laughed. "That will make a good story for the newspaper."

Chapter Ten

Mel

"Did you have a good lunch?"

Mel's assistant, Imogene, was all smiles when Mel walked through the door of the Visitors Bureau.

"I wasn't as hungry as I thought." Mel looked down at the box in her hand. "Do I have any messages?"

"I've stuck a couple on your corkboard. Nothing pressing, I don't think." Imogene took in a deep breath. "You may want to fire me though."

"Why in the world would I want to do that?"

Mel sighed. Imogene was fresh out of college. This was her first job. For the most part, Imogene was quite mature for her age. Sometimes, Mel forgot how young she was.

"Well, after you left for lunch, I decided that it would be a good time to take everything off my desk and give it a good cleaning. Tucked under my standing file holder, I found this message for you. It's from about two weeks ago." Imogene held out a pink message slip.

"Oh, Imogene, the world will not come to an end because of one missed message. If it was important, the person has probably called back by now."

"I sure hope so. You know how methodical I am when our visitors call in requesting brochures mailed to them. You taught me from my very first day that if someone makes the effort to request information about our town, that it's our job to send it out that same day, if possible."

Mel didn't hear anything else Imogene said. The name on the message was 'Sinclair Lewis.'

Holding her breath until she reached her office and closed the door, Mel let out a sob that had been building since Randy first said Sinclair's name in the diner. She'd not dared to even release it in the restroom of the restaurant for fear that she would not be able to stop the crying once it started.

Thankful that her assistant's chair faced toward the front door instead of Mel's office, she didn't try to stop the deep sobs or flood of tears that were now flowing. It had been many years since she'd allowed these old wounds to be opened. She couldn't deny that even though over thirty years had passed, the hurt was still there. The fact that Mel had not found a lasting love since her young heartbreak didn't ease the sorrow. It was like the chicken or the egg scenario. Was Sinclair her one chance at true love? Or did the damage to her soul from the breakup prevent her from allowing love in?

Wiping her tear-stained face and runny nose with a tissue, Mel stared at the pink slip with a name that was imbedded on her heart and a phone number she never expected to have. *What am I going to do?*

Like an answer to a prayer, the ding of a text message drew Mel's eyes away from the message. It was Jenn checking on her. Mel would never have survived that first year after Sinclair broke up with her and immediately married Dana without Jenn. The irony that Jenn was so close by when Sinclair reappeared did not escape Mel's thoughts.

"I need my friend tonight." Mel typed the short response.

"Why don't you pack a bag for you and Mia, and we'll have a sleepover?"

"Perfect."

The remaining hours of the afternoon passed slowly. Somehow, Mel managed to conceal her swollen eyes with a little makeup. Imogene was never the wiser, or at least never let on, if she was. Enough tasks demanded Mel's attention to distract her thoughts until five o'clock finally came and the closed sign could be hung on the door.

At home, Mia's welcomed wagging brought a smile to Mel's face.

"We're going to see Auntie Jenn and Mr. Jasper. Mommy needs therapy."

Mia cocked up her head like she didn't understand the last word.

After packing a few essentials, Mel made a quick call to check on her parents and let them know she would be staying at Jenn's. Driving the back streets from her house to Jenn's oceanfront property, Mel found herself looking at every vehicle she passed, wondering if it might contain Sinclair. The coincidence of the day might not be over. Now, Mel would have to be on guard. It gave her an anxious feeling in her stomach.

Pulling into Jenn's driveway, it hit Mel that she'd not even asked Jenn if she needed her to bring anything. Jenn came out on the side deck with Jasper in her arms.

"My southern manners are on hiatus." Mel closed the car door after letting Mia out. "I didn't even ask you if you needed me to pick anything up."

"No worries. I've got plenty of food and beverages for all of us as well as some extra snacks appropriate for an occasion such as this." Jenn let

Jasper down to join Mia. "Remember, I'm newly divorced. I understand what foods are therapeutic."

"Wine and chocolate." Mel proclaimed loudly.

"And any item produced by Little Debbie."

"You do speak fluent heartbreak, my friend."

Mel climbed the steps up to Jenn's back door. Dropping the bags at the door, she allowed Jenn to engulf her in a strong hug.

"I've wanted to do this all afternoon." Jenn did not let go.

"I've needed it even longer than that." Mel let out a small sob. "It got worse this afternoon."

"You've had too much time to think about it."

"I had a message to call him."

Jenn stepped back to make eye contact with Mel. "What?"

"Apparently, Sinclair called me two weeks ago. Imogene misplaced the message and found it today, while we were at lunch."

"No way."

"Oh, yes. I have his phone number on a little pink slip. How's that for irony? A pink slip from Sinclair."

"Come on in. We've got a lot to talk about."

Jenn called for the dogs to come inside while Mel carried in her bags. Setting them at the edge of the living room, Mel glanced around, resting her gaze on the ocean in the distance.

"Before we do anything else, can we please take a walk with our feet in the ocean?"

"I can't think of anything I'd rather do. I know our babies will love it, too. Let's go."

Mia and Jasper heard 'go' and were instantly running in circles. The sight brought joy to Mel's tired heart. She knew that being with her best friend combined with the soothing ocean would help her make sense of the curveball that was flying toward her head.

Walking arm in arm, Mel and Jenn followed their puppies down the steps leading to the beach. It would be another hour before the sun would set. The sound of the crashing waves hinted that a storm might be brewing.

Once at the ocean, Jenn frolicked in the water with the dogs. Mel began walking along the water's edge. Her mind was racing with the emotions of the day. She longed for a blissful calm. She allowed her mind to focus on her surroundings—the squish of the sand between her toes, the gentle force of the breeze that tousled her hair, the warmth of the sun. With only the moving water to hinder her, Mel walked at a steady, rhythmic pace, leaving Jenn and their pets behind. She could see the glow of beginnings of a sunset. Slowly, the tightness in her shoulders eased. Her heart rate lowered. While her tears flowed freely, it was a release instead of a sorrow. It was relief that was years in the making.

Mel didn't realize she wasn't alone until she heard splashing behind her. Thinking it was Jenn, she turned to speak. Shocked to find a man behind her, Mel quickly wiped her tears in order to see him. It was Jenn's neighbor.

"I tried to make a little noise with the water. I didn't want to startle you and disturb your thoughts."

Parker Bentley made eye contact with Mel but didn't hold it. Mel thought perhaps he saw her tears and did not want to be intrusive.

"I heard you. I thought it was Jenn and our dogs."

"They are still in front of Jenn's house."

"I decided to walk alone."

"This beach is a healing experience."

Parker made eye contact again. Mel thought she saw understanding.

"I'll not bother you further. I still plan to visit your office soon. I need a well-rounded perspective before I reach a decision."

"I imagine it would be hard to give up something so beautiful." Mel looked back in the direction of the Oasis.

"That is true of many things. We do not always make wise choices."

Mel turned her gaze to Parker. He was staring intently at her. She wondered if his words had a double meaning.

"Sometimes choices are made for us."

"Indeed. I am acquainted with that reality. I faced it from an early age." Parker stretched, rotating his shoulders. "It is one reason why I want to clearly know all sides of the decision I am about to make. I've lived with the regrets of others. I don't want to live with my own."

"I hope you are successful." Mel began to walk toward Jenn's house.

"We make our own success. It's our happiness that often falls in the hands of others. Good evening, Mel."

Without another word, Parker began running in the opposite direction. Mel was left with a surreal feeling that this stranger had glimpsed her life without even knowing her.

"Something smells divine."

With her wavy hair still wet, Mel walked into Jenn's living room after her shower. Worn out from their beach frolic, Jasper and Mia were curled up on Jasper's oversized pillow bed.

"Zuppa Toscana! My favorite comfort food." Jenn pulled out a baguette from the oven. "It's a contradictory combination of healthy and not—kale, potatoes, and garlic paired with Italian sausage and heavy cream. It's the most delicious soup I make. My kids call it 'the good stuff.'"

"Yum." Mel stirred the soup, still in a large pot on the stove. "Those aromas are intoxicating."

"We will pair it with a dry Riesling. Renee left me Mom's wine stash."

"What can I do? Have the children been fed?"

"Yes, they dined on some wet and dry food with a grilled chicken appetizer."

"Sounds delightful."

"I think they will mostly be making snores for the rest of the evening from Jasper's king-size bed. They are worn out."

"The beach can be energizing and draining simultaneously." Mel turned back to the stove. "Can I fill our soup bowls now?"

"That would be great. I'm going to quickly slice up this baguette. I've already placed some assorted cheeses on the table and a small green salad."

"My stomach is roaring. I am realizing that I haven't eaten since breakfast."

"You never ate your lunch, did you?"

"I pulled the bacon off the sandwich this afternoon, thinking maybe a protein boost would help."

Jenn laughed heartily, causing the dogs to raise their heads.

"We convince ourselves of many things when we are sad. I didn't end up eating it. I couldn't stomach anything this afternoon."

"I hope that feeling has changed." Jenn walked into the dining room with a bottle of wine in one hand and a basket of bread in the other.

"My stomach is more than ready to receive food now." Mel followed Jenn with two steaming bowls, in quilted cozies, of the soup. "I feel like the ocean has cleansed me. I've given it my salty tears and it has lifted my spirits with its soothing breeze."

"Sometimes you've got to cry everything out." Jenn sat down at the table.

"Is that what you did after Simon made his revelation to you?" Mel joined her on the opposite side. "It still amazes me how you have gotten through this year with such strength."

"One of my long-time friends in Atlanta who had her own challenges with life's curveballs gave me some good advice. She told me that a breakup or divorce was like the death of someone in your life. You needed to go through all the stages of grief in order to heal." Jenn filled each of their wineglasses.

"At first, I scoffed a little at the idea. Simon was still out there walking around. The breakup of our marriage wasn't as final as a death. As the weeks passed, I saw that she was right. I went through what they say are the five stages of grief—denial, anger, bargaining, depression, and acceptance. It was almost like clockwork how it progressed. It was then that I realized that divorce, especially after a long marriage, is like death. The tie is severed. I suppose there are those rare people who reconcile, but let's face it, even if they did, it would not be the same."

"It would have been helpful if I understood this when I was eighteen. Maybe I wouldn't have spent our entire freshman year of college thinking I did something horribly wrong. I guess that's a curse of youth." Mel lifted the glass and took her first drink. "Paisley had excellent taste in wine."

"I'm not so sure that the knowledge of these stages helped with the process of going through them. I spent a couple of months blaming myself for the divorce. Maybe if I'd done this or maybe if I'd done that.

Looking back, it was ridiculous. It takes two people to stay married. I can now see that Simon checked out mentally years ago."

"You are being the kind hostess by avoiding the topic of the elephant in the room. I need you to go ahead and be my best friend now. I'm a twisted ball of emotions."

"First, I want to see you eat. Don't let your soup get cold."

Mel slipped her spoon into the creamy soup. One spoonful told her what she already knew—her body and soul needed comfort. The ingredients were a symphony on her tongue. Once she started eating, she couldn't stop. The bowl was almost empty before she even looked up and found Jenn watching her with an expression of happy surprise.

"I think you must like it." Jenn laughed, beginning to eat her own bowl. "There's plenty more in the pot."

"Jenn, I would tell you that it is the best thing I've ever eaten, if it hadn't been that I've had it before. I remember you making this when I would visit when your kids were young. We'd go see one of them playing some sport or at a recital. When we returned to your house, there would be a pot of this in the slow cooker."

"That's been a lot of years ago. You stopped coming to visit as often somewhere through the years. Over the last decade, we've seen more of each other on my visits here than by you travelling in my direction. Why is that?"

Mel ate more of her salad while she pondered how to answer the question. She and Jenn did not make a habit of keeping secrets. This was one that she'd never revealed.

"You've gotten too quiet. Is there something I don't know about?"

Mel took a sip of water before she spoke. Stalling was not going to make what she had to say any easier.

"First of all, please don't be mad at me for not telling you about this when it happened. I didn't want to cause any issues for you."

"Mel, you're scaring me. Just tell me."

"I stopped coming to visit you because of Simon. During the last time I stayed at your house, he had a conversation with me that made me understand that it would be better if he and I were only in the same room when it was absolutely necessary."

"What did he do?" Jenn's eyes narrowed.

"He had made a few snide remarks through the previous years. When I was there for Emily's thirteenth birthday, he made it clear what he thought about me. He said that I should quit trying to live my life through your family and go get a family of my own."

"Simon said that to you, in our house?"

"Yes. We were in the backyard. It was right before everyone was supposed to be arriving. He was grilling hamburgers and hotdogs." Mel made eye contact with Jenn. She could almost see steam coming out of her ears. "Simon finally told me what he thought of me. He was your husband and you loved him. I needed to respect that. I decided then that I wouldn't visit as often and would stay in a hotel when I did."

"I saw the change in your behavior. You still were that faithful 'Aunt Mel' with all the birthday cards and Christmas presents. They started coming through the mail instead of being personally delivered. I thought that you were getting busier at work, maybe more responsibility. I even thought that you might be seeing someone and weren't ready to talk about him." Jenn reached across the table and squeezed Mel's hand. "I should have known that something had changed."

"There's a part of me that regrets allowing him to affect my visits. You were so busy with the kids then. All three of them were teenagers going in a million different directions. I didn't want to be part of your stress."

"You were never part of my stress, Mel. I was only beginning to learn what a jerk Simon could be at times. There were some of my local friends who he rubbed the wrong way, too. Some were the wives of his business associates or clients."

"I would never have allowed him to come between our friendship. We had plenty of time to visit when you came to see your parents. Paisley always made sure that we had a least a day or two to ourselves. We would chat about it in advance."

"Did Mom know what happened?"

"Yes." Mel scowled. "She pretty much figured it out when I wasn't planning trips to Atlanta. She stopped by the office one day and cornered me until I told her the truth. Keeping something from Paisley was like hiding something from my own mother. She knew me too well."

"Mom never cared for Simon. Dad didn't either. Like you, they tolerated him for my benefit and the children's. I had my rose-colored glasses too attached to my face to see what was crystal clear to everyone else. Even my children have talked to me about it. They felt his love toward them. They said that I did not get treated as well as I should have."

"It's true. Jenn, you can't dwell on it now. It's in the past, and you need to concentrate on your glaringly bright future."

"So says the woman who had a meltdown today over a breakup from her teenage years. How did this conversation become about me? I'm supposed to be counseling you."

"It felt good to not think about myself for a few minutes." Mel chuckled. "Even if it was because of your rotten ex-husband."

"If it's any satisfaction, he's getting his karma served back to him. I cannot even imagine how this new child situation will play out. I'll keep you informed though. Emily will give us a play-by-play. Let's have more soup and wine."

Jenn picked up both soup bowls and headed back to the kitchen. Mel poured another glass of wine for them. Once Jenn returned to the table, they ate in silence for a few minutes.

"It's been a long time since you mentioned hearing anything about Sinclair. Have you even seen him during the years he lived in Raleigh?" Jenn ate most of her second bowl of soup before she resumed the conversation.

"Not really. Sinclair and Dana moved away from Serendipity before we finished college. You know that I didn't come home very often and got summer jobs near the campus. I didn't want to run into him. If he'd still been living here when we graduated, I doubt I would have moved back to Serendipity."

"I remember us sneaking into town on our trips home like we were secret agents."

"Mom and Dad went to the funerals of both of Sinclair's parents. According to Mom, he just shook their hands. I laid low both times. I thought that I had dodged the 'Sinclair bullet' after his last parent passed. The family home was sold. I never imagined he would return to live here."

"So, tell me more about this message from him."

"There's nothing much to tell. The date on the message is ten days ago. His name and phone number are written on it. Imogene says that he didn't leave any other message. He only asked for her to tell me that he called."

"I would imagine by now that he doesn't think you will be calling."

"I guess not."

"What do you think you would have done if you'd gotten the message the day he called?"

"I would have had a heart attack. I'm sure that I would have called a couple of people to try and find out where he was and what he might want."

"And?"

"I honestly don't know. The professional side of me always calls people back. The professional side of me doesn't want to talk to Sinclair though. I might have asked Imogene to call back and say I was out of town or something."

"To see if he would ask her for help?"

"Yes. Then, he could have been handled without me getting involved." Mel shook her head. "But I also know that if it was work-related information he needed, Sinclair could have asked Imogene in the first place. I don't think there's much doubt that he called to speak to me personally. Perhaps, it was the courtesy of telling me he'd moved back."

"I thought about that. But that's a big assumption on his part."

"What do you mean?"

"Sinclair would have to be assuming that you even cared if he was living in Serendipity. It's been decades since you broke up. You two were kids. He would have to assume that you'd been carrying a torch for him. Sinclair wasn't that cocky when he was a popular teenager. I somehow doubt he is now."

"What's your theory then?" Mel moved her bowl out of the way and put her elbows on the table, giving Jenn her complete attention.

"Maybe he wants to try and make amends. A lot of years have passed, people change. Maybe Sinclair wants to apologize and see if he can mend a friendship."

Jenn bit her bottom lip. Mel knew from experience that usually meant Jenn had something more to say and was debating whether to say it.

"Go ahead. Spit it out."

"Randy told me that he's talked to Sinclair since he moved back."

"When did he tell you this?"

"While you were in the restroom at the diner."

"Are you going to tell me what he found out?"

"Some of it I think you probably already know. After they married, Sinclair and Dana moved to Raleigh because her uncle had a dealership there and offered Sinclair a job. Sinclair did well in the car business and eventually became a partner."

"Get to the part about why he's back here."

"I'm not sure that Randy said anything specifically about why Sinclair chose Serendipity as his new home. But he did tell Randy why he's divorced."

"And?"

"Apparently he found out that Dana had been having an affair for ten years with someone who worked at the dealership."

"Ten years!"

"I guess it was happening right under his nose."

"Why would anyone cheat on Sinclair?" Mel closed her eyes and shook her head. "Did I just say that aloud?"

"You did. It's okay. I could see it on your face anyway." Jenn smiled. "Because of the circumstances, I think the uncle offered Sinclair a generous buyout from the dealership. As luck would have it, there was a dealership for sale near Sinclair's hometown."

"And, now, Sinclair Lewis is living back in *my* town."

"And he's called you."

"And I don't want to call him back."

"Maybe I can help with that."

Chapter Eleven

Jenn

Gathering up the dishes, Jenn headed to the kitchen.

"Hold on, girlfriend. You can't drop that bombshell and leave the room." Mel followed carrying the cheeseboard.

"I thought we could continue the conversation on the deck once I put the food away and load the dishwasher."

"We can do all that except the continuing the conversation part. The conversation needs to continue now."

"Patience has never been your strong point, Mel." Jenn couldn't torture her friend any longer. "I thought I would go see Sinclair at this dealership. I'd take one of my ad reps who could present him with an advertising package."

"That sounds logical except why you would be going along? I don't remember Mr. Sebastian going on sales calls very often."

"Perhaps, but I thought I could say that, like him, I am newly back in the area. Even before this, I'd been thinking about having a series of articles about people who grew up in Serendipity and then returned years later. People like me, Randy, *and* Sinclair. I could call the series 'Coming Home.'"

"That sounds legit. How would you find out why he called me?"

"I think he would immediately associate me with you. It would be a golden opportunity for him to find out about you. I think the topic would come up in the conversation."

"I'm not sure if I want him to know about me."

"Mel, you operate the Visitors Bureau. People know you. How do you think he found out where to call you?"

"Okay. You've got a point. It is better than me returning his call blindly, two weeks late."

"Now that we have that settled. Will you help me clean things up so that we can watch the rest of the sunset on the deck?" Jenn finished transferring the remaining soup into a storage container.

"Certainly. I have one question."

"What's that?" Jenn put the soup pot into the dishwasher.

"Can you go tomorrow?"

"Why wait?" Jenn chuckled. "Why don't I go tonight?" Jenn shook her head, laughing

"It's okay. Tomorrow is soon enough."

Jenn and Mel spent the remainder of the evening on the deck—watching the sunset, listening to the waves crash, and relaxing. The beautiful mixture of colors was like a painting coming to life. Jenn could not think of anything more relaxing than the whish-whish of the waves saying goodnight.

"I think I'm going to go to bed." Jenn sat up in the lounge chair. "I have a busy day of detective work tomorrow." Jenn stood up, looking in the direction of the Oasis. "Maybe later in the week, I will cook something for Parker as a neighborly gesture."

"Oh, Parker!" Mel sat up on her lounger. "I saw him earlier while I was walking on the beach. It was a kind of a strange conversation. Part of that was my fault since I'd been crying, and my face probably looked all puffy and swollen."

"So, what was strange about the conversation?"

"He was talking to me like he knew what I was upset about. It gave me an eerie feeling." Mel rubbed her arms, like she was chilled. "Parker said something that was quite wise, but also ominous. He said that our happiness is often in the hands of others. I thought it was a strange statement."

"Parker certainly had some decisions made for him at an early age. I suppose you could say that his parents' choices impacted Parker's happiness. It is an unusual way of putting it."

"That's what I mean. It's a strange statement, almost like you don't have a say in your own happiness."

"That is eerie considering who you saw today. Sinclair was forced into a choice that I'm sure he didn't want to make. It obviously affected his happiness and yours."

"See! It's like Parker knew what happened today."

"Well, maybe he bought a car from Sinclair today." Jenn rose from the lounger.

"Stop that!" Mel hit Jenn in the arm. "You are making fun. Today was not funny. Today was like all the imagined scenarios of the worst way I could see Sinclair again in one horror movie."

"Oh, Mel, I'm sorry. I promise that tomorrow I'm going to find out some useful information so you can figure out how to handle the situation going forward." Jenn pulled Mel into a hug. "Please try to get some sleep."

"My stomach is so full of soup and wine; I'm almost comatose as it is."

"I forgot that I had some dessert for us. I picked up a couple of different flavors of cupcakes from The Frosted Goddess."

"We can have those for breakfast. Have you met Jasmine Rider, the owner?"

"I don't think so. Both times I have been in there, I've been waited on by a teenager with orange hair."

"That's Jasmine's niece, Porcha. She's a sweet kid. She's been accepted into Juilliard."

"*The* Juilliard?" Jenn turned out the lights in the kitchen and followed Mel down the hallway to the bedrooms.

"Yep. Apparently, she is a musical prodigy."

"That's good, because I had to tell her how to make change. She looked at me so strangely when I paid with cash. It was like I was handing her a poisonous substance."

"I think that's one of the reasons that Porcha is working there. Jasmine said something the last time I was in about wanting her niece to understand the real world."

"The real world. Sometimes I wonder what that really is."

"You and me both, girlfriend."

*****

"Good morning, Doris." Jenn handed Doris a small bag.

"Good morning, Jenn. What's this?" Doris raised her eyebrows, smiling.

"I made some soup last night for Mel. I thought you might enjoy some for lunch today."

"Thank you." Doris opened the bag, reaching in to investigate the contents. "This is a full meal. There's bread, salad, and a cupcake, too. I might save this for dinner."

"That's even better. When Ellie gets in, will you have her come to my office?"

"Certainly. She should be here soon. Is everything okay?"

"Yes. I have a potential new client for us. I'd like to accompany her when she makes the call."

Jenn headed to her office. Her phone beeped with a text before she had time to sit down. Pulling the phone out of her purse, she saw the message was from her son, Foster.

Sending him a quick response, moments later her phone lit up with a call from him.

"Good morning, Foster. How's my favorite son today?"

"That joke is just as funny as the first time you made it years ago, Mom."

"Sorry, Foster. How are things with you?"

"I'm good. I wanted to talk to you for a few minutes to see how you are doing in your new adventure and to tell you that I'm about to start a new one of my own."

"My adventure is an overwhelming learning experience with an ocean in the background."

"Cool. You deserve something wonderful in your life, Mom. Claire told me Dad's latest news. I still don't get it."

"Don't worry about me, Foster. I'm embracing my life with both hands and ready for this challenge. Now, tell me your news."

"I've been offered a promotion."

"That's wonderful. Do you have to move?"

"I don't have to, but I'm thinking about it. The job is fully remote with travel, of course."

"Does that mean you could live anywhere?" Jenn's motherly mind immediately imagined her only son moving halfway around the world.

"In theory, yes. That's probably limited to the United States since I still need to make business trips within the country."

"Whew! I'm relieved. I was imagining you living in some remote corner of the globe." Jenn laughed. "When does this promotion begin?"

"It already has. I was sort of given a test run of doing the job for about the last sixty days or so. I didn't mention it because I wanted to make sure that I liked it and that my bosses thought I could do the job. Michelle and I have been thinking that we could make a move, if we wanted to."

"Is Michelle interested in changing jobs?"

Foster and Michelle married shortly after they graduated college two years earlier. Both had degrees in marketing, but their careers were opposites. Michelle was a goal-breaking sales rep for a mega real estate agency in Atlanta. Foster worked on the marketing team for one of the biggest soda companies in the world, specializing in social media.

"Michelle is getting a little burnt out selling real estate. It's such a high-pressure career in a city like Atlanta. She's been thinking about trying a different type of sales."

"You've both excelled. You spend most of your life working; you should enjoy it, if you can. Where have you been thinking about geographically?"

"Both of us have dreamed of living at the beach. You know how much we enjoy water sports."

"I know someone who lives at the beach." Jenn got a little excited.

"I think that would be my favorite mother. What if we came to visit and didn't leave?"

A shocked Jenn was not sure how to answer.

"Mom, that's not the reaction I was expecting."

"Foster, I'm shocked. I would be thrilled for you to move to Serendipity."

"That's better. We aren't asking to move in with you. Michelle has already been looking at real estate online and talking to an agent. We are thinking about looking at a couple of fixer-uppers that are on the canal side. There are several rental properties in our price range that we could pay outright for."

"Wow! I didn't realize you had that kind of savings."

"Michelle and I have managed to live rather cheaply. We've both done quite well these first two years of our jobs. We've stashed away quite a bit thinking that we would be needing a hefty down payment to buy a house in Atlanta."

"I'm so proud of you, Foster. You and Michelle both. That's quite some mature financial habits you two are forming. How fun it would be for you two to remodel a home."

"The only thing we are concerned about is finding a job for Michelle. There are certainly lots of online or remote positions she could do, but she loves face-to-face interaction with clients."

"Oh, Foster! I think I know of a job that would be perfect for Michelle!" Jenn couldn't believe it hadn't occurred to her sooner.

"That would be great. Where is it?"

"Working at the *Serendipity Sun* with me. I need to hire a new advertising sales rep. I have some big plans for expansion of the newspaper. I need to build revenue to do that."

"Give her a goal and Michelle will exceed it. I'm sure she would love to be a part of an expansion. It would challenge her creativity."

Jenn looked up and saw that Ellie was in her doorway.

"This is all wonderful news, Foster. Let's talk again this evening if you have time. I have someone in my doorway that I need to talk to. Give Michelle my love. I'm so excited about this."

"Me, too, Mom. We'll call you soon. Love you."

"Love you."

"Hello, Ellie, I'm sorry that I was on the phone."

"You wanted to see me, Ms. Halston."

"Jenn wanted to see you. I've got a lead on a potential new advertising client for us."

"That's great! Give me the name and I'll head over to see them."

Jenn was pleased to see that Ellie had come to her office with a pen and pad in hand.

"You and I are going to have to do some detective work to find out the name of the business. I would like to go with you on this call. I'm thinking that we might do a story on the new owner."

"Sure, we can double team to clinch the sale! Most clients would love having the exposure of an article to pair with their advertising. What type of business is it?"

"It's a car dealership in Tyrell County. The new owner's name is Sinclair Lewis."

"Okay. Let me do some research and call around. It shouldn't be hard to find out which dealership it is. How did you learn about the change in ownership?"

"Chief Nave told me. The Chief and I went to high school with Sinclair Lewis. He's recently moved back to Serendipity and bought the dealership in Tyrell County. That would be the angle of the story."

"That sounds great. Car dealerships make awesome clients. When would you like to go?"

"I was thinking that if you could confirm the dealership name and get the phone number, I would call and make an appointment, preferably for this afternoon, if Sinclair is available."

"I'll email you the information as soon as I can." Ellie left the room.

Jenn's phone was blowing up with text messages. She had multiple messages from Mel wanting to know when she was going to see Sinclair. One from Foster thanking her for their talk. Short ones from Claire and Emily. Even one from Randy, checking to see how Mel was doing. One person was glaringly missing, Renee.

Jenn dialed her sister's number hoping to hear Renee's cheerful voice. After several rings, it went to voicemail.

"Hey, Renee. I hadn't heard from you and was wondering how those tests went. Please call me when you have time. Love you."

Jenn pressed the button to end the call. A feeling of dread passed over her. Something wasn't right about the situation. Renee would be furious if Jenn went around her and called Neil, Renee's husband. Renee and Neil were very close. They'd been through so much together. Most couples would not have survived the tragedy that tore their family apart.

Jenn reached into her purse and pulled out her wallet. She knew it was a rare thing for anyone to do in the digital age they lived in, but Jenn kept a couple of actual photos tucked inside. Little dog-eared school photos of her own children when they were small. A photo of her parents when they were first married. And a photo of a little boy who went to school one day and never came home.

Jenn felt emotion well inside of her as she pulled the small photo out from a compartment behind the others. The sweet little boy with the light red curls, green eyes, and freckles across his nose. Her precious nephew, Jonah.

"Jenn. Jenn, are you okay?"

Doris' voice grew louder, pulling Jenn back from the past. Jenn wiped a tear from her eye when she raised her head and found Doris standing in the middle of Jenn's office.

"I'm sorry, Doris. I didn't hear you. Lost in my thoughts, I guess."

"What's wrong? You've been crying."

"My tears are not for the present. It's a sadness from long ago." Jenn handed the photo to Doris. "Do you remember this sweet face?"

Doris took the photo. A gasp escaped her lips as a realization crossed her face.

"I remember. This is Renee's son, yes?"

"Yes, it's Jonah. This was his only school photo. He was five years old. It was taken at the beginning of the school year. A few weeks later he was gone."

"Some of the details are blurry now. Do you mind refreshing my memory?"

Jenn took a deep breath, staring at the photo after Doris handed it back to her. A few moments later, a smile crossed her face.

"It was the weekend before Halloween. A beautiful warm fall. The leaves were spectacular. Simon and I brought the kids to visit my parents for a long weekend at the beach. Claire was six and Foster was three. They were a handful. Renee, Neil and Jonah came for a couple of days, too. Claire, Foster, and Jonah played on the beach from sunrise to sunset. Throwing Frisbees. Building sandcastles. Frolicking in the water. It was as happy of a time as we ever had as a family."

Jenn stood up from her desk, walking around it. She began to pace in front of her desk.

"They headed back to Raleigh early on Sunday morning because Neil needed to meet a potential client to quote a big job. That was about the time that Dad first expanded the construction business to Raleigh. Neil had already landed a couple of contracts to build dozens of homes in a subdivision. The job he was bidding that day was similar, only it was for patio apartments near a university. Jonah begged his parents to let him stay with us until we traveled home midday on Monday. Renee would not hear of it. She told him that he could not miss school."

"I'm not sure I knew this part of the story." Doris furrowed her brow. "If Jonah had stayed with you, he wouldn't have been at school on the day—"

"No. He wouldn't have been. Renee will never forgive herself for telling him no." Jenn stopped pacing and leaned on the front of her desk, in a half-seated position, rubbing her forehead. "They went back to Raleigh on Sunday. Neil met the client. Jonah went to school on Monday morning. On Monday afternoon, we began the six-hour plus drive back to Atlanta. It was another beautiful day."

"Everything you've said so far sounds so normal. It's not the part of the story that most people heard."

"No, it's not. The story the public heard was anything but normal. For Renee and Neil, normal ended that morning." Jenn held back tears. "Renee took Jonah to school. She went to the grocery store. She ran other errands. She decorated her front porch with pumpkins, skeletons, and spider webs, for the little ghouls and goblins she expected to arrive on her doorstep a few days later. She was outside when her phone first started ringing."

"That was a time long before cell phones or even portable landlines. If you weren't in the house with your phone, you didn't know it was ringing."

"True. Because of Neil's work with the construction company, they did have an answering machine. Looking back, I'm not sure that was a good thing. Renee still has that message on a tiny little cassette." Jenn took a deep breath. "The school had called. They couldn't find Jonah. The police had been called. They asked for Renee and Neil to come to the school."

"And so it began, the longest day of their lives." Doris reached out and squeezed Jenn's hand.

"That day has never ended, not for Renee and Neil. Other days have come and gone, but that October day will never be over."

"I remember the headline that Mr. Sebastian wrote—'Vanished Without A Trace.'"

"Looking back, I've often wondered how many newspapers, and television and radio stations ran stories." Jenn walked back around her desk and sat down in front of her computer. "I've wondered if the internet had existed then, if Jonah would have been found. If a universe of mothers connected by social media would have found that little red-haired boy who called me Aunt J."

"It's hard to say, Jenn. People are still disappearing. Little children are still being taken."

"Every single day."

"What has made you remember this today, Jenn? A few minutes ago, you were chatting with Ellie."

"I've been worried about Renee. She's not seemed like herself when I've talked to her. She said she was having some medical tests done. I tried to call and check on her. I got her voicemail. I always worry when she gets quiet. I know where her mind has gone. Renee and Neil have learned how to cope. That's a far cry from being happy. I don't know if that will ever be an emotion that either one of them fully feels again."

"Many marriages would not have survived such a loss."

"There were times when it was quite rocky. In the end, I think they are better together than apart. Despite the constant reminder, they understand each other in a way that another person in either of their lives never would."

"It's extra hard that they've never had closure, isn't it?"

"Yes. At that same time, I know for a certainty that they've never given up hope that Jonah may be alive."

"I can't imagine." Doris rose to leave the room. "I hope Renee calls you back soon. Maybe she's having a rough day."

"Thanks, Doris. Ellie and I will probably be going over to Tyrell County this afternoon, if she can make an appointment with the new owner of a car dealership there."

"Would that be Sinclair Lewis?" Doris looked back over her shoulder as she walked through the doorway.

"Why, yes, how did you know?"

"He called for you while Ellie was in here. That's what I came in here to tell you. I forgot when I saw that you were upset."

"There's been one coincidence like that after another since I returned to Serendipity."

"Well, you know it's said that serendipity is a happy accident."

"Indeed."

Jenn sat back down at her desk, looking at her email. One of the most recent was from Ellie confirming an afternoon appointment with Sinclair Lewis.

"I'm meeting with Sinclair at three o'clock." Jenn typed the text to Mel.

A few moments later, Mel's reply consisted of a video of an animated little dog trembling in fear.

"It's going to be fine. I'll bring some takeout. You come to the house this evening. Let yourself in with the key I gave you, if I've not gotten home yet."

Jenn hoped that Mel would not torture herself until they met again.

"Jennifer Halston, it's been a long, long time."

As Sinclair Lewis closed his hand around Jenn's to shake it in greeting, Jenn remembered the word she always associated with him in school—smooth. Even as a teenager, Sinclair was smooth in everything he said and did. Jenn could see that characteristic had only grown stronger into adulthood.

"We are proof, you and I, that you can go home again."

"Indeed. We are stepping into the future with both feet."

"Sometimes we need to take a leap of faith. For me, this is one of those times." Jenn turned to Ellie. "This young lady is a key person on my advertising team. We are hoping that one of Serendipity's favorite sons will see the opportunity of showcasing his new business to his hometown and the value of using the newspaper as the conduit to do so."

"Very eloquent, Jenn. You could always turn a word. Did this young lady bring a proposal?"

"I certainly did, Mr. Lewis."

Ellie pulled out a folder and handed it to him, then opened her laptop. Twenty minutes later, Ellie's presentation was complete. Jenn was amazed at the young woman's sales prowess in thoroughly showing Sinclair an inclusive advertising package.

"I think you've made a sale, Ellie." Sinclair closed the folder. "This old car salesman isn't even going to try to negotiate it. You've offered me quite a few discounts to commit long term. In the operation of a car dealership, advertising is crucial. We must get eyes on our product."

"Thank you, Mr. Sinclair." Ellie handed the contract to Sinclair for his signature.

"Sinclair, I appreciate your willingness to meet with us and listen to our proposal." Jenn watched Sinclair sign the contract and return it to Ellie. "One of the reasons I came with Ellie today was to also talk to you about possibly doing an article about your business venture and returning to your hometown. Would you be agreeable to that?"

"Absolutely."

For the first time in the conversation, Sinclair flashed the broad smile that Jenn remembered from their youth. The smile that stole many hearts, especially Mel's.

"Excellent. We will arrange an interview soon."

Sinclair rose within the glass office that was common in so many dealerships. He motioned to a young man on the showroom floor who immediately came into the office.

"Jeffrey, Ellie is our new advertising rep with the *Serendipity Sun*. I'd like for you to show her around our lot and give her the necessary photos and price information for a full-page ad in their next edition. Jenn and I will continue our conversation while you two are doing that."

"Yes, sir. Right this way, Ellie. I believe I have all the photos you will need on a jump drive in my office."

Jeffrey stepped back for Ellie to leave the office in front of him, nodding to Sinclair and pulling the door closed when he left.

"Thank you, Sinclair. We will do our utmost to secure our position as a trusted and valuable member of your marketing team."

"I have no doubt. I congratulate you on the brave step of purchasing a newspaper. I believe you may have taken on more risk than I have, despite the inventory you see on this lot." Sinclair stopped for a moment, staring off into space. "I'm sure you can probably imagine the real reason that I took this meeting with you rather than having my sales manager handle it."

"A reunion with an old classmate?" Jenn raised her eyebrows and smiled. "Or, perhaps, you have a set of questions of your own."

"That's why you were one of the smartest in our class. You see past the obvious." Sinclair took a deep breath. "Too many years ago, a stupid kid made the mistake of a lifetime. Doing the right thing isn't always an option, it's the choice decided for you. When is it too late to choose what you really wanted?"

Jenn was shocked by the bluntness of Sinclair's words. Her speculation with Mel that Sinclair reached out to her to make amends might only be the beginning of his intentions.

"That's a deep question, Sinclair. I'm going to assume that you aren't being hypothetical."

"I have no interest in beating around the bush at this point in my life, Jenn. I've had a good life with success and basic happiness. I'm as proud of my children as a father can be. Up until a couple of years ago, I would have said that I spent my life with a decent human being with whom I was reasonably compatible. We had many happy years. Then, I found out that for the last decade I was living a lie, the lie my wife created. It made me also face the fact that I may have allowed myself to live a lie of my own creation for a whole lot longer. A lie about my own happiness. We're in our fifties now. I don't know about you, but I don't want to spend the rest of my life that way. I want to be happy."

"Sinclair, you certainly aren't holding anything back. Why are you telling me this?"

"You know why, Jenn. You were Mel's best friend then. I have no doubt that you two are still as tight as sisters. A couple of weeks ago, after I got settled, I called Mel's office and left her a message. I realize that all those years ago, I broke her heart. What many people don't understand is that I broke my own heart, too. That was my problem though. If I had moved back to Serendipity and found out that Mel was happily married with a couple of kids enjoying a wonderful life, I would never have bothered her. I did a little snooping around. Truthfully, I've kept up with her life ever since I left here. First through things my parents would tell me. Later, with the help of technology, I would keep tabs via the internet. Please correct me if I am wrong. Mel has never been married. I cannot even find evidence that she's been engaged or in anything more than a temporary relationship. I don't want you to think that my ego is so big that I think that is all because of me. I wish that I would have found Mel in her own happily ever after. I didn't."

Sinclair stopped talking and looked Jenn straight in the eyes. *I can't tell him that he is right.* Jenn couldn't betray Mel's trust. Yet, she knew Mel still harbored feelings for Sinclair. It was at the core of why her relationships didn't work. Jenn knew this even if Mel would not admit it.

"It puts me in a tough place to discuss Mel's life with you. But I cannot truthfully say that the only reason I came here was to introduce my new business to your new business. I will say what I feel I can without breaking Mel's trust."

"Fair enough. I don't want you to tell me anything about her life that you don't think Mel would want me to know."

"First of all, Mel only became aware that you called her yesterday. Your phone message became accidentally hidden under something on Mel's assistant's desk. It wasn't discovered until yesterday afternoon after we saw you."

"Saw me? Where did you see me?"

"Mel and I were having lunch with Randy Nave yesterday."

"Oh, I had no idea. I didn't see who he was with."

Jenn thought that Sinclair looked like he was going to say something else, but he remained silent.

"Neither of us even knew you had moved back here until Randy told us. Ironically, when Mel returned from shockingly seeing you, her assistant had been cleaning her desk and found your lost message."

"She still hasn't called me though."

"Sinclair, the shock was quite profound. Combined with the time that has passed since you left the message, I'm not sure Mel knows what to do."

"Jenn, the last thing I want to do is hurt Mel any further. I don't want to mess up her life." Sinclair rubbed his forehead and frowned. "I would like the chance to talk to her. I'd like to apologize. I'd give anything to be her friend again. I don't deserve any more than that as much as I would like to have it. Can you help me?"

"I think it would be good for the two of you to talk. I think it would be healthy for Mel. She needs to hear what you have to say and tell you how she feels. You need to be prepared though. You might get an earful."

"Jenn, I deserve it." Sinclair raised his hands in the air. "I was a coward back then. I'm ready to take my punishment. It's the only way I have a chance to be in her life again."

Jenn heard some desperation in Sinclair's voice. She saw a vulnerability in his expression that reminded her of the young man she knew all those years ago. It touched her heart. He was truly remorseful.

"You're serious about this, aren't you?"

"There are few people I can talk to about Mel. Few people are left in my life who even know about her." Sinclair scowled. "I had one foolish intoxicated night with Dana that changed my entire future. I wouldn't trade my children for anything in this world. I'd be a liar if I said that I haven't wished that someone else was their mother. If not for that one encounter of poor judgment, I have no doubt in my mind that Mel would have been their mother."

Jenn started to speak. Sinclair held up his hand to stop her.

"Please let me finish. I am fully aware that Mel might have gotten rid of my sorry self by now. She deserves better than me. I don't doubt for a minute that I could have convinced her to marry me though. She knew I loved her."

"That's the reason her life has never been the same, Sinclair. She had a sample of true love. It left a bad taste in her mouth. It made her distrust her ability to find it again."

"Thanks to me."

"I'm not sure that I can give you any other reason."

"Just convince her to talk to me. I promise that I will never bother her again, if she doesn't want me to."

Jenn heard her phone buzzing. Reaching into her purse, she saw that she missed a call from Renee. She also saw that it was almost five o'clock. She and Ellie needed to get back to Serendipity.

"Sinclair, I will talk to her. I'm not making any promises. I will try my best though because I believe she needs closure."

Jenn rose from her chair, looking behind her through the glass to see if she could see Ellie.

"Can a beginning follow closure?" Sinclair walked around his desk, putting his hand on the knob of the door.

"I suppose that depends on whether or not both parties want to open another door."

"I appreciate your visit, Jenn, professionally and personally. It's good to see you." Sinclair opened the door. "I can't help but wonder if you are having your own reunion with someone from your past."

Sinclair raised his eyes, smirking while Jenn passed in front of him. Jenn turned around.

"Are you referring to our Police Chief? Like you, he is an old friend."

"That's how he referred to you, too. I saw some smiling behind his eyes though. I remember, back in the day, no one could understand why you two didn't end up together."

Jenn's eyes bugged in a shocked expression. *What was he talking about?*

"Really? Are you shocked by that? I remember Mel and me talking about it. I think it must have been obvious to everyone but the two of you."

"Excuse me, Mr. Lewis." A woman approached them. "That phone call you've been waiting for is on line two."

"Thank you, Nancy. I'm sorry, Jenn, I need to take this call. Thank you again for everything. Let me know when you want to do the article. I'll have my fingers crossed on the rest."

The decades faded away as Sinclair Lewis gave Jenn the perfect beaming smile that he was known for in his youth. As he walked back into his office, Jenn could see Ellie standing in the parking lot with Jeffrey. Several salespeople nodded as Jenn made her way across the showroom and outside.

"It was nice to meet you, Ellie, and you, also, ma'am." Jeffrey grinned.

Jenn couldn't help but notice that Ellie was smiling broadly as well. She wondered if this visit hadn't sparked all types of business.

"Thank you, Jeffrey. Ellie, we've got to get going. Did you get the information we need for the first ad?"

"Yes, ma'am. I've already emailed the details. We've also set up an account for billing." Jeffrey glanced over Jenn's shoulder. "I'm excited to sell some vehicles to the good people of Serendipity."

Jenn and Ellie began heading for their vehicle, waving goodbye to Jeffrey. Jenn was about to put her Jeep into drive when Jeffrey knocked on her window.

"Mr. Lewis asked me to give this to you." Jeffrey handed Jenn a card. "Bye, Ellie."

Jenn looked at it. It was Sinclair's business card. On the back were the words 'Here's my cell number. I'm counting on you.' Jenn laughed and shook her head.

"Mr. Lewis is a character. I bet he was something in high school." Ellie waved at Jeffrey.

"He was Mr. Popularity, that's for sure. Charming and quite athletic. I'm not surprised that he's done well at business." Jenn pulled out of the parking lot and onto the road.

"This is going to be a wonderful account, Jenn. This will give a great boost to our sales. Maybe we can drum up some more accounts over here, especially when we hire a new sales rep."

"Speaking of that, I know someone who may be interested in the position. But we will treat this applicant like any other one."

"Oh, is it someone local?"

"She is not. My son and daughter-in-law are considering relocating to our area. Michelle has been a record-breaking real estate agent in Atlanta. My son recently received a promotion, and his job can be done remotely. For some reason, they like the idea of moving to the beach."

"I can't imagine why anyone would want to do that." Ellie laughed. "Your daughter-in-law sounds like a great candidate."

"Again, she does not get any special treatment. We will hire the best candidate for the position. You, Betsy, and I will make that decision together. I have no doubt that Michelle can find a position somewhere. It doesn't have to be with us."

"That's very fair of you, Jenn. I'm thrilled that we will have another rep, whoever it turns out to be. I feel like we can have some solid growth with another person helping to develop more clients."

"I'm counting on it, Ellie."

Chapter Twelve

Mel

"Hello, Jasper! Princess Mia and I have come to visit you again."

Jasper eagerly ran to her when Mel opened the door of Jenn's beach house. After a little romp with Mia, he quickly went outside in the yard to do his business. Eager to explore, both dogs then scampered down the path heading to the beach.

"Yes, if you insist, we shall walk on the beach." Mel talked to the dogs, taking off her shoes and following them. "I'm sure Jenn will know where to find us if she arrives before we get back."

Even though Mel grew up in the little coastal town, it was not often that she walked on the beach. Life was busy. If you didn't live within walking distance of the sand, you rarely walked in it. Just because she was responsible for luring travelers to the area didn't mean that she had the opportunity to experience everything they did on a regular basis. Having a best friend who owned a beach house was going to be a serious perk in the years to come.

Anticipating that she might be taking the dogs for a walk, Mel had changed into comfort clothes when she stopped at her house to pick up

Mia. Mel was realizing that one of the best things about a private beach was that it was *private*. She let the dogs roam and frolic while she sat at the edge of the beach and let the waves splash her toes. In the distance, the sun was beginning a slow descent with a purply orange hue, an unusual color.

The gentle warm breeze mixing with the relaxing sound of the waves began to lull Mel into relaxation. All afternoon, she was a ball of nerves thinking about Jenn's meeting with Sinclair. The last two days had awakened feelings and memories in her which she'd spent many years trying to lock into the deep recesses of her memory. Snippets of the past came barreling into her thoughts today until she finally gave up concentrating and took the afternoon off.

So many years had passed, Mel hadn't expected to ever see Sinclair again. With his parents deceased, she presumed that there was no longer a reason for him to visit Serendipity. Even if he was planning his retirement, Mel imagined he would either stay in Raleigh or move nearer to his children. She also didn't expect him to get divorced. After he and Dana had been married a decade or more, it seemed that their marriage of necessity had turned into one of love.

Mel never got to know Dana in high school. They ran in different circles and had different friends. After the sudden marriage of Sinclair and Dana, too many people decided that Mel needed to know 'the truth' about Dana. Apparently, it was a common opinion that Dana had been after Sinclair, or one of the other popular boys, for quite some time. It was Dana's goal to find a man with a future. Some thought Dana did not care how she got him.

Mel grew tired of hearing everyone's theories. No matter what the truth was, it would not change what transpired. Dana became pregnant and Sinclair married her. End of story for Mel.

Mel knew that trauma was the underlying reason why she never let herself go too far in a relationship. There were a few men along the way who began to steal Mel's heart. Invariably something would happen between them that would raise suspicion in Mel's mind. Her mother continually told her that she had to allow herself to trust. What was once the easiest thing in the world for her became almost impossible.

At the age of seventeen, Mel fell head over heels for Sinclair. If she told the truth, that love was still alive within her heart. Mel spent most of her life being disappointed in and not liking Sinclair much. He'd broken her heart, but her heart still loved him. It was a feeling as much a part of her as her sarcastic personality.

The barking of both dogs drew Mel's attention from her thoughts. Looking around to see what they might be agitated about, she saw Parker walking in her direction. Both pooches ran in his direction, tails wagging. He stopped, bending down to give each one some attention. *That's the kind of guy I should find—handsome, friendly, independently rich.* Mel cackled.

"I have about as much chance of finding a man like Parker as I have of getting Sinclair back." Mel mumbled. "What am I saying? Sinclair is divorced, living in my town, and he called me. Maybe Parker will ask me out."

Mel put her hand over her mouth. She needed to stop having conversations with herself. Someone was going to hear her.

"Hey, Mel. We meet again." Parker flashed his toothpaste commercial smile.

"Hi, Parker. Yes, we are going to have to stop, or people will start talking." Mel looked around. "Oh, wait, we are on a private beach, there are no people."

"At least, there's not supposed to be. I came by to see you this afternoon. Your assistant said you had just left."

"I'm sorry, Parker. I took the afternoon off. Was Imogene able to help you?"

"Imogene is a young woman with an old name. I don't believe I've known many 'Imogenes' in my life. The ones I have met were all over seventy."

"That may be true, Parker, but I'm fairly certain that those older ladies named Imogene were once young women."

"You got me, Mel!" Parker roared with laughter. "May I sit with you?"

"Sure." A nervous awkward feeling passed over Mel. "You didn't answer my question. Did Imogene help you?"

"Young Imogene endeavored to help me. She gave me lots of information about the area including business directories, maps, and real estate guides. I believe though that you would be able to answer my questions better. I want to know about the real estate climate here for selling and for rental properties."

"I would have more information about those topics than Imogene. I could also put you in touch with some of the best real estate agents in the area."

"That's what I don't want to do, Mel. My financial advisor is strongly encouraging me to sell. He doesn't think I should hold onto a property that he doubts I will live in or visit often. He thinks I only want to keep it for sentimental reasons."

"What do you think?"

"I think that I spent the better part of my life halfway around the world, as far away from here as you can imagine. I left part of my heart here when I was a little boy. Do you know what it's like, Mel, to have part of your heart somewhere else? Especially when it was beyond your control?"

Mel's heart skipped a beat. *Is this man reading my soul?*

"I'm familiar with that type of experience."

"Then you know that when you don't feel whole it messes with everything in your life. Nothing ever seems to be enough. Something is always missing, lacking, or wrong. Coming back here and spending time with my grandfather was life changing. It's crazy to think that a little boy had a grasp on what he wanted at such a young age. I can't even put it into words."

"You were a puzzle with a missing piece. It doesn't matter if it was only one of a thousand pieces. Without it, the rest wasn't right."

"Mel, you have just read my soul."

Mel's eyes locked with Parker's. It was like time stood still. Chills covered Mel's body. It was the strangest feeling under the warmth of a beach sky. For a split second, Mel wondered if this feeling was like fire meeting ice.

"There you are!"

Jenn's voice broke the spell. Parker immediately turned in Jenn's direction. Mel felt dizzy, sick on her stomach, like she was walking away from a roller coaster ride. Only she hadn't moved. She was sitting in the same spot on the sand. Mia came to her, licking her ankle.

"Yes, I've been bothering Mel again." Parker jumped up, joining Jenn a few feet away.

"It's another lovely evening in paradise."

Mel could feel Jenn staring at her. She needed to get up and act as if everything was fine. *Everything was fine.*

"Would you ladies like to join me for some grilled fish on my veranda?" Parker looked back and forth from Jenn to Mel.

"Thank you for the invitation, Parker. I've brought some food home. I need to discuss something with Mel. It's a rather time sensitive issue. Let's plan to all have dinner together soon though."

"I understand. Yes, we must plan a nice seafood dinner. I'm going to leave you ladies to your evening." Parker stepped closer to Mel before he headed to his house. "Always a pleasure chatting with you, Mel."

Mel and Jenn walked back to the house in silence after saying goodbye to Parker. Mel felt a combination of feelings—relaxation, wonderment, confusion. She focused on feeding the dogs to keep her mind occupied while Jenn changed clothes and made a phone call.

Jenn's brow was furrowed, and she seemed tense when she came into the kitchen where Mel was opening the packages of takeout Jenn had brought.

"Are you okay?"

"Not really. It doesn't have anything to do with my meeting with Sinclair. I'm concerned about Renee." Jenn picked up a couple of plates to carry to the table.

"Haven't you been able to reach her?"

"We seem to be playing phone tag. I had a missed call from her while I was with Sinclair. She didn't leave a message. I tried to call her back a few minutes ago and got her voicemail again."

Jenn sat down at the table. Her shoulders were slumped. Mel thought she looked extra tired.

"Have you considered calling Neil?" Mel brought in the remaining food and a pitcher of iced tea.

"It crossed my mind. Renee would be mad, if she found out. My main hesitation is because I don't know if Neil is aware that Renee was having medical tests. Renee never interfered in my marriage. Even though I'm sure there were times when she might have considered it. I've got to show her the same respect. Sometimes Renee doesn't tell things until she's ready."

"We are all that way." Mel filled their glasses with tea before sitting down.

"I've got to learn to not worry about things before I know the whole story."

"If you can figure out that secret, you could be a millionaire." Mel looked at the different containers of food. "Where did you get this food?"

"Oh, on our way back from Tyrell County, Ellie mentioned a Thai restaurant that she liked there. We found it and the service was incredibly fast. You like Thai food, right?" Jenn began to serve herself some of the food.

"I love Thai food. I think I know the restaurant you are talking about. I'm a little concerned that you may be trying to ply me with yummy food before you tell me something horrible about your meeting with Sinclair."

"I'm doing no such thing. Please do your part and start eating. I've got to get a little food in me before I start telling you about my time with Sinclair. I'm afraid if I don't eat before I begin, the food will all be cold before I'm done."

After a few minutes of eating, Jenn dived into describing the meeting with Sinclair, including the amazing proposal that Ellie made and Sinclair's acceptance of all she proposed.

"Wow. That sounds like some high dollar business for the newspaper. Bravo, Jenn!"

"All the credit goes to Ellie. She worked hard in a quick time frame to put together a package that has the potential to get the attention of our subscribers while motivating them to become buyers for Sinclair."

"It's really an open market. There hasn't been a car dealership in Serendipity since we were young. Most people go to dealerships an hour north of us to buy a vehicle. I don't ever remember seeing an advertisement in the *Serendipity Sun* for a dealership in Tyrell County. Since it's less than an hour south of here, I think if we can get a few other businesses to advertise from that area, we might even change some of the shopping patterns of our residents."

"The added factor of Sinclair Lewis being a name that some people will still remember, I think, will make this a home run."

"Sinclair has a lot of home runs in his history here."

Mel let her mind drift back to all the afternoons she watched Sinclair play baseball. Even before they began dating, Mel went to most games. Looking back, it was probably one of the reasons he noticed her. She was always in the stands, cheering on the team.

"He also struck out, big time." Jenn poured herself another glass of tea. "Mel, he knows that. I think that is a key reason he moved back here. Sinclair wants to make amends with you."

"It's mighty late." Mel looked down at her plate, not wanting Jenn to see the tears that were forming in her eyes.

"I agree. The question is, is it too late?" Jenn held up her hand. "I don't expect you to answer that. I do believe you should think about it. It would be a healthy step for you to talk to Sinclair and allow him to apologize. The breakup was as hurtful of an experience as I hope you ever go through. But it cannot be undone. All Sinclair can do now is explain and apologize. He was very humble and sincere today in everything he said. He realizes that you have every reason to not allow him an opportunity to make amends." Jenn paused. "Please look at me, Mel."

Slowly Mel raised her head. Tears spilled out of her eyes, running down her cheeks.

"Oh, my friend, I am so sorry." Jenn reached and took hold of Mel's hand.

"It's silly to have this much emotion over something that happened so long ago." Mel's voice cracked. "I'm still a silly teenager who thought this great guy really loved her."

"Mel, you are not silly. I'm your best friend in the world. I do not want to see you hurt further. But I cannot keep this information hidden from you. Sinclair did love you. Sinclair still loves you. You are the reason he moved back to Serendipity."

"Oh, Jenn." Mel began to sob. "How can I possibly let myself go through that again?"

Jenn got up from her chair and pulled Mel into a hug. After a few minutes, Mel's sobs had slowed. Jenn pulled away, looking Mel in the eyes.

"Mel, you've continued to go through this breakup for almost forty years. Don't try to tell me any different. You've not had another love, because your heart was still too full of your first one. It worries everyone who loves you. I concluded after the first decade that you had to be the one to choose to move on." Jenn shook her head. "I couldn't understand what you were waiting on. Maybe now we know. Maybe there was some part of you that knew he would eventually return."

"It makes me a pitiful human. Waiting a lifetime on someone who broke my heart." Mel wiped her eyes with her napkin.

"It makes you a human who loves intensely. I've felt that same dedication from you about our friendship. You are my friend no matter what. It's obvious that your heart made a commitment to Sinclair that it wasn't ready to give up."

"Would I be a fool to let him waltz back into my life? He was married to Dana for so many years."

"The man I saw today takes his responsibilities seriously. He made a mistake, he took responsibility. He had a family; he honored that responsibility. Everything you loved about him then is still in there somewhere." Jenn paused, looking away from Mel in thought. "This may sound strange. I honestly feel better about him coming to you now than if he had a few years after you broke up. I say that because it probably would have been easy, in some ways, for him to have gotten divorced then and come running back. I'm not so sure it would have been as genuine as it is now. Sinclair was responsible. He saw the situation through. Dana ended that with her actions. Sinclair is truly free from the marriage and the potential guilt of ending it for someone else."

"What are you trying to say?" Mel's mind was going in many confusing directions.

"Sinclair Lewis fell in love with you a long time ago. I'm pretty sure that he never fell out of love. Now, though, he doesn't have to feel guilty about it anymore. Just like he took responsibility for the child he created with Dana, he took responsibility for a life he built. He's fulfilled that responsibility and is free to do what he wants."

"I cannot imagine how I am going to wrap my mind around this." Mel let out a deep breath, putting her head in her hands.

"You need to take some time to think about this whole situation. I think the first aspect for you to consider is if you agree to meet with Sinclair and talk."

"You think that is a good idea, don't you?"

"I think it is a healthy step. I think it should be on your terms though. Somewhere that you feel comfortable. That may not be a public place where people could be watching."

"Oh, that's a good thought, Jenn. I wouldn't feel comfortable with that. With my luck, we would go to a restaurant where every table around us is filled with people we went to school with."

"In a town as small as Serendipity, that would certainly be possible."

"I wouldn't want to be at his house or my house either. Offices don't seem appropriate." Mel frowned, thinking about places.

"Would you feel comfortable here?"

"I think so. It would sort of be on my turf, since it's your house." Mel shook her head affirmatively.

"Absolutely. I could be here or not, whichever you preferred."

"Since you've interacted with him recently, I think that would make you a neutral person. It would probably be comfortable for both of us."

"I'm not sure that 'neutral' is the right word to use for me. I'm on Team Mel and Sinclair knows that. I could go for a walk on the beach or be working out on the deck."

"What would I do without you?" Mel pulled Jenn back into a quick hug. "I can't imagine going through this with you six hours away."

"Everything happens for a reason, my friend. I don't want to influence you. This is your decision. But I've got to say that Sinclair seemed so sincere. Only you can decide if you can get past the old hurt. I think that same good guy we knew, once upon a time, is still there. He's had a lifetime of experience to jade him, as we all have. There was a mighty hopeful glimmer in his eyes though. When he was talking about you, the years fell away. I saw the young baseball star who had a sweet girl in the stands watching every game."

Mel's eyes filled with tears again. "I miss that girl. She was so full of hope. Now, she's full of Thai food and sarcasm." A cross between a sob and a giggle came out. "She still dreams of happily ever after."

"It's not too late. It might be closer than she thinks."

Chapter Thirteen

Jenn

"I'm so glad you called me back."

About thirty minutes after Mel went home, Jenn's cell phone lit up with a call from Renee.

"Jenn, it's Neil."

"Neil, why are you calling on Renee's phone?" A sudden feeling of fear gripped every muscle in Jenn's body.

"Jenn, Renee's in the hospital."

"What's going on? She told me that she was having some tests run. She called me back earlier today."

"Jenn, I called you earlier today from Renee's phone. She's been keeping something from you. I told her repeatedly that she should tell you. She said you have enough to worry about in your life."

"Oh, Neil. I knew something was wrong. Renee can be so private. Even as her sister, I don't like to pry." Jenn sat down in the nearest chair. "Please tell me that she is okay."

In her mind's eye, Jenn saw the brother-in-law who decades previously became more like a brother. Tall and slender, Neil's amber hair now was whiter than red. Time and heartache turned his boyish good looks into those of a man who had looked older than his age for too many years.

"She's okay, Jenn. It's been a difficult couple of days though. Renee went through a bunch of tests over the last six weeks that revealed colon cancer. She was scheduled to have surgery in about three weeks to remove the tumor."

"Neil, no, not like Daddy."

Jenn's father battled cancer for eight years. It began in the colon.

"Your sister is stubborn. You remember that your father's doctor recommended for all three of you girls to begin colon cancer screenings by your early forties. Renee had one when she was forty-three and that's it. She never had another. She kept telling me that she didn't have any symptoms. Finally, her family doctor insisted she have one. There was indeed a problem."

Jenn could hear exhaustion in Neil's voice. It scared her.

"I'm sorry, Neil. I don't understand why she's in the hospital now, if her surgery is several weeks away."

"The colonoscopy revealed a large tumor. That was about three weeks ago. Apparently since then an abscess developed. She had to have emergency surgery to get the infection under control. While they were in there, they went ahead and removed the tumor."

"Is she okay?"

"She's going to be. The doctor assures me that they do not see any evidence at this point that the cancer is anywhere else."

"I can come tomorrow." Jenn's mind raced, thinking about her schedule.

"Jenn, Renee will be in the hospital for several days, perhaps a week. I told her before she was taken into surgery that I was going to call you.

Through the painkiller she'd been given, she made a face at me. I think she will be mad if you show up before she gets home."

"Are you scared, Neil?"

From the first time Renee brought Neil home, Jenn liked him. He always treated her with love and respect, like an important human, not just Renee's sister. Jenn cared about this man who stood beside her sister during the worst possible thing that could have happened to them.

"Jenn, I've been scared for a long time. I've been scared since we lost Jonah. I'm constantly worried that I will lose Renee. This is one possible way. There have been many."

Jenn felt a pain in her heart. She understood what he was saying. She felt his fear, too. Renee was strong as steel and fragile as an eggshell.

"Okay, Neil, I will do what you advise. I'm so worried and feel helpless. Remember, I am much closer than I once was. I can be in Raleigh quickly."

"That is great. Renee is happy that you are now only a couple of hours away. Maybe after she gets some of her initial recovery over with, she could come visit you. I'm sure she would enjoy resting at the beach."

"That would be wonderful. Please encourage her to do that."

"Jenn, I'm going to check on Renee and then head home. I'll call or text tomorrow and let you know how she's doing."

"Thanks, Neil. You get some rest. Tell Renee I love her. Thanks for calling."

Jenn put down her phone and leaned back in her chair. A surge of emotion came streaming out of her eyes, remembering her father's cancer diagnosis and the surgeries and treatments that followed. It was a hard road that led to a sad and painful ending for him.

After sending Mel a brief text about Renee, Jenn walked through the kitchen to make sure she'd put everything left from dinner away. Pouring herself a glass of wine, she went out to the deck to sit in the moonlight. Looking in the direction of the Oasis, Jenn noticed that she could see one corner of Parker's deck from the place she was sitting. She was surprised to see him walk outside and look in her direction. He made a motion asking if he could come over. Jenn was exhausted but didn't want to be rude.

Jenn went back into the kitchen while Parker was making his way over, getting another wine glass and the bottle to offer him. He was already climbing the stairs to the deck when she went back outside.

"Hi, neighbor!" Parker didn't look the least bit tired.

"Good evening, Parker. I was enjoying a glass of wine and listening to the waves. Would you like a glass?"

"That would be lovely. I promise to only stay for one glass. I realize that newspaper publishers must get to work early." Parker smiled, accepting the glass that Jenn handed him.

"Thank you for understanding that. I didn't want to have to kick you off the deck or fall asleep while you were talking. It's been a long day."

They sat in silence for a few minutes, sipping the wine and relaxing.

"I've been meaning to ask you, Parker. How did you recognize me on the beach? We were children when we last saw each other."

"I came over here once before your mother passed away. We had a brief chat. I asked about you. She told me that you were living in Atlanta. She also mentioned your married name. With that combined information, I was able to find you on social media. You've got a great profile photo. I've been watching for you to move in."

"Glad to know that you weren't stalking me or anything!" Jenn laughed.

"Stalking is a strong word. I would describe it more as researching an old friend."

Parker grew silent again. Jenn turned slightly, watching his profile in the moonlight. For a split second, she remembered sitting on the beach with Parker on a similar evening and watching him the same way. Even as a little boy, he could look serious beyond his years, like he'd seen more in his young life than he should have.

"You're trying to figure me out, aren't you?"

"You look like you're in deep serious thought. I remember a little boy who used to get a similar expression."

"That little fellow didn't have a care in the world. He was oblivious to what was going on in his family. He had no clue that he could be whisked thousands of miles away from the only home he'd known. He didn't realize that a father could die and a new one would expect to live in his place."

"How old were you when he passed?"

"Thirteen."

"Hard age."

"A life forever changed. Here I am again at another crossroads. You seem to be as well. It's not any easier than it was in childhood to know what the right choices are."

"You're right. I think your heart ultimately leads you in the right direction, at least I hope so."

"My heart says for me to keep the Oasis. My mind doesn't know what I will do with it."

"What do you do for a living, Parker?"

"I own several businesses. Most are run by others. My professional strength is in software development."

"Business software? Programs and such?"

"Actually, gaming is my strength."

"Games like the kids play?"

"No, the gambling kind. My biggest clients are casinos."

"That's interesting. I went with Simon on a business trip to Vegas a few years ago. I spent some time in the casino while he was in his meetings. It amazed me how many different types of slots that were available. There are so many creative themes and concepts."

"It's big business for sure. There always needs to be something new to grab the consumer's attention. It's not limited to casinos either. Online gambling is huge. Internet gambling is a world of its own."

"Can't you do that type of design work from anywhere?"

"Certainly. I've traveled the world and worked from my laptop."

"Then why not make the Oasis your home base? Wouldn't this view spark your creativity?" Jenn pointed to the ocean. "Forgive me for being forward, but I do not get the impression that you need to sell it for financial reasons."

"I do not. Being the sole heir to my grandparents' estate left enough to take care of this property for many years. My financial advisor thinks everything I own should make money."

"It would seem to me that selling your family home should not be made as a hasty decision. There could be great regrets if you didn't take time to think it through."

"I agree with you, Jenn. We have both found ourselves in places that are filled with family memories. I imagine it would be difficult for you to let go of this property that you have spent time in your entire life." Parker finished the last sip of wine, setting the glass on a small table next to his chair. "It's amazing how we have both ended up back in Serendipity at the same time, fifty years later. Maybe that's a sign."

Jenn continued to look out on the horizon, thinking about Parker's words. She wondered if they might contain a message she hadn't realized he was trying to convey. She was tired. It would be best not to start another conversation topic so late. Jenn yawned, stretching her arms above her head.

"I think that's a sign that I need some sleep."

"Absolutely. I said I would only stay for one glass of wine, and I have finished it." Parker rose from the chair. "Thank you for the nightcap and the conversation, Jenn. I hope we can have more of these times together. Until then, I will bid you goodnight."

Parker made a little bow before quickly going down the steps. A few moments later, he waved from his own deck.

"Is this what happens when you return to your hometown, Jasper?" Her precious pooch wagged his tail in response. "Is it one person after another from your history? The past week has been a strange series of events, an exhausting one."

Turning off the lights, Jenn walked through the dark house, wondering who the next person from the past would be to make an appearance in her future.

―――ellie―――

"Ellie was here bright and early this morning, chatting excitedly about our new advertising client." Doris greeted Jenn when she arrived mid-morning. "Sounds like you two had a successful afternoon in Tyrell County."

"We certainly did. I'm hoping that we might be able to drum up a few more new advertisers from that area, once we have another sales rep to help."

"Speaking of that, Betsy began posting the position yesterday, we already have three applications."

"That's great! Maybe we will have enough to go ahead and begin interviewing next week."

Jenn walked past Doris' desk and into her office. She put her things down and turned on her computer before returning to the lobby area.

"Doris, you are going to be surprised by this after the conversation you and I had yesterday. Neil called me last night. Renee is in the hospital. Apparently, she had emergency surgery yesterday because of an abscess that formed in her colon area."

"Oh, dear, that sounds serious." Doris frowned.

"It's even more serious than that. Renee has colon cancer. She was scheduled to have a tumor removed in a couple of weeks. Neil said that they went ahead and did that as part of this emergency surgery."

"Jenn, did you know that Renee had cancer?"

"I didn't have a clue."

"I know this must be extra frightening for you after what you saw your father go through."

"It is. I hate to think that she's been carrying around this worry. I wish she would have told me. If nothing else, I could have listened to her talk it out." Jenn sighed. "Renee used to be an open book. After what happened to Jonah and how that shoved her family into the public eye, she's been the exact opposite. It's like my beautiful fluttering butterfly of a sister reverted into her cocoon and refuses to come out. Neil sounds so stressed. He won't let me come to Raleigh though. He says that it took enough convincing for Renee to allow him to call me. I've got to respect that."

"Hard as it may be, I think that is the right decision. We cannot judge Renee or Neil for what they must do to survive. I cannot imagine that I would be able to keep my sanity at all."

"That is true. Renee and Neil have shown my children nothing but devotion through the years. I can see the pain in their eyes each time we've had a milestone, a graduation, a wedding, even a soccer game. They see what they have missed. They must do whatever they have to in order to cope."

Someone came through the front door. Jenn stepped away, allowing Doris to greet the customer. Returning to her office, Jenn could hear her phone beeping. It was a missed call from Claire. Looking at the time, Jenn decided to give her a quick call back. Claire needed to know what was going on with her Aunt Renee.

"Hey, Mom. My family radar is buzzing this morning. Is something going on?"

For as long as Jenn could remember, her oldest child had a powerful sixth sense regarding things that occurred in the family. It was like the universe communicated with her, minutes or hours before everyone else. The phenomenon had frightened Jenn at first. She'd since learned to embrace it like any other talent her children exhibited.

"Your radar is amazingly correct once again, Claire. I'm afraid it's not something positive though."

Jenn could hear Claire holding her breath. Another distinct characteristic of her oldest child.

"Aunt Renee is in the hospital."

"Oh, no! What's wrong?"

"Apparently Renee has been hiding some health issues from us. Neil called last night and caught me up. Renee was diagnosed with cancer a few weeks ago." Jenn heard Claire gasp. "She was scheduled to have surgery to remove a tumor in her colon. Before that time arrived, an abscess formed causing the doctors to perform emergency surgery on her yesterday. They also removed the tumor while they were in there. Neil says she's going to be okay."

"Does this mean the cancer is gone?"

"I don't know the answer to that. I'm not sure that Neil knows either. From what he said, everything happened quickly."

"Are you in Raleigh?"

One of the most interesting things about having cell phones was that you never knew where a person was when you called. Claire knew that Jenn's inclination would have been to immediately jump in a vehicle and get to Renee.

"Despite my desire to be, I am still in Serendipity. Neil advised that Renee would not like me rushing to her bedside."

"That doesn't surprise me. Aunt Renee doesn't want the focus on her. She's had her fill of attention."

"Exactly. So, I'm listening to Neil. Maybe I can convince her to come stay with me during her recovery."

"That would be wonderful, Mom. Maybe I could come and help take care of her."

"I would love that, but you don't have to disrupt your life. Renee and I can manage. I'm a boss now, remember? In theory, I should be able to take off whenever I want."

"My life is already disrupted. A change of scenery would be great."

"Claire, I sensed something wasn't right when we last talked. Is everything okay?"

"It's a long story, Mom. I've got to get back to work. We can talk later. Don't worry. I've got some things I need to figure out. Would it be okay for me to text Aunt Renee?"

"I think it would probably be best for you to wait until this evening. I would bet she's still rather medicated right now."

"Okay. Love you, Mom. Don't worry. Aunt Renee is strong. We will help her heal."

"Love you, Claire."

Jenn spent the next couple of hours answering emails and reviewing financial reports for the previous five years. She was looking for time frames in the past several years when the newspaper had fewer pages of news and advertising. She wanted to use some of the ideas the staff had suggested for special sections, during these slower periods, which could provide interesting feature articles combined with advertising. If they were done right, these could be strong revenue generators and help pay additional staff.

She wondered about Mel a few times during the day but decided to not bother her. Jenn knew that her friend had a lot of thinking to do, deciding if she wanted to talk to Sinclair.

After eating lunch at her desk, Jenn called Betsy and Ellie into her office to brainstorm a special section plan for the next six months. It was important for a plan to be in place before an additional ad rep was hired. An organized plan would also help the next Editor to quickly put together article ideas to assign the reporters.

"It's time to go home, Jenn." Doris came to Jenn's door.

"How can that be possible?" Jenn looked at the clock on her computer.

"You've been sitting at that desk all day. Your mind has done enough. Go home and soak up a little sunshine. Tomorrow is another day."

"You're absolutely right, Doris." Jenn turned off her computer. "I'm not even going to take home any files. I need to check on Renee, eat something healthy, and chill out."

"I'm saying extra prayers for Renee. Have you told Rachel?"

"No, I haven't. Honestly, Doris, I've not spoken with Aunt Rachel since I moved back to town."

"I know, Jenn. She mentioned that to me. I've covered for you. I can't hold her off much longer." Doris waved, walking out the door.

Jenn stuck her head into the newsroom, saying goodbye to Shaun and Tyler. Leaving the building, she saw a familiar looking vehicle pulling in front to park. Randy waved from behind the wheel before he got out and joined her on the sidewalk.

"Hey, Jenn. I saw your Jeep was still here. I thought I would stop and see how Mel was doing."

"Hey, Randy. I haven't talked to Mel today. Trying to give her some time to think. I went to see Sinclair yesterday."

"Oh, I bet that was an interesting conversation."

"Ellie and I went to his dealership and sold him an advertising package to introduce his new business to our readers."

"That's great! I think that will work well for him. A lot of people have been talking about Sinclair returning to town. I think people like the idea of dealing with a hometown boy, even if he's been away for a few decades."

"I think you're right, Chief. Good to see you. I'm heading home."

"Would you like to grab some dinner? I was on my way to get some takeout but would enjoy some company."

"Thank you, Randy. I'm tired. It's been a tough couple of days. Lots of surprising news from different places. I need to rest and be alone with my thoughts."

"I understand. Just know that I'm here, if you need someone to listen."

"I appreciate that, old friend. I really do."

Chapter Fourteen
Randy

Randy watched Jenn pull out of the parking lot, waving before she drove away. Something was troubling her; he could see it in her eyes. He sensed that it was more than a business worry bothering her. Something was heavy on her heart. She called him *old friend*. He hoped one day she might see him in a different light.

Pulling away from the curb, Randy pondered what was left in his refrigerator, the thought of takeout seemed less appealing now. A bowl of cereal wasn't a bad dinner after a long day. Tired as he was, it would certainly make his sleep easier than a heavy meal.

At the next stop light, he was surprised to see Sinclair Lewis pull up next to him. Sinclair waved, rolling down his window. Randy lowered the passenger window to speak.

"Good evening, Chief." Sinclair yelled. "Are you still on duty?"

"Nope, heading home."

"Do you have time for a beer and burger with an old friend?"

Randy laughed under his breath, so much for a little healthier dinner.

"Sure, man. Meet you at O'Reilly's."

Sinclair nodded as the traffic light turned green. Randy pulled in behind, following him to the popular local pub. The parking lot was already half full. Hopefully, his usual booth in the corner would be available. Randy remembered one of the first times that he was ever at the local hangout after a state championship baseball game when Sinclair hit the winning home run.

"I remember the first time I ever got to drink a beer here." Sinclair got out of his vehicle when Randy approached.

"I was thinking about that night when I drove up. Seems like a hundred years ago."

"You got that right. I sure would love to have a talk with my younger self. I would steer him in another direction than the one he went in." Sinclair patted Randy on the back while they walked toward O'Reilly's front door. "What would you tell your teenage self?"

"I don't know, man. Probably to take better care of his teeth and try harder to not get shot."

"Well, that's important, too, old buddy."

Randy's preferred booth was available, and his favorite server was on duty. After placing their food orders and sipping on their beers, their conversation turned from sports and weather to two women they knew as girls.

"Have you talked to Mel since you've been back?" Randy decided he would use his detective skills. "She runs the Visitors Bureau, if you didn't know."

"Yes, I tried calling her office a couple of weeks ago. Mel didn't return my call. When Jenn visited me earlier in the week to sell the dealership some advertising, she said that Mel's assistant lost the message. Mel still has not called me though. She probably doesn't want to talk to me. I blew my chance a long time ago."

"I'm not going to argue with you, Sinclair. You messed up that relationship pretty good. We didn't tell you at the time, but how that situation played out amazed a lot of us back then. We all thought you were head over heels for Mel."

"I was, Randy. More than I would have ever admitted to myself. That trip to the beach was ridiculous. I should have known better. I knew that Dana had a thing for me. I didn't realize she was so intent on getting me."

"Do you think Dana intentionally set you up to marry her?"

"I know she did. She told me after we'd had our second child."

"Whoa!" Randy's eyes bugged out in surprise. "I think I would have had a hard time staying married to someone who confessed that to me."

"It was a hard pill to swallow, Randy. I had two young kids though. I knew that I would lose the life I wanted with my children if I divorced their mother."

Randy shook his head in agreement. He knew that he had missed a lot of time with Bryson because of the divorce.

"As time went on, I realized that Dana loved me. She was a good mother to our kids. We got along most of the time. Enjoyed a lot of the same activities. Agreed on how to raise our kids." Sinclair took a deep breath, peeling off the label on the bottle of beer, seemingly lost in thought. "I'd be a liar if I told you that I didn't wonder about Mel. No one here seemed to want to tell me anything about her. I never ran into her when we visited our families here. It's like she disappeared when I came to town."

"Sinclair, I was in the Army by then, Jenn wrote to me for a while. She and Mel were roommates in college. Mel had it rough for a long time. The best thing was that she didn't have to live in Serendipity then. I'm not sure that she came home that first semester until Christmas."

"I was a jerk, no doubt."

"I guess you're right. It was a hard reality at the young age of eighteen."

"I made decisions I was too young to make. Professionally, sales and the car business were good to me. I sure would have liked to go to college though."

"It's a shame that you couldn't still use that scholarship."

"It was a different time. Colleges were less flexible with their requirements. I had to earn a living to support a wife and child." Sinclair nodded at the server when she placed the food in front of him and Randy. "If I had known that Dana would reward my loyalty with an affair with one of my employees, I would have been single sooner and maybe I would have had a chance with Mel."

"Don't give up, pal. Mel is still in shock. Give her time to adjust to the idea of you living here, to the possibility of you two being friends again. It's a lot for her to process. Considering how long you and Dana were married, she probably never thought that would be a possibility."

"You're right. I guess I'm in a hurry to catch up on lost time."

"You never stopped loving her, did you?" Randy looked down at his food, giving his friend time to consider how he would answer.

"A few years ago, I would have been ashamed to truthfully answer that question, Randy. My answer now is I never stopped. I don't expect her to feel the same. I hope though that Mel will at least let me talk to her and explain. Maybe let me be her friend again."

"Don't give up. I'm rooting for you. I can't say for a certainty, because I know her loyalty is to Mel, but I think Jenn is rooting for you, too."

"There's another situation we can discuss. When are you going to admit that you've been in love with Jenn all your life?"

"What are you talking about, man?" Randy became interested in his food again, dipping a French fry in ketchup.

"I came clean with you, buddy. It's your turn. We all knew back in the day that you had a thing for Jenn. I never understood why you weren't dating her. She obviously liked you."

"Jenn was out of my league, Sinclair. I was a jock with a questionable future. Jenn was smart and pretty. She was going to find someone who would give her a good life."

"How did that work out for her?" Sinclair raised his eyebrows, chuckling. "I believe she's divorced, too. Her Prince Charming didn't guarantee a happily ever after, it would appear."

"I guess you're right. I couldn't imagine she would have wanted a life with me back then."

"What about now?"

"Okay, Sinclair, if we're being honest. Yes, I would love to have a chance with her now. I'm not sure she's ready yet for a relationship with anyone. She's not been divorced long."

"Have you given her any hints?"

"You might say that." Randy shook his head, rolling his eyes.

"How did she respond?"

"She was nice, polite, and noncommittal. I think she isn't ready. I don't know what she told you when you two met the other day. Jenn and her husband were divorcing when her mother passed away suddenly. Mrs. Halston left Jenn the beachfront house that the family owned. Do you remember that place?"

"Oh, yeah. Prime Serendipity property for sure. Did she sell it to buy the newspaper?"

"No, I understand that her divorce settlement provided the money for that. She still owns the house."

"That's a lot of change at once. Maybe you're right. Jenn needs time to adjust to her new life. You hang in there, Randy."

"Dating wasn't this hard when we were young." Randy took another swig of his beer.

"We need to work hard to not make the same kind of mistakes this time though. We don't have many chances left."

"Let's concentrate on not making any mistakes at all."

The two men lifted their beer bottles and clinked them together in agreement.

Randy hoped that both could make good on their vow. Their lives would be better with Jenn and Mel in them.

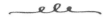

A life of police work meant you never had the same day twice. It provided Randy with a wealth of stories from his career. Today would be no different.

Randy stood in front of Sew What. The fabric and quilting store had been a fixture on Main Street since Randy was a child. Originally owned by Pearl Lowe, Randy had often stood uncomfortably in the store's foyer as a kid while his mother picked out fabric. Mrs. Lowe was strict, keeping a close eye on children who came with their mothers. 'Don't touch anything,' his mother would counsel before entering the store. Once, he picked up a spool of thread and swore he heard Mrs. Lowe growl.

Currently, the store was operated by Pearl's daughter, Amelia. Randy went to school with the woman. She was the opposite of her mother most of the time. Today, Amelia had a problem, and her Pearl side was showing.

"Every evening I clean the front window and door." Amelia stood on the sidewalk with Randy. "Every morning I come in and find all of these handprints." The woman pointed.

"It would appear that there are some young folks who like to leave their mark."

"I want you to do something about it."

"Amelia, I don't think it is against the law for someone to touch your window or door."

"I have them on camera. You can see their faces."

"Are they children?"

"Yes."

"I guess they are being children then." Randy shook his head.

"It causes me double work every day in glass cleaning."

"Why don't you skip cleaning in the evening? The glass probably isn't that dirty anyway. Then, clean first thing in the morning. It will be sparkling for a new day."

"Randy, this is ticking me off."

For a moment, Randy was back in his childhood with Mrs. Lowe's voice ringing in his ears.

"I'll have my patrol officers monitor the area. If they see the kids, they can tell them to stop doing this."

"Thank you." Amelia's normal voice returned. "I'm only trying to keep a nice business for our downtown community. I get a lot of travelers in my store with the Visitors Bureau next door."

Randy looked at the storefront that housed Mel's office. Maybe he would pay her a visit since he was nearby.

"If one of my officers talks to the kids, I'll have him or her stop by and tell you."

"Thanks, Randy. Did you hear that Jennifer Halston bought the newspaper? I'm so glad that someone with a local connection owns it. Do you think she will run it, too? I think she used to be a reporter."

"Yes, I think Jenn intends to be the Publisher. I agree it is good for our town. Look at all the members of our high school class who have businesses in our downtown."

"Or are leaders like you, Randy. I guess I should be calling you Chief Nave."

"You should always call me Randy." Randy tipped his hat. "I'm going to stop in and see Mel while I'm close by. See how our tourism business is doing these days. We'll report back to you about the children."

"Thanks. I guess I better clean these windows."

Randy thought he heard a low growl when Amelia began spraying glass cleaner. He shook his head, laughing under his breath while he walked toward the door of the Serendipity Visitors Bureau.

"Good morning, Chief Nave." Imogene greeted Randy with a big smile and cheerful sounding voice.

"Hello, Imogene. How are things going?"

Randy approached the front desk, giving the area a 'police sweep,' taking in the surroundings. In this case, he was trying to see if Mel was around.

"Things are fine."

Mel spoke from behind him. It almost made Randy jump. Almost.

"Good morning, Mel. I didn't see you there." Randy turned, spying Mel in the right-hand corner where a tall brochure rack hid a small hallway. Randy had forgotten about that hallway.

"What brings you to our office this morning?"

"I was next door at Sew What. There have been some kids leaving handprints on Amelia's window and door at night."

"Yes. We've heard about that." Mel smirked. "I can't help but wonder if she hasn't done something to make the kids mad. There haven't been any prints on our doors, or anyone else's on this side of the street that I've heard."

"That's interesting." Randy looked out the window toward the street.

"I think there might be a little of Mrs. Lowe's personality that comes out in Amelia sometimes. You were a kid in Miss Pearl's store. You know what that felt like. I was a little girl with clean hands. I can't imagine what a little boy who'd been playing might provoke in her."

"Honestly, Mel, I thought the same thing. I noticed that your windows looked nice and clean. I'm going to have my officers patrol by this evening though. If they see any kids messing around Sew What, they will give them a stern talking to. That should fix the problem."

"Indeed."

"Could I speak with you privately for a few minutes, Mel?"

"Sure. Let's go back to my office. Hold my calls, Imogene."

Imogene nodded as Mel and Randy walked around her desk toward Mel's office. It always amazed Randy at how efficiently Mel used a small space. Most of the travel brochures were in acrylic holders around the perimeter walls of the office. Several tall vertical displays filled the rest of the small floor space with information about local attractions, including touchscreens for visitors to watch videos or see advertisements of upcoming events.

The ding of the bell on the door caused both Mel and Randy to turn back toward the front. Imogene stood, greeting a couple who immediately started asking questions.

"How many visitors does Imogene greet in a day?" Randy followed Mel through her office door.

"At least one hundred and fifty on an average day. During busy times leading up to some of the festival weekends, it can easily pass three hundred." Mel sat down behind her desk, motioning for Randy to sit in a chair across from her.

"That's a lot of questions for one cheerful young woman." Randy sat.

"I go out on the floor and help, when needed. Imogene is like a well-oiled machine though. You would be amazed at the efficiency of her information giving. She runs a tight front desk."

"I've heard nothing to the contrary. She makes sure that all our patrol vehicles have a pad of those tear-off maps so that we can give directions. My officers are asked a lot of questions."

"It's all part of Imogene's efficiency. I don't know what I would do without her." Mel took a deep breath. "Somehow, Chief, I don't think you've come by to check the windows and Imogene's greeting skills. What did you want to talk about?"

"Something that is none of my business. But we've been friends for a long time, and I can't just stand on the sidelines on this one."

Mel remained silent. Her gaze was unflinching.

"I had dinner last night with Sinclair."

Randy looked for changes in Mel's expression. He saw none. The conversation might be harder than he expected.

"I'm not trying to make any excuses whatsoever for his behavior in the past. Everything that happened back then was inexcusable. You've had every right to be angry and heartbroken."

Still no change in her expression. It was a little unnerving.

"I remember Sinclair back then. I'm getting to know Sinclair again now. There are a lot of differences between the two versions. One thing is crystal clear to me though. He cared about you then and he still does. I saw your initial reaction when you first learned he was back in town. It seems to me that there's still a little caring on your part as well."

Randy stopped talking. He learned long ago when interviewing suspects, if you were quiet long enough, someone would speak. He could wait Mel out. The minutes seemed like hours before Mel finally spoke.

"Why is it that you and Jenn, and probably half the town, if they knew about it, are so sure that I should allow Sinclair to explain himself after all these years? Who's on my side in this situation?"

"We are all on your side, resoundingly so. Mel, during my time in the Army and now in Public Safety, I've seen more than my share of lives cut short. There's one thing that you learn from that above all else. Life is fragile and short, even if you live to be one hundred. Second chances don't come for everyone. Sometimes the first chance is the only one and it passes you by. Sometimes you take the first chance and discover that it was worse than having no chance at all."

"You're talking in circles, Randy." Mel put her head in her hands. "There is no right answer. I fear that no matter what I do, my heart shall not fare well. Like it did when Sinclair made his choice when we were eighteen."

"If you could go back to the day before Sinclair went on the senior trip, what would you say to him?"

Slowly, Mel raised her head, tears spilling down her face. "I'd say, choose me, even when I'm not there, choose me."

"I never told Jenn this. I didn't want her to know then, she could not have kept it from you." Randy closed his eyes, briefly bowing his head. "Dana told Sinclair she was pregnant on a Friday, right after both of us had finished working that day for Mr. Halston, Jenn's father."

"I remember you both working for him every summer."

"Dana came to the worksite and told Sinclair. She didn't tell us that her parents had already been to see Sinclair's parents that afternoon. I saw Sinclair's father kick up gravel as he sped into the worksite. Mr.

Halston gave him a mouthful. Mr. Lewis didn't hear a word he said. His eyes were daggers on Sinclair. His mother tried to catch up, she was yelling and crying. When Mr. Lewis reached Sinclair, he slapped him across the face with such force that it knocked Sinclair down. Before he could stand up, his father began yelling—'Your life is over! You will marry her.'"

Randy saw horror cross Mel's face. The tears continued.

"Sinclair tried to reason with his father. He kept telling him over and over that he loved Mel, not Dana. Looking back, I might have felt a little sorry for Dana having to stand there and listen to it, were it not for the trouble she'd caused. Sinclair kept saying over and over, 'I love Mel. I love Mel.' It started raining. Sinclair was on his knees, crying, saying that over and over. His father picked him up by the shirt collar and dragged him to their car."

Mel was still crying, a hiccupping sound coming out every so often.

"At lunch that same day, Sinclair had told me that he was going to ask you to marry him." Randy heard Mel gasp. "He was concerned about you going away to college and finding someone else. Ironic, considering what he had done a couple of months before. I wonder if that wasn't part of the reason. At lunch that day was the last time I saw Sinclair smile, a real genuine smile. I've run into him now and then on visits home, his or mine. Sinclair didn't seem to smile anymore, until last night."

Randy made eye contact with Mel. Her gaze grew bigger, stronger.

"Last night as we sat in O'Reilly's, eating hamburgers and drinking beer, Sinclair talked about you and the minute possibility that he might have a chance to win you back. In that moment, I saw that smile, the same smile I saw at lunch during the last happy hours of Sinclair's young life."

Randy didn't wait for a response from Mel this time. He simply got up, put on his police hat, and walked out of her office. When he got to the desk to say goodbye to Imogene, Randy looked behind the receptionist back into Mel's office. He smiled slightly seeing that she had risen from her desk, looking straight at him. Through her tear-stained face, he saw the beginning of a smile.

Chapter Fifteen

Mel

"Answer the phone. Answer the phone. Answer the phone." Mel chanted while listening to Jenn's phone ring. "I need you to answer the phone!"

Mel's magical powers worked as, if on cue, Jenn finally answered.

"Hey, Mel. What's up?"

"I need to know if I can use your house this evening, before I chicken out."

"I'm sorry. What are you talking about?"

"I was just talking to Randy. I think I'm ready to talk to Sinclair."

"Randy? I don't understand. How does talking to Randy make you ready to talk to Sinclair?"

"I can't explain that right now. I can feel my nerve slipping. If I don't call Sinclair in the next few minutes, I may never call him. Do you want me to call him?" Mel knew the answer to her question. It would make Jenn answer hers.

"Yes, I do think that's a good idea. I'd like to understand—"

"My nerve is waning. Can I use your house as a meeting place?"

"Of course, you can. What makes you think that Sinclair will agree to a meeting on such short notice?"

"Because he smiled. Randy says he smiled." Mel paused, letting what she said sink in, for Jenn and herself. "Thanks, Jenn. I'll text you the details."

Mel ended the call before Jenn could say another word. Looking down at the pink message slip that Mel had almost stared a hole through in the last few days, she took a deep breath and began putting Sinclair's cell number into her phone.

"Why haven't you told me anything else? I didn't get any more texts from you except what time he was coming."

Jenn came barreling through the sliding door of her house while Mel sat calmly at the kitchen table.

"I'm trying to remain calm. You're not helping my calm."

"I'm sorry. I've got to straighten up the house. It's a mess."

Mel squinted, looking around the room. Jenn's house was far from being a mess.

"The house looks fine, perfect almost. More importantly, how do I look?"

Mel stood up from behind the table. She'd rushed home and pulled everything out of her closet trying to find the 'perfect' outfit. *Talk about a mess. I've got one at home.* She finally chose a business casual pantsuit in emerald.

"You look beautiful, Mel. Emerald has always been a good color for you." Jenn continued straightening things that weren't messy.

Emerald. *It was her signature color.* The color Mel wore for her job interview when she landed the Director of the Visitors Bureau position. The color she wore when she received the Business Professional of the Year Award. Mel's first piece of clothing she'd worn with the beautiful green hue was a glimmering sequined emerald gown at her Senior Prom. The event that Mel considered the closest thing to a wedding day she'd experienced.

"I remember your prom dress." Jenn seemed to be reading her mind. "Sinclair's cummerbund matched perfectly. You two looked magical."

"I doubt he will show up in a tuxedo with a corsage, but a special memory prompter can't hurt."

"What did he say when you called him?" Jenn moved into the living room, straightening magazines on side tables which were already piled neatly.

"He didn't *say* anything."

Jenn stopped what she was doing, looking at Mel with a scowl.

"I texted him. I didn't trust myself to hear his voice. I figured this was the twenty-first century, everyone texts. I was also afraid I would get his voicemail and chicken out."

"Okay. Good idea. What did his text say?"

"It took him five whole minutes to respond."

"I bet he looked at his phone for four of those minutes in shock."

Mel chuckled. "I hope so. His response said, 'I'm so grateful. Please tell me when and where. I will be there.'"

"Do you feel like you're seventeen again and there's a new guy you're interested in?" Jenn sat down on her couch, resting her head on the back, staring at Mel.

"You look almost exactly like you did then." Mel smiled, remembering so many similar conversations between the two of them in their youth. "Maybe you should invite Randy over and we can double date."

Mel watched Jenn quickly stand up, shaking her head at the idea.

"Randy and I are friends."

"It could be more, and you know it."

"I don't know. He's been very kind since I moved back to town. We were always like siblings growing up."

"Stop ignoring what he has already told you. The man has all but got down on one knee. When are you going to realize that you've had his heart for a long time? This is your chance at happiness. Listen to your own advice."

"I'm not ready to think about any of that. I'm barely divorced." Jenn glanced at her watch. "Sinclair will be here in fifteen minutes. I stopped and got a fruit and cheese tray. Where do you want to have this meeting?"

"It's such a nice day. I was thinking about the deck, if that's okay."

"Perfect. That gives me lots of space to disappear into. I will set up the food and beverages out there." While walking by her, Jenn pulled Mel into a hug. "No matter how this meeting goes, it is the right thing to do. Both of you need closure from the past. It's the only way for you to walk freely into the future, with or without each other."

"I know you're right. I feel like I'm giving someone permission to reach inside me and pull a Band-Aid off my heart. It's way past time. I honestly don't have any expectations. I'm not allowing myself that extravagance. As far as I'm concerned, we are here to say our goodbyes."

"Maybe there can be hellos around the corner."

"We shall see."

Fifteen minutes later, Mel was doing Lamaze-style breathing when she heard a vehicle pull up, followed by the closing of a door. Her heart raced so fast, she wondered if she was too young to consider seeing a cardiologist. Holding her breath, Mel closed her eyes, waiting for the sound of a knock. The knock never came as Jenn opened the side door, greeting Sinclair.

Mel walked up behind Jenn, getting her first in-person glimpse of Sinclair in more years than she could count. She stayed out of sight, watching Jenn make small talk with Sinclair and offering him a seat on the deck.

Mel now had concrete proof that time travel was possible. Taking one look at the middle-aged man on the deck, she immediately saw the young man she was so in love with. The color of his hair, a deeper golden with patches of silver. The broad shoulders, his build more filled out than his once-thin athletic one. The way he turned his head, listening to Jenn. Wringing his hands, a nervous tick Mel remembered from long ago. The reality of the moment hit Mel like a slap—this was Sinclair Lewis standing a few feet away, and he was here to talk to her. Her mouth grew dry. Her knees shook. She grabbed hold of the edge of the kitchen sink in front of her, closed her eyes, and said a silent prayer.

"I'll go get Mel, Sinclair."

Mel looked up when Jenn opened the sliding door, stepping into the kitchen. Jenn didn't say a word. A lifetime of friendship made words unnecessary. Mel shook her head and took a deep breath.

"I'm ready." Mel began to walk, not feeling her feet touch the ground.

"Hello, Sinclair." Still within the open doorway, Mel stopped. Sinclair, still wringing his hands, appeared to be looking at the ocean view. Slowly, he turned around.

"Hello, Mel." The corners of Sinclair's mouth started turning up in a smile.

Everyone has seen that point in the movie when two star-crossed lovers meet and the full orchestra bursts into the most complicated piece of music ever played, ebbing and flowing with emotion. Only that didn't describe the moment. It was total silence. For a few seconds, Mel heard nothing, not the Atlantic Ocean on the horizon, not the whirling of the heat pump from below the deck, not even the beating of her own heart. For that moment, there were only two people in the world. Complete silence. Unrelenting eye contact.

"You look lovely, Mel." Sinclair took a step toward her, and then stopped.

"Time has been kind to you in every way, except your eyesight, Sinclair." Mel cheered inside, amazed at her wit.

"There's the sassy girl I—"

"That girl is long gone."

Mel's shaking legs could stand no longer. She broke their eye contact, sitting down at the table where Jenn had left an assortment of food and drink.

"Too many years have passed." Sinclair followed her lead, sitting on the other side of the table.

"Time has a way of slipping by while we're busy being adults."

Mel poured a glass of iced tea for Sinclair, then one for herself. She was glad that Jenn chose the beverage over wine. It kept the occasion friendly, but not quite social.

"Adulting. It's been my full-time job for too many years.' Sinclair bowed his head.

Mel noticed it was the second time Sinclair had referred to being an adult in the last few moments.

"We could spend this time making idle chatter about the years between then and now. I doubt that is what you had in mind though." The relaxed expression on Sinclair's face turned to a furrowed brow. "I want to thank you, Mel, for agreeing to sit down with me, after all these years. I wish I'd had the gumption to try to have this conversation a long time ago. It would have been more appropriate, and I'm sure appreciated, if it had been sooner."

"I've been told that it's never too late to right a wrong." Mel set her glass down, looking Sinclair straight in the eyes. "I've not quite figured out though how long never is."

Sinclair wrung his hands. Mel heard a soft laugh escape before he started to speak and then stopped himself. She remained silent.

"At the time, I couldn't form the words of a true apology to you. I was too shocked and ashamed that I had to break up with, who I now know was, the only girl my whole heart loved."

Mel felt a pain in her heart. It was a familiar feeling that she'd managed to tuck away for a long time. *This is going to get worse before it gets better.*

Sinclair swallowed hard, as if he'd suddenly lost his voice. "I was stupid and foolish. I drank too much because I was angry that you weren't at the beach with me."

"Are you trying to say that it was my fault?" Mel felt her emotions change. Every hair on her body stood up, ready to fight.

"No, no, no! It was all me, you did nothing wrong. I was trying to explain."

"Why you cheated on me the first time you were out of my sight?" Mel's internal self put on the boxing gloves.

"Doesn't your heart have to be involved for it to be cheating?"

"I don't know, Sinclair. I've never cheated." Mel didn't like the direction the conversation was going. "Maybe this wasn't such a good idea."

"Please hear me out. I did many wrong things. The first one was even going on that stupid trip when you couldn't. I should have stayed right here in Serendipity. We'd be having dinner in our dining room now. We would have had ten thousand dinners together by now."

Mel started to respond but chose to stop.

"I shouldn't have let Dana put me in a compromising position. I should have walked away from her. You know how she got me to even talk to her that night?" Sinclair briefly made eye contact. "She started talking about you. I loved talking about you. Then, she said little things about you not being there. Little by little, she fed my anger and frustration until all my resistance was gone. There's no excuse for it. I was stupid."

"You managed to keep that secret for two months. Did you think that would make it disappear? Dana wasn't keeping it a secret. Multiple people whispered about it. 'Poor Mel,' they would say."

"I thought everything could be forgotten. We were going off to college. Only a few people knew that I'd bought you an engagement ring. I wanted us to be committed before we set foot on any college campus. I wasn't going to lose you."

"Did Dana get that ring?" Mel was thankful Randy had shared that story. She could conceal her shock and have a great comeback.

"No. I never bought Dana an engagement ring." Sinclair bowed his head again.

"But she got a gold band and is the mother of your children."

"She did. Those children have been what's kept me sane. I honored my responsibility like my father told me I would do."

Mel cringed inside thinking about the rest of the story Randy told her. She knew that in Mr. Lewis' mind there was no alternative. It was the only honorable thing to do.

"My children are grown. I was an honorable husband to Dana. I know you may not want to hear this, but I've never cheated on her. Can I tell you the reason why?"

"I'm not sure I want to hear it." Mel closed her eyes, taking a deep breath. "Go ahead."

Sinclair leaned over, putting his elbows on his knees, holding his head in his hands. A few moments passed before he raised his head up and made eye contact. His eyes were filled with tears.

"In my entire life, there's only one woman that I ever wanted to be with, only one. I destroyed that in the most foolish and unforgivable way that I could. I vowed that I would never be intimate with another woman, unless it could one day be you."

Mel tried to make sense of Sinclair's words. Maybe there had been 'too many years,' like he had said. Somehow, his heartfelt confession didn't make her years of heartache disappear. If anything, it might be making it worse.

"We can't turn back the hands of time, Sinclair. What's done is done."

"Sometimes, we get second chances though."

For a split second, Mel saw the face of her young Sinclair, all eager and hopeful. It touched her heart as much as anything he'd said.

"We're not too old for second chances, are we?"

Sinclair reached out to touch her hand. Mel pulled away.

"I don't know. It's a lot to think about. I was doing fine, you know, until you decided to move back here. I have a nice life."

"You've spent your life alone it would appear." Sinclair sat back in his chair; age returned to his face. "I am surprised that you did not marry, have children."

"I suppose I have trust issues."

"I'm sorry about that. I would have liked for you to have a happy family life."

"Did you?"

More age appeared on Sinclair's face. Lines that minutes before were barely visible, now seemed to deepen. The smile that made Mel's heart race was now a frown.

"There are several sides to that answer. I have loved being a father. My children have been the joy in my life."

Mel felt a pain in her heart. Sinclair's joy should have been hers, also.

"I could have married. I've enjoyed my career."

"I've watched from afar as you helped take Serendipity from a sleepy little beach town to a bustling coastal destination. I saw the interviews of you when that movie was filmed here. I was proud."

Mel never considered that Sinclair would have seen those interviews. Serendipity received a lot of positive media in the weeks and months after the movie that was set in their small town became a blockbuster.

"There was quite a bit of real estate development after that. It was unexpected growth." Mel took a deep breath. *It's time to ask my question. Spit it out, Melinda.* "Why did you decide to move back to Serendipity? Most of your family is gone."

"Haven't you figured that out by now?" Sinclair half smiled. "Dana and I separated about two and half years ago. Our divorce was rather messy. Did Jenn tell you about that?"

"Yes, I'm sorry."

"You shouldn't be. I deserved it for what I did to you."

"That's the thing, Sinclair, no one deserves it. Dana treated you far worse than you treated me. Come to think of it, she did so twice."

"You still have a big heart, Mel. You are still a smarter person than I ever deserved."

Sinclair smiled. Mel saw so much love in his eyes she had to break their gaze to keep from crying.

"You know, they say you can't go home again. I guess that phrase was coined about fools like me who leave their hometown in shame. About a year ago, I had a dream. I was playing baseball. I looked up in the stands. There you were, cheering and smiling like you always did. You held up a sign, it said, 'Come Home.' I decided that was my sign to do exactly that. The settlement with Dana's uncle finally came through. A few days later, an old buddy called and told me that there was a dealership for sale in Tyrell County. That's all I needed to hear. I got in my car and drove there. Within a couple of hours of haggling, the former owner and I reached a deal. The rest was up to the bank and the lawyers. I decided there was no use for me to live there when I wanted to be here. I went all in and rolled the dice."

"How's it worked out for you so far?"

"I'm sitting in front of the love of my life. I'd say it's going well."

"Sinclair, I don't know if I can—"

"Mel, I'd like nothing better than to get down on one knee in front of you right now and ask you the question I should have asked years ago. I understand that you aren't ready for that. I must face the reality that you may never be ready for that question. I don't deserve your forgiveness. I don't deserve a second chance. That knowledge isn't going to stop me for asking for another chance anyway. What have I got to lose?"

Mel started to speak. Sinclair held up his hand.

"Let me spend a little time with you. We were friends once. Let's eat a few meals together. Get to know each other again. Maybe spend some time with Jenn and Randy, if they can tolerate my company. If that's all you want, so be it. If I'm luckier than I deserve, maybe I can charm you into dating me again. I might even join a softball team, if you'd come and cheer me on."

Tears burned in Mel's eyes. She knew she'd reached the point where there was no holding them back. Sinclair would see them. They were making streaks down her face.

"Don't cry, Babycakes."

His nickname for her rolled off his lips like he had last said it yesterday. More tears came. Sinclair stood up from his chair, walking around to kneel in front of her. Before Mel knew what was happening, Sinclair reached up and wiped her tears away.

"Just give me a chance."

Chapter Sixteen

Jenn

"Why don't you stay here tonight? We'll order a pizza and talk about boys."

After Sinclair left, Jenn joined Mel on the deck to hug her friend while a seemingly endless stream of sobs left her body. Jasper and Mia were curled together on Jasper's bed, sound asleep.

"I appreciate everything you have done, I'm so glad you are here. I think I should go home. I think I need to crawl into my own fluffy bed with my ridiculous number of pillows and not come out for several days. I already told Imogene that I was taking the rest of the week off."

"That's even more reason why you should stay right here. Mia is already here. I will put more pillows on the guest bed. I might even take some time off, too."

"You, my friend, don't have an ex-boyfriend who wants you back to cry over. *You* have a hunk of a man who has such a good heart and who has loved you from afar. You should be running to him with your arms open."

"Oh, Mel, don't make this about me. I'm here to help you. I was married for the last thirty years, remember?"

"Not so happily married as I recall. I just heard a speech about second chances. This is a big whopping first chance for you."

"That would be the same for you, girlfriend."

"Well, yeah, sort of, but mine is way more complicated. Yours is crystal clear. With a wonderful man who adores you. He never broke your heart. He just wasn't brave enough when he had the chance. Randy's grown some bravery. You've got to go get him!"

"Stop being silly." Jenn began gathering the plates of food that were still on the table. "I think you might have left some clothes from when you stayed here the other night. If not, I'm sure I've got some pajamas you could wear."

"I'm only staying if you agree to hear me out about Randy."

"Okay. I said we could order pizza and talk about boys."

"Let's have a calzone from Babalinos with a bottle of Chianti that's wrapped in straw."

"Is there any other way?" Jenn howled with laughter, hugging her friend. "We shall solve all of our problems with that combination in our bellies."

"And probably create a few more. Oh, Jenn, I'm full of so many emotions, my head is literally spinning. You're right. I don't need to be by myself. I need to laugh and cry with my best friend."

"You made a big step today. No matter what, it was a good one."

Several pieces of calzone later, snuggled in soft pajamas with the taste of wine still on their lips, Jenn told Mel about her conversation with Renee.

"It was a lot like talking to Renee during those early months after Jonah disappeared. She said words and made sentences, but I'm not sure her brain was completely turned on."

"It sounds like it was a serious and scary surgery. Maybe the pain meds have her in a fog."

"Maybe. I'm afraid that she may have raised a wall again. I think that her psyche can only take so much for so long. It goes on autopilot so that she can function."

"How's Neil?"

"Neil sounds tired. Now that Renee's condition has stabilized and with the knowledge that she will probably be recovering in the hospital for several more days, Neil is going home and getting some real rest. He warned me about how she would sound. It worries him, too."

"I don't suppose they have any further prognosis for the cancer?"

"I think it's too early to tell. I'm sure there will be more tests and scans after she's healed. I'm still hoping that she might consider spending a few weeks here while she is healing. Renee will be thrilled to hear about you becoming re-acquainted with Sinclair."

"Yes, that. Did I really spend an hour talking to him this evening?"

"It wasn't quite an hour. It was much shorter than I expected. I was ready to order dinner for all of us from Babalinos."

"I could only handle so much. It was emotionally intense."

Mel spent the next few minutes recounting the details of her conversation with Sinclair.

"I knew he was serious about his intent." Jenn reflected on what Sinclair said to her during their meeting in his office. "I didn't realize he would lead with that."

"He's obviously spent his life being a no-nonsense businessman. He has a direct delivery. He doesn't beat around the bush." Mel chuckled, shaking her head. "I get the impression that he never thought he would have the opportunity to approach me. I think he was trying to say everything at once. While I don't think he had an especially happy marriage, I'm not sure that he would have ended it if he hadn't found out about Dana's affair."

"Despite what happened, we knew back then that he was a solid guy. Even in his teens, he would do the right thing. I remember Dad talking about him as a worker. He wasn't a slacker. He followed the rules."

"Until one night, he didn't." Mel leaned back on the couch where they'd moved after the last piece of calzone was consumed. "I've often wondered what would have happened if Dana hadn't become pregnant. Or even if the child was Sinclair's? This was before paternity tests became mainstream."

"I know the answer."

"Did Sinclair tell you when you met with him?"

"No, my father did. Back then, you had to wait until the child was born to do a paternity test. Dad thought a great deal of Sinclair. He also knew Dana's father and didn't trust him. Dad didn't want Sinclair to be on the hook for something he didn't do. He also loved his 'bonus daughter,' as he used to call you. He arranged for a paternity test to be done after the child was born. The child was Sinclair's."

"Why didn't you ever tell me that?"

"Because Dad didn't like to get in other people's business. I had to be his secret keeper."

"Marshall Halston was such a good man. His daughter is, too." Mel reached over, squeezing Jenn's hand.

"Have you talked to your parents about Sinclair?"

"No. Mom and Dad aren't here long enough most months to do much besides laundry and doctors' appointments."

"Your folks have taken retirement travel to a new level. How many continents have they been to now?"

"All seven. There are still many countries they want to visit. I hope their savings holds out."

"What do you think they would say about the situation?"

"I think they would tell me to be happy and careful. They certainly weren't pleased with what happened. A few years after we broke up, I remember my father saying that mistakes are part of the human experience. All of us make them. It's what we do next that proves who we are. As heartbroken as they were for me, they thought that Sinclair did the right thing."

"Unfortunately, the right thing for some is the wrong thing for others. What does Mel want to do? What does her heart say?"

"It's confused and terrified. It never thought it would be here again." Mel was quiet for a few moments. "There's a part of me that is teenage excited, like I was when Sinclair and I were dating. She's hopeful and only sees a bright future. The older version feels quite differently. She's the one who cried all the tears. She's the one who's had about a thousand first dates without a happily ever after. She's harder to convince."

"Sounds like there needs to be a compromise. Maybe Young Mel would agree to date Sinclair again, with Older Mel chaperoning." Jenn leaned toward her friend, bumping shoulders.

"That might work if Older Mel didn't sit between them." Mel howled with laughter. "All this talking in third person is confusing. Thanks for not calling her Old Mel, that sounds too much like Old Maid."

"I don't want to be Old Jenn either. We are still hip chicks." Jenn stood up and did a little dance.

"Randy thinks so." Mel raised her eyebrows. "I think that Young Jenn should date Older Randy."

"Are you sure about that? That sounds like a May-December romance to me." Jenn walked toward the kitchen. "I think we need some dessert."

"We just ate an entire large calzone. You are trying to change the subject."

"I thought something chocolate would be a good distraction."

"Not working, I'm full. If you think that I should give Heartbreaker Sinclair a second chance after all these years, then you must give Sweetheart Randy a first chance." Mel followed Jenn into the kitchen. "Listen, Jenn, you've heard some of my dating stories through the years. You've not heard all of them. Finding a good guy who is sane, has basic manners, and holds down a job isn't as easy as it may sound. Finding one who is also handsome, charming, and you know his upbringing, that's like hitting the jackpot. There are a hundred women locally who would love to have the chance to date Randy."

"Why isn't he dating any of them then?" Jenn faced Mel with her hands on her hips.

"I'm not only saying this because of this present situation, but it's always seemed to me like Randy was waiting for something. I've not told you about all the times through the years that he's asked about you. He knew you were married. He was respectful of that. It didn't stop him from caring about how you were doing. This isn't something that's just come up because you've moved back here. Your mother told him that you were getting divorced."

"She what?"

"As soon as she told him, he came to my office and asked me about it. I think he was ready to drive to Atlanta and help you pack. He kept his police expression on for most of the conversation, talking about how an old friend can be helpful when someone is going through a difficult time. He didn't fool me. I could see the corners of his mouth turning up. He was genuinely excited. I told him that you needed time to sort things out. I didn't tell him this, but I had a feeling that you might consider moving here, even if temporarily."

"All of this stuff going on behind my back, even from my own mother! I don't know if I like that."

"All of these people who love and care about you so much that they want to see you happy. Do you really have a problem with that?" Mel didn't wait for Jenn to answer. "Hopefully, we've both got many years ahead. But look at what Renee is going through. That should show us that we've got to take advantage of every day and grab all the happiness we can."

"Does that mean that you've decided to give Sinclair a chance?"

Mel stood still for a moment. "I think it means that I'm willing to try."

After staying up late, Jenn and Mel slept in the following morning. Eating a light breakfast with lots of coffee, the two were quiet in their own thoughts.

"As much as I would love to stay here and have a mini vacation, I think I'm going to go back to work this afternoon. We've got a group of travel writers coming next week for a three-day press trip. I've got to make sure all the details are finalized."

"Work. Work. You sound like me. Doris texted me this morning and said that Lyle Livingston called. He's already moved back somewhere close by and is ready to interview. I think I will try to schedule that for Friday morning."

"Speaking of Friday, which I think is tomorrow, what would you think about us having a cookout tomorrow evening here?"

"Who is 'we'?" Jenn raised one eyebrow.

"You and me hosting Sinclair and Randy. It could be a 'break the ice' sort of thing. Four old friends getting together."

"You are relentless. Don't you want your first dinner with Sinclair to be private?"

"Not really. I'd rather it be a no-pressure evening with others to keep the conversation light."

"Well, I suppose there are worse things I could do on a Friday night. Maybe we could do some surf and turf, get some nice steaks and fresh shrimp."

"Sounds awesome. Let me take care of that. You are so much better at side dishes than I am. Keep it simple though. No need for too much work involved. This is a simple dinner. We aren't trying to impress them."

"Okay. So, you will be calling Sinclair and asking him?" Jenn winked.

"Yes, and you will be calling Randy and asking him." Mel winked back. "Could you please tell me when you are going to call Randy? I'd like to ask him to stop by my office about that time, so that I can see his face."

"Not funny."

"Wasn't trying to be." Mel got up from the table, carrying her coffee cup. She kissed Jenn on the top of the head. "I may be more excited about your 'date' than I am about mine."

"I know that would be true for me." Jenn shook her head. "It's not a date."

"It will be an evening to remember though. We can take a little step back in time."

"Hey, Randy, thanks for calling me back."

"No problem, Jenn. It sounded urgent. Is everything okay?"

After Mel left later in the morning, Jenn did a few things around the house, including making a grocery list for items she would need for the Friday evening cookout. She decided to go ahead and call Randy while she was still at home. There were plenty of potential 'listening ears' at the office. The only ones at home were on Jasper.

"Nothing is wrong. More like something is right."

"That's great! I'm always ready for some good news."

"Sinclair and Mel met last evening at my house. They talked for almost an hour. I think it was good for both."

"That's an interesting piece of news. I'm shocked that it happened so quickly."

"Once Mel gets an idea in her head, she doesn't let loose until she does something about it. There were more tears than laughter, but it was a big step for her. I think she may finally be able to heal from some very old heartbreak."

"It had to be a big step for Sinclair, too. He's wanted to talk to Mel for years. I don't think Sinclair ever thought that he would be talking to her again as a single man."

"I respect him for his commitment to his marriage, despite the circumstances that led up to it."

"Yes, I have no doubt that Sinclair wanted to be a family man. The family he ended up with wasn't the one he planned on."

Jenn could hear Randy take a drink of something.

"Still working on your morning pot of coffee?"

"Yes." Randy laughed. "I had to come in extra early this morning. This is my second pot. I appreciate you letting me know about Sinclair and Mel."

"Certainly. We are partners in that crime, Chief. That's not the only reason I called you though." Jenn took a deep breath. "Mel wants to have a cookout at my house and invite Sinclair. She thought you might want to come, too."

"Mel wants me to chaperone her first date with Sinclair?"

"I'll be there, too."

"Are you a chaperone, too?"

Jenn could tell that Randy was making fun and poking around for another question.

"I would like for you to come and have dinner with us, me." Jenn closed her eyes and shook her head. *I sound like a teenager.*

"That sounds like you're asking me out, Jenny Halston. Is that what you're doing?"

Jenn could hear laughter in Randy's voice. He was enjoying the moment too much.

"Yes, Randy Nave, I am asking you if you would like to have dinner with me and our two friends tomorrow night."

"I'll have to check my calendar."

Jenn could hear paper rustling. She would call his bluff.

"Of course, if you have other plans, I'm sure I could—"

"I would love to have dinner with you, Jenn. If others are there, it's fine, too. But I can't wait to have dinner with *you*. I finally get to see if you learned anything about cooking since Home Ec."

"Touché, Chief. Come hungry. I'll see you about seven."

"This is an opportunity I've been looking forward to for a long time. I won't be late."

"It's a dinner, Randy, keep it in perspective. I won't be asking to wear your class ring."

"I'll bring it, just in case. I'll tell Sinclair to do the same." Randy chuckled. "Seriously, I couldn't be happier that our friends are renewing their friendship. It's nice that all four of us are finally in the same town. I see some enjoyable evenings in our future."

Jenn ended the call. Taking a deep breath, she smiled, letting a little feeling of excitement run through her. Spending another evening with Randy would be wonderful. She dared not allow herself to see it as anything more than friendship. The ink was barely dry on her divorce papers. She needed to stay focused on her new business.

Looking back at her phone, Jenn saw there was another text from Doris about Lyle Livingston. Apparently, he was in the lobby of the newspaper office waiting to see her. She hadn't had a chance yet to ask him to come in on Friday.

"Hello, Doris, I got your text. Mr. Livingston is eager, isn't he?" Jenn decided that phoning Doris would be the quickest way to handle the situation.

"It would appear so. We've been having a nice chat. Are you coming into the office today?"

"I am. I'll be there within the hour. Why don't you encourage Mr. Livingston to go to Quincy's and have a cup of coffee?"

"Good idea. I'll tell him. See you soon."

Jenn's lazy morning was turning into a busy day. She smiled. That was the way she liked it.

"You made some quick progress on your moving, Mr. Livingston."

Jenn had barely sat down at her desk before Doris informed her that Lyle Livingston was back from Quincy's Diner.

"Please call me Lyle. Being close to the same age, I feel like we should have been friends growing up."

"I remember your name and your athletic record. I believe there's a few years difference in our ages."

Jenn also remembered his wavy blonde hair and blue eyes. Most of her teenage friends thought Lyle looked like TV actor and heartthrob singer Shaun Cassidy. Jenn could see that, like Mr. Cassidy, Lyle's looks fared well with age.

"I was able to reconnect with many I remembered from the area when I was Editor previously. Got to know Randy Nave, the current Police Chief, Melinda Snow at the Visitors Bureau, and others."

"I've read some of the articles and editorials you wrote from your previous years here. As we talked about on the phone, you weren't afraid to tackle controversial topics. I'm also interested to hear how you feel about more advertorial-type sections that focus on local and regional interests. I would also like for the newspaper to be actively involved in the growth of Serendipity."

"Those are some intriguing ideas."

"Let's talk about them."

For the next hour, Jenn listened to Lyle give his ideas and viewpoints on some of the changes Jenn was considering making in the newspaper. Their dialogue was fast paced, sometimes argumentative, but positive in most regards.

"Lyle, I've enjoyed our conversation. If you are still interested in the position, please email your salary requirements and we can continue this discussion. I'm very interested in you rejoining the newspaper and being part of my new team."

"I'm happy to hear you say that. I moved to the area specifically hoping that I could rejoin this staff. I promise you I will work hard to help make your goals become a reality. I will email you this evening."

Jenn followed Lyle to the front desk. She watched him give Doris a thumbs up and a big smile, waving when he walked out the door.

"That appears to have gone well." Doris stood up. "Is everything old new again?"

"Maybe not everything, but everyone seems to be." Jenn moved closer to Doris. "We've got to work out a salary, but I believe Lyle will be joining us soon. Isn't it amazing how things work out?"

"Lyle will run a tight newsroom, but his staff will love him. They will learn and grow."

"It's all coming together. We've got a great new advertiser, a new Editor, and, hopefully, soon we will have a new salesperson."

"There was another application in today's mail for that position. I believe that Betsy has also received a couple via email. How long do you plan to wait before you begin interviewing?"

"I don't want to wait too long. We need another revenue producer if we are going to grow this newspaper. I hope that we will have someone onboard within sixty days, thirty would be wonderful."

"It will happen. There will be another dynamic individual who will walk through our front door and be the next piece in this puzzle."

"I've made several sides that I hope will go well with surf and turf."

By mid-afternoon on Friday, both Jenn and Mel were preparing food in Jenn's kitchen for their dinner with Randy and Sinclair.

"Whatever you are baking in the oven smells divine." Mel put shrimp in a plastic bag with a marinade.

"In the oven are twice-baked potatoes with sour cream, bacon, and cheese. Not the healthiest item, but I think the guys will like them with the steaks. The other sides are a mixed green salad with pecans, strawberries, and bleu cheese, and stuffed squash. The rolls came from The Frosted Goddess."

"What about dessert?" Mel looked a little panicked.

"Covered. I gave Randy the task of picking up ice cream from Dippers."

"Ice cream from Dippers that officially makes this a high school date." Mel finished adding marinade to the steaks, putting them into the refrigerator.

"I don't remember cooking for a high school date. If that had been a prerequisite, I probably wouldn't have gone on any." Jenn stood back, watching a change in Mel's mood.

"I'm so nervous, Jenn." Mel's voice quivered. "I've dreamed of having the opportunity to see Sinclair again. I never thought I would have the chance."

"I know it's scary. This may be a turning point for you."

"Why do you say that?"

"It's a chance to reconcile a friendship, to clear the air. It may turn into a second chance for you and Sinclair. Or, you two might not hit it off. You might have grown past your first love. If that happens, I think you will once and for all be free from what happened between you. You will finally be able to put Sinclair behind you and *allow* yourself to find someone new."

For several minutes Mel was silent, she just stared at Jenn with her head tilted.

"That is freaking brilliant, Jenn! You've unblocked a mind block that's been in my head since I was eighteen. I love you!" Mel ran to where Jenn was standing, pulling her into a hug.

"You've got to remember this. The romance-loving side of me wants you to have a chance to live happily ever after with Sinclair. The lifelong best friend side of me wants you to live happily ever after, period, with whomever your heart chooses. Bottom line is that I want you to be happy."

"I feel sorry for people who don't have at least one lifelong best friend. Who do they share their deepest darkest secrets with?"

"I knew a few people like that in Atlanta. They didn't have any good stories from childhood. It was sad."

"Look at the time!" Mel's voice was almost a scream. "We are sweaty cooking messes. We've got to get ready."

"Despite your deeming it is a date for all of us, this is a casual evening." Jenn looked down at her food-stained outfit. "I will be taking a shower and changing clothes though."

"You may have been married for years, but I see a little dating spark coming out in you." Mel bumped Jenn when she walked by her. "I'm heading to the boudoir in my suite. I shall return in an hour or two."

"Someone is going to need to start the grill." Jenn called after her.

"I asked Randy to come early and do that." Mel yelled back.

"Early! How early is he coming? I've got to get ready, too." Jenn looked at the kitchen clock.

"See, it is a date, after all." Mel peeked around the corner. "You better hustle. The most popular boy in our senior class is going to light your fire." Mel howled with laughter as Jenn chased her down the hallway.

Chapter Seventeen

Sinclair

"I don't know if it's such a good idea for me to arrive early." Sinclair paced inside Dippers Creamery while Randy purchased several different flavors of ice cream. "Mel invited you to come early, not me."

"If you will recall, I didn't ask you to come early, you told me that you wanted to ride with me. If it makes you feel better, you can sit in the vehicle until it's time for *you* to be there." Randy paid the cashier for the ice cream.

"What are you so grumpy about? I thought you would be happy to be spending an evening with Jenn. If my recollection is correct, you wanted to do this since you were a teenager, maybe before that." Sinclair held the door open while Randy carried two bags of ice cream. "Did you buy some of every flavor?"

"I wanted to make sure everyone had a flavor they liked. You picked at least four yourself."

"In my defense, it's been a long time since I've had Dippers ice cream."

Sinclair stood on the passenger side of Randy's vehicle while Randy put the ice cream in a cooler. Both got into the vehicle and were quiet for the first mile or so of the trip to Jenn's house.

"Seriously, Randy, what's bothering you? You seem stressed."

"I'm happy to be having this evening with everyone. I get the feeling though that Jenn has been forced into it. I invited her to my house for dinner the first weekend after Jenn moved back. I think I may have revealed too much in that dinner conversation." Randy tightened his grip on the steering wheel. "I always told myself that if I ever got the chance again, I would tell Jenn how I felt all those years ago. I would tell her that I regretted not asking her out. I told her some of that the other night. I don't think she believed me."

"You were a popular fellow back in the day. There was a long list of the most popular girls who were vying for a date with Randy Nave. I don't think Jenn put herself on that list. You two had been friends since you were toddlers. Despite the way some of us knew how you felt, you treated her like a sister."

"I know. I thought a girl as wonderful as Jenn was out of my league. Back then, guys put girls in categories. It wasn't right, but that's what we did."

"I know. There were pretty girls and there were smart girls. Girls who you dated, girls who were your friends."

"Jenn was the whole package to me. I thought she'd find someone far better than me someday."

"I hoped the same for Mel, frankly. She deserved better than the likes of me. From what I've heard, it sounds like Jenn's husband was 'good on paper,' as they say."

"We still don't deserve these girls, Sinclair."

"That's not going to stop us from trying to get them this time, buddy. This is the championship game; we've got to play hard and win!"

"Do you still compare everything to sports?" Randy chuckled.

"Probably more than I should. Those were good days for me. I'm ready to have an older version of some of them. Since I'm back in town, I might even see if they will let me do a little coaching. I was a volunteer coach for my son's little league. I enjoyed it. Have you done any coaching since you've been back here?"

"The police department had a softball team that I played on in my early years back here. The bullets I took put an end to that."

"My folks told me about that. I tried to keep up with your recovery. That was a serious incident."

"That on top of the injuries I got in the military did some work on my body. You talk about the old days, I'd tell those young bucks a thing or two about taking care of themselves, if I could. I'd not feel so old if I didn't have so many aches and pains."

Randy turned into Jenn's driveway. From their parking place, Sinclair could see Jenn arranging some things at the table on the deck. He looked over at Randy. His old friend was staring at Jenn. Sinclair saw love mixed with fear in Randy's eyes.

"Stop worrying. You didn't break her heart like I did Mel's."

"I think Jenn's heart is broken though."

"Randy, you weren't the one who caused that. But you can be the one to heal it. I think Jenn just needs time. She went from being a daughter to a wife to a mother. For the first time, she gets to be her own independent person. Let Jenn get her feet underneath her. Show her that you're interested but give her time and space. I know she loved you once."

"Good advice. We're not here for me though. Tonight's your night, Sinclair Lewis. Go knock this one out of the park."

"If only this was as easy as a home run. This time around, I'm the one out of my league."

"You don't suppose that Mel climbed out the window and went home, do you?"

Sinclair whispered to Jenn. He and Randy had been there for about a half hour and still hadn't seen Mel.

"It always takes Mel a long time to get ready." Jenn gave Sinclair a reassuring pat on the back when she walked by him in the kitchen. "You don't have to hang out with me in here. Go sit on the deck and supervise Randy."

"No, ma'am, he barked at me when I was out there earlier. Randy must have some grill master certification they hand out in the Army or the Police Department. He did not appreciate my grilling suggestions. I think he's a little nervous about the date."

"He doesn't need to be nervous. It's not like it's a real date." Jenn responded quickly. "It's a casual dinner with old friends."

"I got the impression from Mel that this was a date."

"Maybe it is for you two. Randy and I are your chaperones."

"Jenn, I realize that you haven't been divorced long. I understand that feeling; it's strange after being married a long time. I hope you will allow yourself to get past that and try again."

"I'm sure I will eventually. Randy has been very kind to me since I moved back to Serendipity. His friendship is important."

"I feel like there is a 'but' coming."

"I don't want to confuse kindness and friendship with something more. I don't want him to feel obligated to date the divorced friend. I'm sure Randy has many lady friends."

Sinclair shook his head. This beautiful and smart woman in front of him was still an insecure young girl who had no idea of her worth in the eyes of a man.

"You were kind enough to be honest with me the other day. I'm going to do the same for you. Then, I'm going to back off and mind my own business. That successful man out there who broke athletic records in his teens, served his country for a couple of decades, and has protected his community ever since, taking a bullet in the process, probably has a list of ladies pursuing him like he did in high school. Then and now, he's got his heart set on one special woman, but he's never had the nerve to act on it because he doesn't consider himself worthy. You may not see him as anything more than a friend, and that's your choice. But if your heart has any of the devotion to Randy Nave that I *know* it once did, please do something about it. I would hate to see the two of you waste the last few decades of your life being nice when you could spend it together being in love."

Sinclair watched Jenn's eyes bug out and her mouth open in a shocked expression.

"I'm glad I got your attention. I'm not going to waste another minute of my life beating around the bush. I'm going to pursue Melinda Snow with the determination of a hound dog on a hunting trip."

"Good to know. I might have to kennel you."

Sinclair closed his eyes and made a face when he heard Mel's voice behind him. *So much for taking it slow.* He cringed to think what her expression might be. Slowly, he turned around. Gasping when he finally saw her, Mel looked almost exactly like she did when they were teens.

Cute summer outfit in a beautiful shade of blue, her hair was pulled back in a ponytail. Sinclair always loved how Mel looked when she wore her hair that way. She was breathtaking. His heart lurched with a sensation akin to what he imagined a heart attack might feel like. His heart literally hurt with love. Sinclair's emotions took control. While a smile crossed his lips, a tear fell down his cheek. He couldn't control it. Sinclair was helpless under Mel's spell.

"Beautiful."

It was the only word Sinclair could say. He watched a dozen emotions cross Mel's face in less than sixty seconds. He wanted to turn away and wipe the tears from his face. All he could do was gaze at her and feel a sadness that he'd not let himself admit for over half of his life. Time seemed to be in suspension. The only sound he heard was his heart beating like a race car.

"The steaks are ready!"

Randy opened the sliding glass door behind Sinclair. The sound was jarring, causing Jenn to yelp. The spell was broken. Mel dropped her gaze. Sinclair turned toward Randy. The two friends locked eyes for a moment. Randy had a perplexed look as if he sensed he'd interrupted something.

When Sinclair turned around, he saw that Mel was now standing at the sink with her back to him. He wondered if she too was caught up in the emotion of it all. Sinclair's eyes met Jenn's. She gave him a slight smile, handing him a bowl of salad.

"Why don't you take this outside? We'll bring the rest of the side dishes out in a few minutes."

Sinclair took the bowl and followed Randy outside, closing the sliding door behind him.

"I'm sorry, man. I think I interrupted something." Randy frowned.

"It's okay. We needed an interruption. I think that Mel and I were back in another time. It's probably best we stay in the here and now. I need to watch my emotions. I'll scare her off." Sinclair glanced back to the house. "This is harder than I expected, Randy. All these years, I've not allowed myself to think about Mel too often. I was a married man. My heart didn't need to be remembering my first love. Now that she's right here and I'm free, I've got to get control of myself."

"Jenn and I will keep the conversation light."

"That sounds good. I'm going to need all the help I can get, my friend."

"I've been meaning to ask this ever since Randy told me the story." Jenn passed a basket of rolls around the table. "Mel, why do your parents take food to the police department every Christmas?"

Sinclair was thankful that Jenn and Randy jumped in and kept the conversation focused on local news while they enjoyed dinner. Sinclair knew that both he and Mel didn't need to go down memory lane. Talking about their youth would make Mel remember all the things that went wrong.

"Because Randy rescued Christopher Robin."

Mel answered Jenn's questions between chews.

"Your Cocker Spaniel?" Jenn and Sinclair said simultaneously. They laughed at each other.

"You two both have a short memory. The Cocker Spaniel that I got when I was thirteen was named Charlie Brown."

"That's right." Again, Jenn and Sinclair responded together.

"Christopher Robin was a Siamese cat with one blue eye and one black eye that escaped from Mr. and Mrs. Snow's house on the coldest night of the year." Randy began to tell the story. "He was cornered in a tree by their neighbor's Doberman. I climbed the tree and got him out with the Doberman's sharp teeth in my leg."

"That's exactly right. Randy is a hero." Mel beamed. "My mother loved Christopher Robin more than she loves my father."

"Loved? Is this cat gone now?" Sinclair asked.

"Yes, Christopher Robin used up his nine lives at the ripe old age of seventeen. He was quite traumatized after his experience with Elvis."

"Elvis? What?" Sinclair was still on his first glass of wine, but he felt a little confused.

"Elvis was the name of the neighbor's Doberman." Randy answered.

"I love a good story and a delicious meal." Sinclair began to spread butter on the roll he'd taken from the basket that Jenn passed. "It's wonderful to be here and share this meal with all of you. I was wary of returning to Serendipity to live. But I thought that the opportunity to buy a dealership so close by was maybe a sign that I should come home." Sinclair glanced at Mel. She was intently watching him. He took a deep breath. "I thought it was time that I took a chance. I never imagined that I would gain so many other blessings as well. I'm very happy to be here."

"On behalf of the Serendipity Visitors Bureau, I would like to welcome you to Serendipity, 'Our Sunsets are Our Welcome Mat.'" Mel's eyes twinkled as she laughed. "Seriously, it's good to have you and Jenn home."

Sinclair took a deep breath, closing his eyes. He wanted to remember the moment. It was his chance to start over, and he would take it.

Chapter Eighteen

Jenn

WAKING UP THE FOLLOWING morning, Jenn had a surreal feeling. The past few weeks of being reintroduced to life in her hometown had been full of twists and turns and more surprises than she imagined. Even though the road which brought her back to Serendipity was mired in potholes of life-changing sadness, Jenn was beginning to understand that the next chapter of her life was going to include experiences beyond her imagination.

Sipping a strong cup of coffee as the sun rose over the Atlantic Ocean, Jenn reflected on how fortunate she was to have been given the gift of her family's beautiful beachfront property. While Jenn knew that she would always come back to Serendipity to visit, she never realized that her parents wanted to ensure that one day she came back to the coastal town to live. Marshall and Paisley Halston were detailed planners of their own lives. Jenn doubted that they would have imagined that their hometown newspaper would be for sale at the precise time that their middle daughter would find her way home. She knew without a shadow of a doubt that they both would approve of her pursuing a lifelong dream by taking a chance and purchasing it.

Jenn was beginning to see that the plans she was formulating for her new business could become reality. Her childhood self who dreamed of owning a newspaper was present in every decision of the challenging journey. Giving her the determination to take risks and move forward.

Jenn wasn't the only one experiencing change. Her phone lit up with a call from her best friend, Mel.

"Good morning, Melinda Snow. How did you sleep last night?" Jenn chuckled remembering the evening. It's relaxed simplicity. The comfortable feeling of the four of them being together, despite the decades in between.

"When my mind finally stopped reviewing each conversation, my sleep was restful. It was full of dreams though, reliving everything that happened this past week. I woke up a few minutes ago, wondering if any of it really happened. I can't believe that I shared a meal with Sinclair. That we had a relaxed conversation, like no time had passed."

"That's exactly what I was thinking before you called. It was a comfortable evening. It felt very natural. I can't imagine how you must feel though. How is that broken heart?"

"Honestly, it doesn't feel near as broken as it once did. I can't say that I've forgiven Sinclair. It's too soon for that. I can say that I enjoyed being in his company. It didn't hurt like I thought it would. I think my mind allowed me to think past the hurt." Mel was quiet for a moment. "I'm trying not to feel impetuous, like when we were young. Remember making a split-second decision as a teenager? We often said or did exactly what was on our minds. Sometimes, regretting it later. Other times, amazed that we were brave enough to even try."

"That's a great way to describe it. I felt a little of that when I signed the documents to buy the newspaper."

"Last evening, I had to maintain control of my teenage self. At one point, she wanted to lean over and kiss Sinclair. The adult version had to remind her that Sinclair broke her heart."

"Yes, that could have been as costly of a transaction as my buying the newspaper. Your heart is your collateral. After all you have been through, I know this interaction is truly priceless and incredibly scary."

"I'm not going to argue with you, my friend. Having dinner with Sinclair was a huge, and maybe crazy, leap of faith. I'm honestly surprised that I didn't run in the opposite direction."

There was a pause in the conversation. Jenn waited for Mel to gather her thoughts.

"I've spent decades of my life overthinking everything, especially potential relationships and my past one with Sinclair. I heard such emotion in his voice last night, such conviction. I believe he has true regrets. As afraid as I am that my heart will be broken again, I'm more afraid of not taking a chance to get to know the man who has held my heart for my whole life."

"Spoken like the brave soul I know you are. None of us can predict what the future will hold. If we knew what was going to happen in our lives, we most certainly wouldn't live life worrying about each step. Second chances are often the best part of life."

"If we let them. You've got a second chance looming on your horizon, too, Jenn. I'm not referring to your new business either. Serendipity may mean happy accident, there's nothing accidental about Randy's feelings for you. You have the same in your heart as well, if you will allow yourself to remember. That young girl inside can't believe that Randy's attentions are coming in her direction. The grown-up version needs to open her eyes to see what most of us knew was there all along."

"I hear what you are saying, Mel. I'm not blind; I can see Randy's attention. You've got to understand that it's an exciting thought in one way. I still haven't unpacked my 'Simon baggage' yet. I've not fully separated myself from the psychological side of being his wife. It's not about the lack of desire to move on; I want to be free of the mental side of that time. Packing up my house and the legal aspects were the easier part of the divorce. I feel like I need to shed some layers of my mental skin before I'm ready to embrace the thought of loving someone else."

"That's deep, Jenn. You have a process of healing to go through. If you have any interest in exploring a future with him, communicate that with Randy. Don't lose the chance for a tomorrow by only acknowledging today."

"That's a good point. I know he is a wonderful man. My mind can't grasp that I am the one he's interested in."

"You spent too long being the 'Randy whisperer' in school. Even then, you only saw all those girls' eyes for Randy. You didn't see what the rest of us did. That Randy only had eyes for you." Mel paused. "I'm not going to lecture you any further. It's time for me to get out of my pajamas and slay some dust bunnies. The crazy woman who has lived here all week has neglected her home fiercely. There are still outfits in the floor of my bedroom closet from when I was trying to decide what to wear to my first meeting with Sinclair this week. That feels like weeks ago."

"Time has been doing some strange things since I arrived in Serendipity. It speeds along at an incredibly fast pace at some points. Yet, in some ways, for all that has occurred, it feels like I've been back for years. I can only imagine what the next few months will bring."

"Lots of good things, my friend. I'd like to whisper in the ears of our younger selves. I'd like to tell those girls that the best days of their lives might be so far away that they won't even recognize them."

"I think you're right, Mel. There's a calm inside me now that I've not felt for a very long time."

"That's the 'serene' in serendipity, Jenn. We've got to accept what comes our way and enjoy it."

About the Author

Attributing her limitless imagination to growing up as an only child, Liza Lanter enjoys creating heartwarming fiction with characters who instantly seem like friends and have bonds that feel like family. Every aspect of her life has involved writing of a non-fiction variety. Her heart is most at home spinning yarns of a fictional nature.

To sign up for Liza's newsletter and learn more about her writing adventures,
visit www.LizaLanter.com.

Visit the Liza Lanter author page on Amazon
at www.amazon.com/author/lizalanter

Visit the Liza Lanter Facebook page
at http://www.facebook.com/lizalanter

Did you enjoy this book? You can make a big difference by leaving a short review. Honest reviews help convince prospective readers to take a chance on an author they do not know. Thank you.

Made in United States
Orlando, FL
01 April 2024

45342048R00150